The Tsathoggua Cycle

Terror Tales of the Toad God

More Titles from Chaosium

Call of Cthulhu® Fiction
The Book of Eibon

Disciples of Cthulhu II

Encyclopedia Cthulhiana, 2nd Ed.

The Ithaqua Cycle

The Klarkash-Ton Cycle: The Lovecraftian Fiction of
Clark Ashton Smith (Forthcoming)
Singers of Strange Songs

Song of Cthulhu

R. W. Chambers' The Yellow Sign (his complete weird fiction)

Robert E. Howard's Nameless Cults
(his Cthulhu Mythos fiction)

Arthur Machen's The Three Impostors & Other Stories

Arthur Machen's The White People & Other Tales

Arthur Machen's The Terror & Other Tales

Call of Cthulhu® Fiction

The Tsathoggua Cycle

Terror Tales of The Toad God

By

JAMES AMBUEHL

JAMES ANDERSON

TERRY DALE

JOHN S. GLASBY

LOAY HALL

ROD HEATHER

RON HILGER

GARY MYERS

STANLEY C. SARGENT

CLARK ASHTON SMITH

HENRY J. VESTER III

EDITED AND INTRODUCED BY ROBERT M. PRICE

Cover Art by Harry Fassl

A Chaosium Book
2005

This book is printed on 100% acid-free paper.

FIRST EDITION

10 9 8 7 6 5 4 3 2 1

Chaosium Publication 6029. Published in 2005.

ISBN 1-56882-131-X

Printed in Canada

Contents

This book of batrachian beastliness is for
The Pulverizer,
my dear friend and colleague.

Bat/rachian

Introduction to The Tsathoggua Cycle

Saint Toad

Many of us can vividly recall (if someone there in our old folks' home nudges us from our semi-permanent drowsing and inquires) what an impression Lovecraft's Great Old Ones, initially probably Cthulhu or Yog-Sothoth, made upon us. We never got over it, became life-long cultists. One can observe precisely the same reaction on HPL's own part when he discovered Clark Ashton Smith's protegé Tsathoggua, reading Smith's "The Tale of Satampra Zeiros" in manuscript. He announced to Smith, "As for me — Tsathoggua made such an impression on my fancy that I am using him in the 'revision' (i.e., 'ghost-writing') job I am now doing — telling of some things connected with his worship before he appeared on the earth's surface" (December 19, 1929). Smith was, of course, flattered: "I was delighted by your additions to the Tsathoggua myth. Too bad you aren't publishing the story under your own name. It sounds fascinating!" (January 9, 1930).

As it happened, Smith's own "Tale of Satampra Zeiros" would not see print till the November 1931 issue of *Weird Tales*, while Tsathoggua himself would debut a season earlier in a Lovecraft story, but not the one Smith and Lovecraft referred to in the exchange just quoted. They were talking about "The Mound," published only in the November 1940 issue. But the first mention of Tsathoggua came in *Weird Tales*, August 1931, in "The Whisperer in Darkness." Thus the irony of HPL's comment to Robert E. Howard (August 14, 1930): "Clark Ashton Smith is launching another mock mythology revolving around the black, furry toad-god Tsathoggua, whose name had variant forms amongst the Atlanteans, Lemurians, and Hyperboreans who worshipped him after he emerged from inner Earth (whither he came from Outer Space, with Saturn as a stepping stone)." In reality it was HPL himself who launched the Tsathoggua cycle. He quickly appropriated Tsathoggua, informing August Derleth (May 16, 1931), "I have adopted [him] into our malignly leering family pantheon."

xii The Tsathoggua Cycle

Tsathoggua versus Zhothaqquah

Though ostensibly Lovecraft was borrowing Smith's invented deity, it might be closer to the truth to say he hijacked him, for Lovecraft, much as he had done with Richard F. Searight's *Eltdown Shards*, went on to develop Tsathoggua in an entirely different direction from that pursued by Smith.

The two conceptions are the same in name only. Lovecraft recorded his pronunciation of the name in this bit of pseudo-research: it was "a terrible cosmic name — that which the mildewed palimpsests of Commoriom, confirmed by the unmentionable Pnakotic manuscripts, more or less liberally render as Tsathoggua, or Sath-og-gwah" (to Clark Ashton Smith, Christmas Day, 1930). He can never have heard Smith pronounce the name, but since Smith did not correct him, we must assume Lovecraft had got it right. He appreciated Smith's device of varying the god's name in the different cultures that worshipped him, calling him Sadogua in medieval France and Zhothaqquah in Hyperborea. Lovecraft added another version in "Winged Death," where we learn that Africans called the god "Tsadogua," and still another in his fragment "Of Evil Sorceries donne in New England by Daemons in no Humane Shape": the American Indians knew Tsathoggua as "Sadogowah," which may imply an original pronunciation one sometimes hears from fans, "Sath-o-goo-ah." By analogy with other Lovecraftian coinages, a suffix like "-gwah" often implies a contraction.

Lovecraft's Tsathoggua and Smith's differ at practically every point. In appearance Smith's Zhothaqquah is said twice to have a roughly toad-shaped head, but in general to be small and fat and to look like something between a bat and a sloth. Lovecraft's Tsathoggua is never said to be batlike but is always called toadlike or amorphous or somehow both at the same time. Lovecraft seems to have derived Tsathoggua's essential shapelessness from the unstable plasticity of Tsathoggua's "Protean spawn" ("The Testament of Athammaus"), though Smith does not describe Tsathoggua himself this way. (Smith has these amoeboids appear again in "The Tale of Satampra Zeiros," while Lovecraft has them appear in subterranean N'kai in "The Mound.")

Smith calls his deity "nonanthropomorphic," but he is hardly nonanthropopathic, since he seems to converse quite congenially with his protegé Eibon in "The Door to Saturn." For Lovecraft, such chats would seem to be out of the question; his Tsathoggua is utterly unhuman.

Both writers place Tsathoggua among the Old Ones' ranks. But here all resemblance, as Lovecraft once said in another context, leaves off. Smith and Lovecraft posit altogether different relations between Tsathoggua and Cthulhu. Both men actually went so far as to draw up genealogical charts of the Old Ones, but these agree as little as do Matthew's and Luke's genealogies of Jesus. According to Smith, Cthulhu is the cousin of Hzioulquoigmnzhah, the god of Cykranosh (Saturn) whom Smith in turn makes the paternal uncle of Tsathoggua. Lovecraft, however, has Cthulhu and Tsathoggua descend as cousins, sons of Nug and Yeb respectively, these two "evil twins" being the sons of Yog-Sothoth and Shub-Niggurath.

In what order did Cthulhu and Tsathoggua descend to the earth? Smith once quipped how a sculpture he fashioned must represent "a divinity who must have come down from the ulterior stars and planets with Cthulhu and Tsathoggua" (to HPL, October 1930). In a spontaneous hymn, the idolater Lovecraft, having received an image of the god from Smith, ascribes the priority to Tsathoggua:

> Homage, Lord Tsathoggua, Father of Night!
>
> Glory, Elder One, First-Born of Outer Entity!
>
> Hail, Thou Who wast Ancient beyond Memory
>
> Ere the Stars Spawned Great Cthulhu!
>
> Power, Hoary Crawler over Mu's fungoid places!
>
> Iä! Iä! G'noth-ykagga-ha!
>
> Iä, Iä, Tsathoggua!! (October 7, 1930)

"First-Born of Outer Entity" might refer either to his prior birth or to his prior advent on earth, since being "born of outer reality" might easily denote "appeared on earth from space." So Smith has Tsathoggua younger than Cthulhu, but coming to the earth simultaneously, whereas Lovecraft has them coeval cousins, and/or Tsathoggua being much older than Cthulhu and/or here long before him.

Whence came Tsathoggua? In "The Door to Saturn" Smith has him descend to the earth from Saturn, landing in Hyperborea. Lovecraft did not know this, so in "The Whisperer in Darkness," written the same year, 1930, he has the pseudo-Akeley confide that "It's from N'kai that frightful Tsathoggua came — you know, the amorphous toad-like god-creature mentioned in the Pnakotic manuscripts and the Necronomicon and the Commoriom myth-cycle preserved by the Atlantean high priest Klarkash-Ton." And yet, strangely enough, in the same tale Lovecraft does imply some extraterrestrial frame of reference for Tsathoggua, since he has the Plutonian Yuggoth-spawn worshipping him! As if to confuse things further, in "The Mound" Lovecraft does not quite even locate Tsathoggua himself as ever having been in N'kai, only locating his cult, spawn, and images there.

Smith took it upon himself, in his "The Family Tree of the Gods," to reconcile all these data. In a contemporaneous letter to HPL Smith explains that his own "account of Ts[athoggua] can be reconciled with the legendry told to Zamacona in 'The Mound.' The myth, through aeons, was varied in the usual mythopoeic fashion by the cavern-dwellers, who came at last to believe that merely the images of Tsathoggua, and not the god himself, had

emerged in former cycles from the inner gulf. Ts[athoggua] travelling
fourth-dimensionally from Saturn, first entered the Earth through the lightless abyss of N'kai; and, not unnaturally, the Yothians regarded N'kai as his
place of origin. Undoubtedly the god now resides in N'kai, to which he
returned when the ice overwhelmed Hyperborea" (to HPL, ca. June 16,
1934). Actually, here Smith is harmonizing not only "The Mound" with
"The Door to Saturn," but also "The Mound" (which does not place
Tsathoggua in N'kai) with "The Whisperer in Darkness" (which does). In
"The Family Tree of the Gods" he harmonizes "The Door to Saturn" with
"The Whisperer in Darkness" by having Tsathoggua live long upon
Yuggoth (where his adoration might well have been adopted by the
Fungoid-Crustaceans) before hopping over to Neptune and then Saturn.

This Our Dreadful Toadying

Who was it that worshipped Tsathoggua in Hyperborea? Lovecraft has emi-
grees from "Kythanil, the double planet that once revolved around
Arcturus" dwelling in Hyperborea (presumably after the destruction of their
world) and worshipping "black, plastic Tsathoggua" in "Through the Gates
of the Silver Key." Of this, of course, Smith knows nothing. He restricts the
cult, first to the savage Voormis, then to a wider public of human
Hyperboreans who came to believe that by saving Eibon from Morghi's
inquisition, Tsathoggua had shown himself more powerful than the official
Hyperborean pantheon.

Lovecraft seems to preserve Smith's schema intact in "The Shadow out
of Time," when he numbers among the captive minds of the Great Race
"three from the furry pre-human Hyperborean worshippers of Tsathoggua."
These must be the Voormis. At this time Lovecraft kept quite separate his
own cycle of ancient polar civilizations. Also in "The Shadow out of Time"
the narrator "talked with the mind . . . of a king of Lomar who had ruled
that terrible polar land one hundred thousand years before the squat, yellow
Inutos came from the west to engulf it." This is a reference to Lovecraft's
early tale "Polaris," in which we read of the final, failed struggle of the men
of Olathoë in Lomar to resist the incursion of the Inutos just as their glorious Aryan ancestors had once "swept aside" the "hairy, long-armed, canni-
bal Gnophkhehs that stood in their way" when the descent of the glaciers
forced them to move south to the site of Olathoë. The Inutos are not some
imaginary race; they are none other than the very real Inuits, or Eskimos.
Lovecraft elsewhere has the Eskimos preserve legends of Rhan-Tegoth ("The
Horror in the Museum") and the actual worship of Cthulhu (the renegade
"Eskimo diabolists" in "The Call of Cthulhu").

Lovecraft had already begun confusing his own primal history of
Lomar: in *The Dream Quest of Unknown Kadath* he has Olathoë and Lomar

overrun not by the Eskimos/Inutos but by their remote primordial counter-parts the Neanderthal Gnophkehs! He has confused the two.

In a letter to Smith, Lovecraft expressed his conviction that "immemo-rial Commoriom . . . must lie buried today in glacial ice near Olathoë in the land of Lomar!" (December 3, 1929). Similarly, he told Derleth (May 16, 1931), "I shall identify Smith's Hyperborea with my Olathoë in the land of Lomar." He did this in "The Mound": "one branch of the race [of K'n-yan] even took [the Tsathoggua cult derived from the Yothians] to the outer world, where the smallest of the images eventually found a shrine at Olathoë, in the land of Lomar near the earth's north pole. It was rumoured that this outer-world cult survived even after the great ice-sheet and the hairy Gnophkehs destroyed Lomar." Evidence of this survival would be the magical conjuration of the demon Ossadogowah which the Indians learned from "the tribes of Lamah to ye North" ("Of Evill Sorceries Donne in New England of Daemons in no Humane Shape"). And notice, again, the Inutos have been confused with the Gnophkehs.

Does any of this fit Smith's picture? Who forms the counterpart to Smith's pre-human Voormis? It would have to be the Gnophkehs, not the Inutos, since the latter are true humans. And yet Lovecraft attributes the worship of Tsathoggua to the clean-limbed men of Olathoë and Lomar!

True, in "The Door to Saturn," as in "The Mound," the worship of Tsathoggua is borrowed by humanoids from pre-human races (the Voormis and the Yothians), but Lovecraft has the men of Lomar (whom he equates with the Hyperboreans) receive Tsathogguanism directly from the mission-aries of K'n-yan, fellow humanoids, unlike Smith who has the Hyperboreans borrow it from the Voormis. Again, Lovecraft and Smith do not agree.

We might be able to cobble together a few of the Lovecraft references if we supposed that the alien worshippers of Tsathoggua in "primal Hyperborea" in "Through the Gates of the Silver Key" were the humans of Olathoë/Lomar, but that these were in turn to be identified with missionaries from K'n-yan. We learn in "The Mound" that the first K'n-yanians had come with Tulu from the stars. Can it be that they came with him specifically from Kythanil? Thus the primordial worshippers from Kythanil, the men of Lomar, and the missionar-ies from K'n-yan would all be the same group. But even so, this

Idol of Tsathoggua as rendered by
Clark Ashton Smith

wouldn't help smooth out things with Smith, whose Voormis would have to be the same as Lovecraft's Gnophkehs.

Sleepy Little God

What are we to make of the yawning gap between Lovecraft's Tsathoggua and Smith's? It is not too much to say that the distance between the two Tsathogguas is no less wide than that separating Bierce's original Hastur the shepherds' god (in "Haïta the Shepherd") and Derleth's Hastur the Unspeakable. And it is significant that, in linking Smith's Hyperborea with his own narrative world, Lovecraft identified Smith's universe with that of his own Dunsanian dream-sagas. Thus Smith's Tsathoggua stories bear exactly the same relation to Lovecraft's Cthulhu Mythos tales as do HPL's own Dunsanian dream fantasies. They are part of a parallel sub-universe. Just as the Nyarlathotep of the *Dream Quest* is not quite like that in the "The Whisperer in Darkness," "The Haunter of the Dark," or "Clarendon's Last Test," neither is Smith's Tsathoggua quite the same being as the Tsathoggua who appears in Lovecraft's Cthulhu Mythos tales.

This is also why I have chosen to segregate the Tsathoggua stories of Smith from his Cthulhu Mythos tales proper, which appear collected in *The Klarkash-Ton Cycle: The Lovecraftian Fiction of Clark Ashton Smith*. His "The Coming of the White Worm" and "The Door to Saturn" appear in yet a third collection, *The Book of Eibon* by Clark Ashton Smith, Lin Carter and Divers Hands.

Robert M. Price

Guardian of the Idol

April 16, 1997

The Tsathoggua Cycle

About "From the Parchments of Pnom"

While not strictly speaking a story, "From the Parchments of Pnom" is nonetheless an important piece of fiction in the Tsathoggua cycle. It represents an expanded version of something published in *The Acolyte* (Summer, 1934) as "The Family Tree of the Gods" (title supplied by editor Francis T. Laney, one imagines) and reprinted, sans title, in August Derleth (ed.) *The Shuttered Room and Other Pieces*, Arkham House, 1959, as well as in Charles K. Wolfe (ed.) *Planets and Dimensions: The Collected Essays of Clark Ashton Smith*, Mirage Press, 1973 (with title restored). This mini-theogony comes from a June 16, 1934 letter to Robert H. Barlow. I have supplemented this material with excerpts from another of Smith's letters to Barlow, dated September 10, 1934, which supplies more fascinating nuggets of Smith's imaginary universe and its harmonization with those of Cabell, Dunsany, and Lovecraft. I have rechristened the piece "From the Parchments of Pnom" (which is at least a Smithian phrase) to differentiate this more complete Smithian theogony from the previous edition. Both epistles to Barlow appear in *The Dark Eidolon: The Journal of Smith Studies*, # 2, July 1989, pp 28-32.

From the Parchments of Pnom

by Clark Ashton Smith

I have filled out the "style-sheet" with such annotations and details concerning Tsathoggua as I am at present able to furnish. Some of these have required considerable delving into *the Parchments of Pnom* (who was the chief genealogist as well as a noted prophet) and I am well aware that certain of my phonetic renderings from the Elder Script are debatable. You raise some interesting points with your questions. Azathoth, the primal nuclear chaos, reproduced of course only by fission; but its progeny, entering various outer planets, often took on attributes of androgynism or bisexuality. The androgynes, curiously, required no coadjutancy in the production of offspring; but their children were commonly unisexual, male or female. Hzioulquoigmnzhah, uncle of Tsathoggua, and Ghizghuth, Tsathoggua's father, were the male progeny of Cxaxukluth, the androgynous spawn of Azathoth. Thus you will note a trend toward biological complexity. It is worthy of record, however, that Knygathin Zhaum, the half-breed Voormi, reverted to the most primitive Azathothian characteristics following the stress of his numerous decapitations. I have yet to translate the terrible and abominable legend telling how a certain doughty citizen of Commoriom (not Athammaus) returned to the city after its public evacuation, and found that it was peopled most exe-

crably and numerously by the fissional spawn of Knygathin
Zhaum, which possessed no vestige of anything human or even
earthly.

Ech-Pi-El, I am sure, can furnish much fuller data concerning the genesis of Tulu (Cthulhu) than I am able to offer. It
would seem, from the rather oblique references of Pnom, that
Tulu was a cousin of Hzioulquoigmnzhah, but was somewhat
closer to the Azathothian archetype than Hzioulquoigmnzhah.
The latter god, I learn, together with Ghizghuth, was born of
Cxaxukluth in a far system. Cxaxukluth came *en famille* (family
already included Ghizguth's wife, Zstylzhemgni, and the infant
Tsathoggua) to Yuggoth (where, I may add, Cxaxukluth has
most mercifully continued to sojourn throughout the aeons).
Hzioulquoigmnzhah, who found its parent slightly unconge-
nial owing to its cannibalistic habits, emigrated to Yaksh
(Neptune) at an early age; but, wearying of the peculiar religious devotions of the Yakshians, went on to Cykranosh, in
which he preceded by several aeons his nephew Tsathoggua.
(Tsathoggua, with his parents, lingered a long while in
Yuggoth, having penetrated certain central caverns beyond the
depredations of Cxaxukluth.) Hzioulquoigmnzhah, a rather
reflective and philosophic deity, was long worshipped by the
quaint peoples of Cykranosh but grew tired of them even as of
the Yakshians; and he had permanently retired from active life
at the time of his encounter with Eibon as related in *The Door
To Saturn*. No doubt he still resides in the columned cavern, and
still quenches his thirst at the lake of liquid metal, a confirmed
bachelor, and sans offspring.

My account of Tsathoggua's advent can readily be reconciled with the references in *The Mound*. Tsathoggua, travelling
through another dimension than the familiar three, first
entered the Earth by means of the lightless inner Gulf of
N'Kai; and he lingered there for cycles, during which his ultra-
terrestrial origin was not suspected. Later, he established himself in caverns nearer to the surface, and his cult thrived; but

after the coming of the ice he returned to N'Kai. Thereafter, much of his legend was forgotten or misunderstood by the dwellers in the red-litten Caverns of Yoth and blue-litten Caverns of K'n-Yan. Through such mythopoetic variations, Gll'-Hathaa-Ynn came to tell the Spaniard Zamarcoma that only the images of Tsathoggua, and not Tsathoggua himself, had emerged from the inner world. . . .

I'll now try to answer your questions, some of which have necessitated research into archives even darker and more obscure than those of the learned Pnom. Chushax, or Zishaik, of whose lineage I can learn only the most meager and dubious details, was the wife of Tsathoggua. Their offspring, Zvilpoggua, was more male than anything else. The immediate parent of Cthulhu and his race (child of Nug) was Ptmâk. The parent of Yhoundeh or Y'houndeh was the androgyne animal Archetype Zyhumë, which still abides in that cavern of the Archetypes which was visited by the ill-starred Ralibar Vooz on his compulsive itinerations through the Hyperborean under-world. Zyhumë is a sort of nebulous and more or less spheroid elk. As to the marriage of Y'houndeh and the flute-player Nyarlathotep, I am inclined to suspect that something of the sort is hinted or adumbrated by Pnom. I quote the reference: "Houndeh in the 3rd cycle of her divinity was covered by that spawn which pipes perennially the dire music of chaos and cor-ruption." If this doesn't refer to the Azathothian flute-player, I'll undertake to drink a straight gallon of the next segur-whiskey that is imported from Mars.

As to the people of your Annals, I think that Yaksh is too bleak and boreal for them. I am inclined to believe that they must have lived on Antanôk, the lost, disrupted planet of which the asteroids are the remnants. This would account for their likeness to humanity, since, in earlier times, there seems to have been a little intercourse between Earth and Antanôk. In fact, there are certain forgotten authorities who claim that mankind as we now know it is descended from Antanôkan colonists. Ulthar, as you have surmised, is indeed conterminous with both Averoigne and Poictesme, the latter lying somewhat to the northeast and the former to the southwest. As to Yondo, I have been told that that country is situated many hundred leagues to the south of Dunsany's lands of Wonder. Thus, you will readily perceive, it lies beyond all chartable regions of Earth without belonging to an alien planet.

Genealogical Chart of the Elder Gods

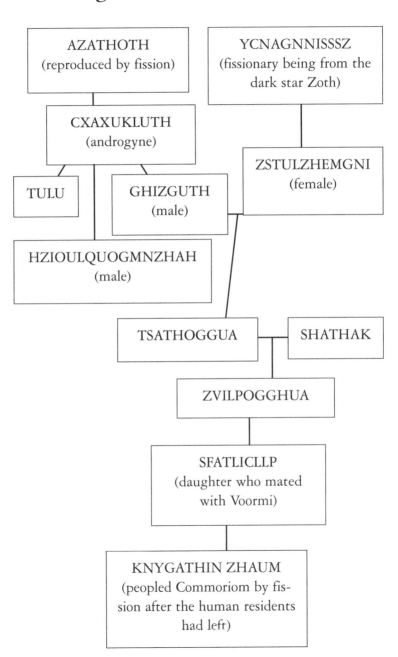

About "The Seven Geases"

Here is Smith's only story in which the godling Tsathoggua actually appears on stage! Smith completed the "outrageously grotesque, sardonic and satiric" tale on October 1, 1933, and was a proud papa: "I am rather partial to that opus. These grotesque and elaborate ironies come all too naturally to me, I fear." It appeared in the October 1934 issue of *Weird Tales*.

"The Seven Geases" features a rogues gallery of Klarkash-Tonian monsters. It fits quite well that the Hyperborean Olympus of the Old Ones should be under a mountain rather than atop one! As for the name of the mountain, we must suppose that Smith is indulging in the broadest of puns; Tsathoggua reposes beneath the mountain on which the degraded Voormis live. Suppose one lisped. Where the Voormis live would be the Voormithadreth, wouldn't it?

We have seen all of the Old Ones before, though some bore aliases. Atlach-Nacha (whose name seems redolent of Mayan or Aztec legendry) seems to recall the eponymous "Weaver in the Vault," while Abhoth the Unclean is obviously a transplanted Ubbo-Sathla, only now the entity is no longer pictured as the Primal Parent of all life-forms.

The story has the structure of a genuine folktale, with the repeated advances to the brink of doom and the repeated fortuitous deliverances. On the whole, it bears some resemblance, too, to Lord Dunsany's "The Distressing Tale of Thangobrind the Jeweler and of the Doom That Befell Him," in which a thief, filled with hubris, runs afoul of a giant spider.

The Seven Geases

by Clark Aston Smith

The Lord Ralibar Vooz, high magistrate of Commoriom and third cousin to King Homquat, had gone forth with six-and-twenty of his most valorous retainers in quest of such game as was afforded by the black Eiglophian Mountains. Leaving to lesser sportsmen the great sloths and vampire-bats of the intermediate jungle, as well as the small but noxious dinosauria, Ralibar Vooz and his followers had pushed rapidly ahead and had covered the distance between the Hyperborean capital and their objective in a day's march. The glassy scaurs and grim ramparts of Mt. Voormithadreth, highest and most formidable of the Eiglophians, had beetled above them, wedging the sun with dark scoriac peaks at mid-afternoon, and walling the blazonries of sunset wholly from view. They had spent the night beneath its lowermost crags, keeping a ceaseless watch, piling dead cryptomeria branches on their fires, and hearing on the grisly heights above them the wild and dog-like ululations of those subhuman savages, the Voormis for which the mountain was named. Also, they heard the bellowing of an alpine catoblepas pursued by the Voormis, and the mad snarling of a saber-toothed tiger assailed and dragged down; and Ralibar Vooz had deemed that these noises boded well for the morrow's hunting.

He and his men rose betimes; and having breakfasted on their provisions of dried bear-meat and a sour dark wine that was noted for its invigorative qualities, they began immediately the ascent of the mountain, whose upper precipices were hollow with caves occupied by the Voormis. Ralibar Vooz had hunted these creatures before, and a certain room of his house in Commoriom was arrayed with their thick and shaggy pelts. They were usually deemed the most dangerous of the Hyperborean fauna; and the mere climbing of Voormithadreth, even without the facing of its inhabitants, would have been a feat attended by more than sufficient peril: but Ralibar Vooz, having tasted of such sport, could now satisfy himself with nothing tamer.

He and his followers were well armed and accoutered. Some of the men bore coils of rope and grappling-hooks to be employed in the escalade of the steeper crags. Some carried heavy crossbows; and many were equipped with long-handled and saber-bladed bills which, from experience, had proved the most effective weapons in close-range fighting with the Voormis. The whole party was variously studded with auxiliary knives, throwing-darts, two-handed scimitars, maces, bodkins, and saw-toothed axes. The men were all clad in jerkins and hose of dinosaur-leather, and were shod with brazen-spiked buskins. Ralibar Vooz himself wore a light suiting of copper chain-mail, which, flexible as cloth, in no wise impeded his movements. In addition he carried a buckler of mammoth hide with a long bronze spike in its center that could be used as a thrusting-sword; and, being a man of huge stature and strength, his shoulders and baldric were hung with a whole arsenal of weaponries.

The mountain was of volcanic origin, though its four craters were supposedly all extinct. For hours the climbers toiled slowly upward on the fearsome scarps of black lava and obsidian, seeing the sheerer heights above them recede interminably into a cloudless zenith, as if not to be approached by man. Far faster than they the sun climbed, blazing torridly upon them and heating the rocks till their hands and feet were

scorched as if by the walls of a furnace. But Ralibar Vooz, eager
to flesh his weapons, would permit no halting in the shady
chasms nor under the scant umbrage of rare junipers.

That day, however, it seemed that the Voormis were not
abroad upon Mt. Voormithadreth. No doubt they had feasted
too well during the night, when their hunting-cries had been
heard by the Commorians. Perhaps it would be necessary to
invade the warren of caves in the loftier crags: a procedure none
too palatable even for a sportsman of such hardihood as Ralibar
Vooz. Few of these caverns could be reached by men without
the use of ropes; and the Voormis, who were possessed of quasi-
human cunning, would hurl blocks and rubble upon the heads
of the assailants. Most of the caves were narrow and darksome,
thus putting at a grave disadvantage the hunters who entered
them; and the Voormis would fight redoubtably in defense of
their young and their females, who dwelt in the inner recesses;
and the females were fiercer and more pernicious, if possible,
than the males.

Such matters as these were debated by Ralibar Vooz and his
henchmen as the escalade became more arduous and hazardous,
and they saw far above them the pitted mouths of the lower
dens. Tales were told of brave hunters who had gone into those
dens and had not returned; and much was said of the vile feed-
ing-habits of the Voormis and the uses to which their captives
were put before death and after it. Also, much was said regarding the genesis of the Voormis, who were popularly believed to
be the offspring of women and certain atrocious creatures that
had come forth in primal days from a tenebrous cavern-world
in the bowels of Voormithadreth. Somewhere beneath that
four-coned mountain, the sluggish and baleful god Tsathoggua,
who had come down from Saturn in years immediately following the Earth's creation, was fabled to reside, and during the
rite of worship at his black altars, the devotees were always
careful to orient themselves toward Voormithadreth. Other and
more doubtful beings than Tsathoggua slept below the extinct

volcanoes, or ranged and ravened throughout that hidden underworld; but of these beings few men, other than the more adept or abandoned wizards, professed to know anything at all.

Ralibar Vooz, who had a thoroughly modern disdain of the supernatural, avowed his skepticism in no equivocal terms when he heard his henchmen regaling each other with these antique legendries. He swore with many ribald blasphemies that there were no gods anywhere, above or under Voormithadreth. As for the Voormis themselves, they were indeed a misbegotten species; but it was hardly necessary, in explaining their generation, to go beyond the familiar laws of nature. They were merely the remnant of a low and degraded tribe of aborigines who sinking further into brutehood, had sought refuge in those volcanic fastnesses after the coming of the true Hyperboreans.

Certain grizzled veterans of the party shook their heads and muttered at these heresies; but because of their respect for the high rank and prowess of Ralibar Vooz, they did not venture to gainsay him openly.

After several hours of heroic climbing, the hunters came within measurable distance of those nether caves. Below them now, in a vast and dizzying prospect, were the wooded hills and fair, fertile plains of Hyperborea. They were alone in a world of black, riven rock, with innumerable precipices and chasms above, beneath and on all sides. Directly overhead, in the face of an almost perpendicular cliff, were three of the cavern-mouths, which had the aspect of volcanic fumaroles. Much of the cliff was glazed with obsidian, and there were few ledges or handgrips. It seemed that even the Voormis, agile as apes, could scarcely climb that wall; and Ralibar Vooz, after studying it with a strategic eye, decided that the only feasible approach to the dens was from above. A diagonal crack, running from a shelf just below them to the summit, no doubt afforded ingress and egress to their occupants.

First, however, it was necessary to gain the precipice above: a difficult and precarious feat in itself. At one side of the long talus on which the hunters were standing, there was a chimney that wound upward in the wall, ceasing thirty feet from the top and leaving a sheer, smooth surface. Working along the chimney to its upper end, a good alpinist could hurl his rope and grappling-hook to the summit-edge.

The advisability of bettering their present vantage was now emphasized by a shower of stones and offal from the caverns. They noted certain human relics, well-gnawed and decayed, amid the offal. Ralibar Vooz, animated by wrath against these miscreants, as well as by the fervour of the huntsman, led his six-and-twenty followers in the escalade. He soon reached the chimney's termination, where a slanting ledge offered bare foothold at one side. After the third cast, his rope held; and he went up hand over hand to the precipice.

He found himself on a broad and comparatively level-topped buttress of the lowest cone of Voormithadreth, which still rose for two thousand feet above him like a steep pyramid. Before him on the buttress, the black lava-stone was gnarled into numberless low ridges and strange masses like the pedestals of gigantic columns. Dry, scanty grasses and withered alpine flowers grew here and there in shallow basins of darkish soil; and a few cedars, levin-struck or stunted, had taken root in the fissured rock. Amid the black ridges, and seemingly close at hand, a thread of pale smoke ascended, serpentining oddly in the still air of noon and reaching an unbelievable height ere it vanished. Ralibar Vooz inferred that the buttress was inhabited by some person nearer to civilized humanity than the Voormis, who were quite ignorant of the use of fire. Surprised by this discovery, he did not wait for his men to join him, but started off at once to investigate the source of the curling smoke-thread.

He had deemed it merely a few steps away, behind the first of those grotesque furrows of lava. But evidently he had been deceived in this: for he climbed ridge after ridge and rounded many broad and curious dolmens and great dolomites which rose inexplicably before him where, an instant previous, he had thought there were only ordinary boulders; and still the pale, sinuous wisp went skyward at the same seeming interval.

Ralibar Vooz, high magistrate and redoubtable hunter, was both puzzled and irritated by this behaviour of the smoke. Likewise, the aspect of the rocks around him was disconcertingly and unpleasantly deceitful. He was wasting too much time in an exploration idle and quite foreign to the real business of the day; but it was not his nature to abandon any enterprise, no matter how trivial, without reaching the set goal. Halloing loudly to his men, who must have climbed the cliff by now and were doubtless wondering what had happened to their master, he went on toward the elusive smoke.

It seemed to him, once or twice, that he heard the answering shouts of his followers, very faint and indistinct, as if across some mile-wide chasm. Again he called lustily, but this time there was no audible reply. Going a little further, he began to detect among the rocks beside him a peculiar conversational droning and muttering in which four or five different voices appeared to take part. Seemingly, they were much nearer at hand than the smoke, which had now receded like a mirage. One of the voices was clearly that of a Hyperborean; but the others possessed a timbre and accent which Ralibar Vooz, in spite of his varied ethnic knowledge, could not associate with any branch or sub-division of mankind. They affected his ears in a most unpleasant fashion, suggesting by turns the hum of great insects, the murmurs of fire and water, and the rasping of metal.

Ralibar Vooz emitted a hearty and somewhat ireful bellow to announce his coming to whatever persons were convened amid the rocks. His weapons and accoutrements clattering loudly, he scrambled over a sharp lava-ridge toward the voices.

Topping the ridge, he looked down on a scene that was both mysterious and unexpected. Below him in a circular hollow there stood a rude hut of boulders and stone fragments roofed with cedar boughs. In front of this hovel, on a large flat block of obsidian, a fire burned with flames alternately blue, green and white; and from it rose the pale thin spiral of smoke whose situation had illuded him so strangely.

An old man, withered and disreputable-looking, in a robe that appeared no less antique and unsavoury than himself, was standing near to the fire. He was not engaged in any visible culinary operations; and, in view of the torrid sun, it hardly seemed that he required the warmth given by the queer-coloured blaze. Aside from this individual, Ralibar Vooz looked in vain for the participants of the muttered conversation he had just overheard. He thought there was an evanescent fluttering of the dim, grotesque shadows around the obsidian block; but the shadows faded and vanished in an instant; and, since there were no objects nor beings that could have cast them, Ralibar Vooz deemed that he had been victimized by another of those highly disagreeable optic illusions in which that part of the mountain Voormithadreth seemed to abound.

The old man eyed the hunter with a fiery gaze and began to curse him in fluent but somewhat archaic diction as he descended into the hollow. At the same time, a lizard-tailed and sooty-feathered bird, which seemed to belong to some night-flying species of archaeopteryx, began to snap its toothed beak and flap its digited wings on the objectionably shapen stela that served it for a perch. This stela, standing on the lee side of the fire and very close to it, had not been perceived by Ralibar Vooz at first glance.

"May the ordure of demons bemire you from heel to crown!" cried the venomous ancient. "O lumbering, bawling idiot! You have ruined a most promising and important evocation. How you came here I cannot imagine. I have surrounded this place with twelve circles of illusion, whose effect is multiplied by their myriad intersections; and the chance that any intruder would ever find his way to my abode was mathematically small and insignificant. Ill was that chance which brought you here: for They that you have frightened away will not return till the high stars repeat a certain rare and quickly passing conjunction; and much wisdom is lost to me in the interim."

"How now, varlet!" said Ralibar Vooz, astonished and angered by this greeting, of which he understood little save that his presence was unwelcome to the old man. "Who are you that speak so churlishly to a magistrate of Commoriom and a cousin to King Homquat? I advise you to curb such insolence; for, if so I wish, it lies in my power to serve you even as I serve the Voormis. Though methinks," he added, "your pelt is far too filthy and verminous to merit room amid my trophies of the chase."

"Know that I am the sorceror Ezdagor," proclaimed the ancient, his voice echoing among the rocks with dreadful sonority. "By choice I have lived remote from cities and men; nor have the Voormis of the mountain troubled me in my magical seclusion. I care not if you are the magistrate of all swinedom or a cousin to the king of dogs. In retribution for the charm you have shattered, the business you have undone by this oafish trespass, I shall put upon you a most dire and calamitous and bitter geas."

"You speak in terms of outmoded superstition," said Ralibar Vooz, who was impressed against his will by the weighty oratorical style in which Ezdagor had delivered these periods.

The old man seemed not to hear him.

"Harken then to your geas, O Ralibar Vooz," he fulminated. "For this is the geas, that you must cast aside all your weapons and go unarmed into the dens of the Voormis; and fighting barehanded against the Voormis and against their females and their young, you must win to that secret cave in the bowels of Voormithadreth, beyond the dens, wherein abides from eldermost aeons the god Tsathoggua. You shall know Tsathoggua by his great girth and his bat-like furriness and the look of a sleepy black paddock which he has eternally. He will rise not from his place, even in the ravening of hunger, but will wait in divine slothfulness for the sacrifice. And, going close to Lord Tsathoggua, you must say to him: 'I am the blood-offering sent by the sorcerer Ezdagor.' Then, if it be his pleasure, Tsathoggua will avail himself of the offering.

"In order that you may not go astray, the bird Raphtontis, who is my familiar, will guide you in your wanderings on the mountainside and through the caverns." He indicated with a peculiar gesture the night-flying archaeopterix on the foully symbolic stela, and added as if in afterthought: "Raphtontis will remain with you till the accomplishment of the geas and the end of your journey below Voormithadreth. He knows the secrets of the underworld and the lairing-places of the Old Ones. If our Lord Tsathoggua should disdain the blood-offering, or, in his generosity, should send you on to his brethren, Raphtontis will be fully competent to lead the way whithersoever is ordained by the god."

Ralibar Vooz found himself unable to answer this more than outrageous peroration in the style which it manifestly deserved. In fact, he could say nothing at all: for it seemed that a sort of lockjaw had afflicted him. Moreover, to his exceeding terror and bewilderment, this vocal paralysis was accompanied by certain involuntary movements of a most alarming type. With a sense of nightmare compulsion, together with the horror of one who feels that he is going mad, he began to divest himself of the various weapons which he carried. His bladed buckler, his mace, broad-sword, hunting-knife, axe and needle-tipped anelace jingled on the ground before the obsidian block.

"I shall permit you to retain your body-armour and helmet," said Ezdagor at this juncture. "Otherwise, I fear that you will not reach Tsathoggua in the state of corporeal intactness proper for a sacrifice. The teeth and nails of the Voormis are sharp even as their appetites."

Muttering certain half-inaudible and doubtful-sounding words, the wizard turned from Ralibar Vooz and began to quench the tricoloured fire with a mixture of dust and blood from a shallow brass basin. Deigning to vouchsafe no farewell or sign of dismissal he kept his back toward the hunter, but waved his left hand obliquely to the bird Raphtontis. This creature, stretching his murky wings and clacking his saw-like beak, abandoned his perch and hung poised in the air with one ember-colored eye malignly fixed on Ralibar Vooz. Then, floating slowly, his long snakish neck reverted and his eye maintaining its vigilance, the bird flew among the lava ridges toward the pyramidal cone of Voormithadreth; and Ralibar Vooz followed, driven by a compulsion that he could neither understand nor resist.

Evidently the demon fowl knew all the turnings of that maze of delusion with which Ezdagor had environed his abode; for the hunter was led with comparatively little indirection across the enchanted buttress. He heard the far-off shouting of his men as he went; but his own voice was faint and thin as that of a flittermouse when he sought to reply. Soon he found himself at the bottom of a great scarp of the upper mountain, pitted with cavern-mouths. It was a part of Voormithadreth that he had never visited before.

Raphtontis rose toward the lowest cave, and hovered at its entrance while Ralibar Vooz climbed precariously behind him amid a heavy barrage of bones and glass-edged flints and other oddments of less mentionable nature hurled by the Voormis. These low, brutal savages, fringing the dark mouths of the dens with their repulsive faces and members, greeted the hunter's progress with ferocious howlings and an inexhaustible supply of garbage. However, they did not molest Raphtontis, and it seemed that they were anxious to avoid hitting him with their missiles; though the presence of this hovering, wide-winged fowl interfered noticeably with their aim as Ralibar Vooz began to near the nethermost den.

Owing to this partial protection, the hunter was able to reach the cavern without serious injury. The entrance was rather strait; and Raphtontis flew upon the Voormis with open beak and flapping wings, compelling them to withdraw into the interior while Ralibar Vooz made firm his position on the threshold-ledge. Some, however, threw themselves on their faces to allow the passage of Raphtontis; and, rising when the bird had gone by, they assailed the Commorian as he followed his guide into the fetid gloom. They stood only half-erect, and their shaggy heads were about his thighs and hips, snarling and snapping like dogs; and they clawed him with hook-shaped nails that caught and held in the links of his chain-armour.

Weaponless he fought them in obedience to his geas, striking down their hideous faces with his mailed fists in a veritable madness that was not akin to the ardour of a huntsman. He felt their nails and teeth break on the close-woven links as he hurled them loose; but others took their place when he won onward a little into the murky cavern; and their females struck at his legs like darting serpents; and their young beslavered his ankles with mouths wherein the fangs were as yet ungrown.

Before him, for his guidance, he heard the clanking of the wings of Raphtontis, and the harsh cries, half hiss, half caw, that were emitted by this bird at intervals. The darkness stifled him with a thousand stenches; and his feet slipped in blood and filth at every step. But anon he knew that the Voormis had ceased to assail him. The cave sloped downward; and he breathed an air that was edged with sharp, acrid mineral odours.

Groping for a while through sightless night and descending a steep incline, he came at length to a sort of underground hall where neither day nor darkness prevailed. Here the archings of rock were visible by an obscure glow such as hidden moons might yield. Thence, through declivitous grottoes and

along perilously skirted gulfs, he was conducted ever downward by Raphtontis into the world beneath the mountain
Voormithadreth. Everywhere was that dim, unnatural light
whose source he could not ascertain. Wings that were too broad
for those of the bat flew vaguely overhead; and at whiles, in the
shadowy caverns, he beheld great fearsome bulks having a likeness to those behemoths and giant reptiles which burdened the
Earth in earlier times; but because of the dimness he could not
tell if these were living shapes or forms that the stone had
taken.

Strong was the compulsion of his geas on Ralibar Vooz; and
a numbness had seized his mind; and he felt only a dulled fear
and a dazed wonder. It seemed that his will and his thoughts
were no longer his own, but were become those of some alien
person. He was going down to some obscure but predestined
end, by a route that was darksome but foreknown.

At last the bird Raphtontis paused and hovered signifi-
cantly in a cave distinguished from the others by a most evil
potpourri of smells. Ralibar Vooz deemed at first that the cave
was empty. Going forward to join Raphtontis, he stumbled
over certain attenuated remnants on the floor, which appeared
to be the skin-clad skeletons of men and various animals. Then,
following the coal-bright gaze of the demon bird, he discerned
in a dark recess the formless bulking of a couchant mass. And
the mass stirred a little at his approach, and put forth with infinite slothfulness a huge and toad-shaped head. And the head
opened its eyes very slightly, as if half-awakened from slumber,
so that they were visible as two slits of oozing phosphor in the
black, browless face.

Ralibar Vooz perceived an odour of fresh blood amid the
many fetors that rose to besiege his nostrils. A horror came
upon him therewith; for, looking down, he beheld lying before
the shadowy monster the lean husk of a thing that was neither
man, beast, nor Voormi. He stood hesitant, fearing to go closer
yet powerless to retreat. But, admonished by an angry hissing

from the archaeopterix, together with a slashing stroke of its beak between his shoulderblades, he went forward till he could see the fine dark fur on the dormant body and sleepily porrected head.

With new horror, and a sense of hideous doom, he heard his own voice speaking without volition: "O Lord Tsathoggua, I am the blood-offering sent by the sorcerer Ezdagor."

There was a sluggish inclination of the toad-like head; and the eyes opened a little wider, and light flowed from them in viscous tricklings on the creased under-lids. Then Ralibar Vooz seemed to hear a deep rumbling sound; but he knew not whether it reverberated in the dusky air or in his own mind. And the sound shaped itself, albeit uncouthly, into syllables and words:

"Thanks are due to Ezdagor for this offering. But, since I have fed lately on a well-blooded sacrifice, my hunger is appeased for the present, and I require not the offering. However, it may be that others of the Old Ones are athirst or famished. And, since you came here with a geas upon you, it is not fitting that you should go hence without another. So I place you under this geas, to betake yourself downward through the caverns till you reach, after long descent, that bottomless gulf over which Atlach-Nacha weaves his eternal webs. And there, calling to Atlach-Nacha, you must say: 'I am the gift sent by Tsathoggua.'"

So, with Raphtontis leading him, Ralibar Vooz departed from the presence of Tsathoggua by another route than that which had brought him there. The way steepened more and more; and it ran through chambers that were too vast for the searching of sight; and along precipices that fell sheer for an unknown distance to the black, sluggish foam and somnolent murmur of underworld seas.

At last, on the verge of a chasm whose farther shore was lost in darkness, the night-flying bird hung motionless with level wings and down-dropping tail. Ralibar Vooz went close to

the verge and saw that great webs were attached to it at intervals, seeming to span the gulf with their multiple crossings and
reticulations of grey, rope-thick strands. Apart from these, the
chasm was bridgeless. Far out on one of the webs he discerned
a darksome form, big as a crouching man but with long spiderlike members. Then, like a dreamer who hears some nightmare
sound, he heard his own voice crying loudly: "O Atlach-Nacha,
I am the gift sent by Tsathoggua."

The dark form ran toward him with incredible swiftness.
When it came near he saw that there was a kind of face on the
squat ebon body, low down amid the several-jointed legs. The
face peered up with a weird expression of doubt and inquiry;
and terror crawled through the veins of the bold huntsman as
he met the small, crafty eyes that were circled about with hair.

Thin, shrill, piercing as a sting, there spoke to him the
voice of the spider-god Atlach-Nacha: "I am duly grateful for
the gift. But, since there is no one else to bridge this chasm, and
since eternity is required for the task, I can not spend my time
in extracting you from those curious shards of metal. However,
it may be that the antehuman sorcerer Haon-Dor, who abides
beyond the gulf in his palace of primal enchantments, can
somehow find a use for you. The bridge I have just now completed runs to the threshold of his abode; and your weight will
serve to test the strength of my weaving. Go then, with this
geas upon you, to cross the bridge and present yourself before
Haon-Dor, saying: 'Atlach-Nacha has sent me.'"

With these words, the spider-god withdrew his bulk from
the web and ran quickly from sight along the chasm-edge,
doubtless to begin the construction of a new bridge at some
remoter point.

Though the third geas was heavy and compulsive upon
him, Ralibar Vooz followed Raphtontis none too willingly over
the night-bound depths. The weaving of Atlach-Nacha was
strong beneath his feet, giving and swaying only a little; but
between the strands, in unfathomable space below, he seemed

to descry the dim flitting of dragons with claw-tipped wings; and, like a seething of the darkness, fearful hulks without name appeared to heave and sink from moment to moment.

However, he and his guide came presently to the gulf's opposite shore, where the web of Atlach-Nacha was joined to the lowest step of a mighty stairway. The stairs were guarded by a coiled snake whose mottlings were broad as bucklers and whose middle volumes exceeded in girth the body of a stout warrior. The horny tail of this serpent rattled like a sistrum, and he thrust forth an evil head with fangs that were long as bill-hooks. But, seeing Raphtontis, he drew his coils aside and permitted Ralibar Vooz to ascend the steps.

Thus, in fulfillment of the third geas, the hunter entered the thousand-columned palace of Haon-Dor. Strange and silent were those halls hewn from the grey, fundamental rock of Earth. In them were faceless forms of smoke and mist that went uneasily to and fro, and statues representing monsters with myriad heads. In the vaults above, as if hung aloof in night, lamps burned with inverse flames that were like the combustion of ice and stone. A chill spirit of evil, ancient beyond all conception of man, was abroad in those halls; and horror and fear crept throughout them like invisible serpents, unknotted from sleep.

Threading the mazy chambers with the surety of one accustomed to all their windings, Raphtontis conducted Ralibar Vooz to a high room whose walls described a circle broken only by the one portal, through which he entered. The room was empty of furnishment, save for a five-pillared seat rising so far aloft without stairs or other means of approach, that it seemed only a winged being could ever attain thereto. But on the seat was a figure shrouded with thick sable darkness, and having over its head and features a caul of grisly shadow.

The bird Raphtontis hovered ominously before the columned chair. And Ralibar Vooz, in astonishment, heard a voice saying: "O Haon-Dor, Atlach-Nacha has sent me." And not till the voice had ceased speaking did he know it for his own.

For a long time the silence seemed infrangible. There was no stirring of the high-seated figure. But Ralibar Vooz, peering trepidantly at the walls about him, beheld their former smoothness embossed with a thousand faces, twisted and awry like those of mad devils. The faces were thrust forward on necks that lengthened; and behind the necks malshapen shoulders and bodies emerged inch by inch from the stone, craning toward the huntsman. And beneath his feet the very floor was now cobbled with other faces, turning and tossing restlessly, and opening ever wider their demoniacal mouths and eyes.

At last the shrouded figure spoke; and though the words were of no mortal tongue, it seemed to the listener that he comprehended them darkly:

"My thanks are due to Atlach-Nacha for this sending. If I appear to hesitate, it is only because I am doubtful regarding what disposition I can make of you. My familiars, who crowd the walls and floors of this chamber, would devour you all too readily; but you would serve only as a morsel amid so many. On the whole, I believe that the best thing I can do is to send you on to my allies, the serpent-people. They are scientists of no ordinary attainment; and perhaps you might provide some special ingredient required in their chemistries. Consider, then, that a geas has been put upon you, and take yourself off to the caverns in which the serpent-people reside."

Obeying this injunction, Ralibar Vooz went down through the darkest strata of that primeval underworld, beneath the palace of Haon-Dor. The guidance of Raphtontis never failed him; and he came anon to the spacious caverns in which the serpent-men were busying themselves with a multitude of tasks. They walked lithely and sinuously erect on pre-mammalian members, their pied, hairless bodies bending with great suppleness. There was a loud and constant hissing of formulae as they went to and fro. Some were smelting the black nether ores; some were blowing molten obsidian into forms of flask and urn; some were measuring chemicals; others were decanting strange liquids and curious colloids. In their intense preoccupation, none of them seemed to notice the arrival of Ralibar Vooz and his guide.

After the hunter had repeated many times a message given him by Haon-Dor, one of the walking reptiles at last perceived his presence. This being eyed him with cold but highly disconcerting curiosity, and then emitted a sonorous hiss that was audible above all the noises of labour and converse. The other serpent-men ceased their toil immediately and began to crowd around Ralibar Vooz. From the tone of their sibilations, it seemed that there was much argument among them. Certain of their number sidled close to the Commorian, touching his face and hands with their chill, scaly digits, and prying beneath his armor. He felt that they were anatomizing him with methodical minuteness. At the same time, he perceived that they paid no attention to Raphtontis, who had perched himself on a large alembic.

After a while, some of the chemists went away and returned quickly, bearing among them two great jars of glass filled with a clear liquid. In one of the jars there floated upright a well-developed and mature male Voormi; in the other, a large and equally perfect specimen of Hyperborean manhood, not without a sort of general likeness to Ralibar Vooz himself. The bearers of these specimens deposited their burdens beside the hunter and then each of them delivered what was doubtless a learned dissertation on comparative biology.

This series of lectures, unlike many such, was quite brief. At the end the reptilian chemists returned to their various labors, and the jars were removed. One of the scientists then addressed himself to Ralibar Vooz with a fair though somewhat sibilant approximation of human speech:

"It was thoughtful of Haon-Dor to send you here. However, as you have seen, we are already supplied with an exemplar of your species; and, in the past, we have thoroughly dissected others and have learned all that there is to learn regarding this very uncouth and aberrant life-form.

"Also, since our chemistry is devoted almost wholly to the production of powerful toxic agents, we can find no use in our tests and manufactures for the extremely ordinary matters of which your body is composed. They are without pharmaceutic value. Moreover, we have long abandoned the eating of impure natural foods, and now confine ourselves to synthetic types of aliment. There is, you must realize, no place for you in our economy.

"However, it may be that the Archetypes can somehow dispose of you. At least you will be a novelty to them, since no example of contemporary human evolution has so far descended to their stratum. Therefore we shall put you under that highly urgent and imperative kind of hypnosis which, in the parlance of warlockry, is known as a geas. And, obeying the hypnosis, you will go down to the Cavern of the Archetypes."

* * *

The region to which the magistrate of Commoriom was now conducted lay at some distance below the ophidian laboratories. The air of the gulfs and grottoes along his way began to increase markedly in warmth, and was moist and steamy as that of some equatorial fen. A primordial luminosity, such as might have dawned before the creation of any sun, seemed to surround and pervade everything.

All about him, in this thick and semi-aqueous light, the hunter discerned the rocks and fauna and vegetable forms of a crassly primitive world. These shapes were dim, uncertain, wavering, and were all composed of loosely organized elements. Even in this bizarre and more than doubtful terrain of the under-Earth, Raphtontis seemed wholly at home, and he flew on amid the sketchy plants and cloudy-looking boulders as if at no loss whatever in orienting himself. But Ralibar Vooz, in spite of the spell that stimulated and compelled him onward, had begun to feel a fatigue by no means unnatural in view of his prolonged and heroic itinerary. Also, he was much troubled by the elasticity of the ground, which sank beneath him at every step like an oversodded marsh, and seemed insubstantial to a quite alarming degree.

To his further disconcertion, the hunter soon found that he had attracted the attention of a huge foggy monster with the rough outlines of a tyrannosaurus. This creature pursued him amid the archetypal ferns and club-mosses; and overtaking him after five or six bounds, it proceeded to ingest him with the celerity of any latter-day saurian of the same species. Luckily, the ingestment was not permanent: for the tyrannosaurus' body-plasm, though fairly opaque, was more astral than material; and Ralibar Vooz, protesting stoutly against his confinement in its maw, felt the dark walls give way before him and tumbled out on the deeply resilient ground.

After its third attempt to devour him, the monster must have decided that he was inedible. It turned and went away with immense leapings in search of eatibles on its own plane of matter. Ralibar Vooz continued his progress through the Cavern of the Archetypes: a progress often delayed by the alimentary designs of crude, misty-stomached allosaurs, pterodactyls, pteranodons, stegosaurs, and other carnivora of the prime.

At last, following his experience with a most persistent megalosaur, he beheld before him two entities of vaguely human outline. These creatures were gigantic, with bodies almost globular in form, and they seemed to float rather than walk. Their features, though shadowy to the point of inchoateness, appeared to express aversion and hostility. They drew near to the Commorian, and he became aware that one of them was addressing him. The language used was wholly a matter of primitive vowel-sounds; but a meaning was forcibly, though indistinctly, conveyed:

"We, the originals of mankind, are dismayed by the sight of a copy so coarse and egregiously perverted from the true model. We disown you with sorrow and indignation. Your presence here is an unwarrantable intrusion; and it is obvious that you are not to be assimilated even by our most esurient dinosaurs. Therefore we put you under a geas: depart without delay from the Cavern of the Archetypes, and seek out the slimy gulf in which Abhoth, father and mother of all cosmic uncleanness, eternally carries on Its repugnant fission. We consider that you are fit only for Abhoth, which will perhaps mistake you for one of Its own progeny and devour you in accordance with that custom which It follows."

* * *

The weary hunter was led by the untirable Raphtontis to a deep cavern on the same level as that of the Archetypes. Possibly it was a kind of annex to the latter. At any rate, the ground was much firmer there, even though the air was murkier; and Ralibar Vooz might have recovered a little of his customary aplomb, if it had not been for the ungodly and disgusting creatures which he soon began to meet. There were things which he could liken only to monstrous one-legged toads, and immense myriad-tailed worms, and miscreated lizards. They came flopping or crawling through the gloom in a ceaseless procession; and there was no end to the loathsome morphologic variations which they displayed. Unlike the Archetypes, they were formed of all too solid matter, and Ralibar Vooz was both fatigued and nauseated by the constant necessity of kicking them away from his shins. He was somewhat relieved to find, however, that these wretched abortions became steadily smaller as he continued his advance.

The dusk about him thickened with hot, evil steam that left an oozy deposit on his armour and bare face and hands. With every breath he inhaled an odour noisome beyond imagining. He stumbled and slipped on the crawling foulnesses underfoot. Then, in that reeky twilight, he saw the pausing of

Raphtontis; and below the demoniac bird he descried a sort of
pool with a margin of mud that was marled with obscene offal;
and in the pool a greyish, horrid mass that nearly choked it
from rim to rim.

Here, it seemed, was the ultimate source of all miscreation
and abomination. For the grey mass quobbed and quivered,
and swelled perpetually; and from it, in manifold fission, were
spawned the anatomies that crept away on every side through
the grotto. There were things like bodiless legs or arms that
flailed in the slime, or heads that rolled, or floundering bellies
with fishes' fins; and all manner of things malformed and monstrous, that grew in size as they departed from the neighbour-
hood of Abhoth. And those that swam not swiftly ashore when
they fell into the pool from Abhoth, were devoured by mouths
that gaped in the parent bulk.

Ralibar Vooz was beyond thought, beyond horror, in his
weariness: else he would have known intolerable shame, seeing
that he had come to the bourn ordained for him by the
Archetypes as most fit and proper. A deadness near to death
was upon all his faculties; and he heard as if remote and high
above him a voice that proclaimed to Abhoth the reason of his
coming; and he did not know that the voice was his own.

There was no sound in answer; but out of the lumpy mass
there grew a member that stretched and lengthened toward
Ralibar Vooz where he stood waiting on the pool's margin. The
member divided to a flat, webby hand, soft and slimy, which
touched the hunter and went over his person slowly from foot
to head. Having done this, it seemed that the thing had served
its use: for it dropped quickly away from Abhoth and wriggled
into the gloom like a serpent together with the other progeny.

Still waiting, Ralibar Vooz felt in his brain a sensation as of
speech heard without words or sound; and the import, rendered in human language, was somewhat as follows:

"I, who am Abhoth, the coeval of the oldest gods, consider
that the Archetypes have shown a questionable taste in thus

recommending you to me. After careful inspection, I fail to recognize you as one of my relatives or progeny; though I must
admit that I was nearly deceived at first by certain biologic sim-
ilarities. You are quite alien to my experience; and I do not care
to endanger my digestion with untried articles of diet.

"Who you are, or whence you have come, I cannot surmise;
nor can I thank the Archetypes for troubling the profound and
placid fertility of my existence with a problem so vexatious as
the one that you offer. Get hence, I adjure you. There is a bleak
and drear and dreadful limbo, known as the Outer World, of
which I have heard dimly; and I think that it might prove a
suitable objective for your journeying. I settle an urgent geas
upon you: go seek this Outer World with all possible
expedition."

* * *

Apparently Raphtontis realized that it was beyond the
physical powers of his charge to fulfill the seventh geas without
an interim of repose. He led the hunter to one of the numerous
exits of the grotto inhabited by Abhoth: an exit giving on
regions altogether unknown, opposite to the Cavern of the
Archetypes. There, with significant gestures of his wings and
beak, the bird indicated a sort of narrow alcove in the rock. The
recess was dry and by no means uncomfortable as a sleeping-
place. Ralibar Vooz was glad to lay himself down; and a black
tide of slumber rolled upon him with the closing of his eyelids.
Raphtontis remained on guard before the alcove, discouraging
with strokes of his bill the wandering progeny of Abhoth that
tried to assail the sleeper.

Since there was neither night nor day in that subterrene
world, the term of oblivion enjoyed by Ralibar Vooz was hardly
to be measured by the usual method of time-telling. He was
aroused by the noise of vigorously flapping wings, and saw
beside him the fowl Raphtontis, holding in his beak an
unsavoury object whose anatomy was that of a fish rather than
anything else. Where or how he had caught this creature dur-

ing his constant vigil, was a more than dubious matter; but
Ralibar Vooz had fasted too long to be squeamish. He accepted
and devoured the proffered breakfast without ceremony.

After that, in conformity with the geas laid upon him by
Abhoth, he resumed his journey back to the outer Earth. The
route chosen by Raphtontis was presumably a short-cut.
Anyhow, it was remote from the cloudy cave of the Archetypes,
and the laboratories in which the serpent-men pursued their
arduous toils and toxicological researches. Also, the enchanted
palace of Haon-Dor was omitted from the itinerary. But, after
long, tedious climbing through a region of desolate crags and
over a sort of underground plateau, the traveller came once
more to the verge of that far-stretching, bottomless chasm
which was bridged only by the webs of the spider-god
Atlach-Nacha.

For some time past he had hurried his pace because of certain of the progeny of Abhoth, who had followed him from the
start and had grown steadily bigger after the fashion of their
kind, till they were now large as young tigers or bears.
However, when he approached the nearest bridge, he saw that
a ponderous and sloth-like entity, preceding him, had already
begun to cross it. The posteriors of this being were studded
with unamiable eyes, and Ralibar Vooz was unsure for a little
regarding its exact orientation. Not wishing to tread too closely
upon the reverted talons of its heels, he waited till the monster
had disappeared in the darkness; and by that time the spawn of
Abhoth were hard upon him.

Raphtontis, with sharp admonitory cawings, floated before
him above the giant web; and he was impelled to a rash haste
by the imminently slavering snouts of the dark abnormalities
behind. Owing to such precipitancy, he failed to notice that the
web had been weakened and some of its strands torn or
stretched by the weight of the sloth-like monster. Coming in
view of the chasm's opposite verge, he thought only of reaching it, and redoubled his pace. But at this point the web gave

way beneath him. He caught wildly at the broken, dangling strands, but could not arrest his fall. With several pieces of Atlach-Nacha's weaving clutched in his fingers, he was precipitated into that gulf which no one had ever voluntarily tried to plumb.

This, unfortunately, was a contingency that had not been provided against by the terms of the seventh geas.

About "The Testament of Athammaus"

This story was plotted out in April of 1930, only four months after Lovecraft's enthusiastic response to "The Tale of Satampra Zeiros" (see below), but it took him a while to get around to writing it out. In mid-February he reported to Lovecraft, "I have drafted a tale from the Commoriom myth-cycle — 'The Testament of Athammaus.'" He finished it on January 22, 1931 and mailed it off to *Weird Tales*, and, while it is almost impossible for us to imagine any editor turning down a tale by Smith (any more than Christians can imagine how anyone who heard Jesus did not immediately become his disciple!), Smith found rejection a lively danger: "I shall feel rather peeved if [*Weird Tales* editor Farnsworth] Wright turns it down; since it is about as good as I can do in the line of unearthly horror." He needn't have worried in this case, though. It appeared in the October 1932 issue of *Weird Tales*. Though it was both written and published after "The Tale of Satampra Zeiros," it is clearly intended as a prequel to that story, and in it we learn the origin and nature of that sticky being of whom Satampra Zeiros and his partner in crime run afoul. In view of this fact, it seemed worth placing "The Testament of Athammaus" before "The Tale of Satampra Zeiros" in the present collection.

As for the misbegotten Knygathin Zhaum, Smith said, "In my more civic moods, I sometimes think of the clean-up which an entity like Knygathin Zhaum would make in a modern town. I really think he (or it) is about my best monster to date" (to Lovecraft, mid-February, 1931).

The Testament of Athammaus

by Clark Ashton Smith

It has become needful for me, who am no wielder of the stylus of bronze or the pen of calamus, and whose only proper tool is the long, double-handed sword, to indite this account of the curious and lamentable happenings which foreran the universal desertion of Commoriom by its king and its people. This I am well-fitted to do, for I played a signal part in these happenings; and I left the city only when all the others had gone.

Now Commoriom, as everyone knows, was aforetime the resplendent, high-built capital, and the marble and granite crown of all Hyperborea. But, concerning the cause of its abandonment, there are now so many warring legends and so many tales of a false and fabulous character, that I, who am old in years and triply old in horrors, I, who have grown weary with no less than eleven lustrums of public service, am compelled to write this record of the truth ere it fade utterly from the tongues and memories of men. And this I do, though the telling thereof will include a confession of my one defeat, my one failure in the dutiful administration of a committed task.

For those who will read the narrative in future years, and haply in future lands, I shall now introduce myself. I am Athammaus, the chief headsman of Uzuldaroum, who held formerly the same office in Commoriom. My father, Manghai Thal, was headsman before me; and the sires of my father, even to the mythic generations of the primal kings, have wielded the great copper sword of justice on the block of *eighon*-wood.

Forgive an aged man if he seem to dwell, as is the habit of the old, among the youthful recollections that have gathered to themselves the kingly purple of removed horizons and the strange glory that illumines irretrievable things. Lo! I am made young again when I recall Commoriom, when in this grey city of the sunken years I behold in retrospect her walls that looked mountainously down upon the jungle, and the alabastrine multitude of her heavenfretting spires. Opulent among cities, and superb and magisterial, and paramount over all was Commoriom, to whom tribute was given from the shores of the Atlantean sea to that sea in which is the immense continent of Mu; to whom the traders came from utmost Thulan that is walled on the north with unknown ice, and from the southern realm of Tscho Vulpanomi which ends in a lake of boiling asphaltum. Ah! proud and lordly was Commoriom, and her humblest dwellings were more than the palaces of other cities. And it was not, as men fable now-adays, because of that maundering prophecy once uttered by the White Sybil from the isle of snow which is named Polarion, that her splendor and spaciousness was delivered over to the spotted vines of the jungle and the spotted snakes. Nay, it was because of a direr thing than this, and a tangible horror against which the law of kings, the wisdom of hierophants and the sharpness of swords were alike impotent. Ah! not lightly was she overcome, not easily were her defenders driven forth. And though others forget, or haply deem her no more than a vain and dubitable tale, I shall never cease to lament Commoriom.

My sinews have dwindled grievously now; and Time has drunken stealthily from my veins; and has touched my hair with the ashes of suns extinct. But in the days whereof I tell, there was no braver and more stalwart headsman than I in the whole of Hyperborea; and my name was a red menace, a loudly spoken warning to the evil-doers of the forest and the town,

and the savage robbers of uncouth outland tribes. Wearing the
blood-bright purple of my office, I stood each morning in the
public square where all might attend and behold, and performed for the edification of all men my allotted task. And each
day the tough, golden-ruddy copper of the huge crescent blade
was darkened not once but many times with a rich and
wine-like sanguine. And because of my never-faltering arm, my
infallible eye, and the clean blow which there was never any
necessity to repeat, I was much honored by the King
Loquamethros and by the populace of Commoriom.

I remember well, on account of their more than unique
atrocity, the earliest rumors that came to me in my active life
regarding the outlaw Knygathin Zhaum. This person belonged
to an obscure and highly unpleasant people called the Voormis,
who dwelt in the black Eiglophian Mountains at a full day's
journey from Commoriom, and inhabited according to their
tribal custom the caves of ferine animals less savage than themselves, which they had slain or otherwise dispossessed. They
were generally looked upon as more beast-like than human,
because of their excessive hairiness and the vile, ungodly rites
and usages to which they were addicted. It was mainly from
among these beings that the notorious Knygathin Zhaum had
recruited his formidable band, who were terrorizing the hills
sub-jacent to the Eiglophian Mountains with daily deeds of the
most infamous and iniquitous rapine. Wholesale robbery was
the least of their crimes; and mere anthropophagism was far
from being the worst.

It will readily be seen, from this, that the Voormis were a
somewhat aboriginal race, with an ethnic heritage of the darkest and most revolting type. And it was commonly said that
Knygathin Zhaum himself possessed an even murkier strain of
ancestry than the others, being related on the maternal side to
that queer, non-anthropomorphic god, Tsathoggua, who was
worshipped so widely during the sub-human cycles. And there
were those who whispered of even stranger blood (if one could

properly call it blood) and a monstrous linkage with the swart
Protean spawn that had come down with Tsathoggua from
elder worlds and exterior dimensions where physiology and
geometry had both assumed an altogether inverse trend of
development. And, because of this mingling of ultra-cosmic
strains, it was said that the body of Knygathin Zhaum, unlike
his shaggy, umber-colored fellow-tribesmen, was hairless from
crown to heel and was pied with great spots of black and yellow; and moreover he himself was reputed to exceed all others
in his cruelty and cunning.

For a long time this execrable outlaw was no more to me
than an horrific name; but inevitably I thought of him with a
certain professional interest. There were many who believed
him invulnerable by any weapon, and who told of his having
escaped in a manner which none could elucidate from more
than one dungeon whose walls were not to be scaled or pierced
by mortal beings. But of course I discounted all such tales, for
my official experience had never yet included anyone with
properties or abilities of a like sort. And I knew well the super-
stitiousness of the vulgar multitude.

From day to day new reports reached me amid the preoc-
cupations of never-slighted duty. This noxious marauder was
not content with the seemingly ample sphere of operations
afforded by his native mountains and the outlying hill-regions
with their fertile valleys and well-peopled towns. His forays
became bolder and more extensive; till one night he descended
on a village so near to Commoriom that it was usually classed
as a suburb. Here he and his fecule crew committed numerous
deeds of an unspecifiable enormity; and bearing with them
many of the villagers for purposes even less designable, they
retired to their caves in the glassy-walled Eiglophian peaks ere
the ministers of justice could overtake them.

It was this audaciously offensive act which prompted the
law to exert its full power and vigilance against Knygathin
Zhaum. Before that, he and his men had been left to the local

officers of the country-side; but now his misdeeds were such as
to demand the rigorous attention of the constabulary of
Commoriom. Henceforth all his movements were followed as
closely as possible; the towns where he might descend were
strictly guarded; and traps were set everywhere.

Even thus, Knygathin Zhaum contrived to evade capture
for month after month; and all the while he repeated his
far-flung raids with an embarrassing frequency. It was almost
by chance, or through his own foolhardiness, that he was eventually taken in broad daylight on the highway near the city's
outskirts. Contrary to all expectation, in view of his renowned
ferocity, he made no resistance whatever; but finding himself
surrounded by mailed archers and bill-bearers, he yielded to
them at once with an oblique, enigmatic smile — a smile that
troubled for many nights thereafter the dreams of all who were
present.

For reasons which were never explained, he was altogether
alone when taken; and none of his fellows were captured either
co-incidentally or subsequently. Nevertheless, there was much
excitement and jubilation in Commoriom, and everyone was
curious to behold the dreaded outlaw. More even than others,
perhaps, I felt the stirrings of interest; for upon me, in due
course, the proper decapitation of Knygathin Zhaum would
devolve.

From hearing the hideous rumors and legends whose
nature I have already outlined, I was prepared for something
out of the ordinary in the way of criminal personality. But even
at first sight, when I watched him as he was borne to prison
through a moiling crowd, Knygathin Zhaum surpassed the
most sinister and disagreeable anticipations. He was naked to
the waist, and wore the fulvous hide of some long-haired animal which hung in filthy tatters to his knees. Such details, however, contributed little to those elements in his appearance
which revolted and even shocked me. His limbs, his body, his
lineaments were outwardly formed like those of aboriginal

man; and one might even have allowed for his utter hairless-
ness, in which there was a remote and blasphemously caricat-
ural suggestion of the shaven priest; and even the broad, formless mottling of his skin, like that of a huge boa, might somehow have been glossed over as a rather extravagant peculiarity
of pigmentation. It was something else, it was the unctuous,
verminous ease, the undulant litheness and fluidity of his every
movement, seeming to hint at an inner structure and vertebration that were less than human — or, one might almost have
said, a sub-ophidian lack of all bony frame-work — which
made me view the captive, and also my incumbent task, with
an unparallelable distaste. He seemed to slither rather than
walk; and the very fashion of his jointure, the placing of knees,
hips, elbows and shoulders, appeared arbitrary and factitious.
One felt that the outward semblance of humanity was a mere
concession to anatomical convention; and that his corporeal
formation might easily have assumed — and might still assume
at any instant — the unheard-of outlines and concept-defying
dimensions that prevail in trans-galactic worlds. Indeed, I
could now believe the outrageous tales concerning his ancestry.
And with equal horror and curiosity I wondered what the
stroke of justice would reveal, and what noisome, mephitic
ichor would befoul the impartial sword in lieu of honest blood.

It is needless to record in circumstantial detail the process
by which Knygathin Zhaum was tried and condemned for his
manifold enormities. The workings of the law were implacably
swift and sure, and their equity permitted of no quibbling or
delay. The captive was confined in an oubliette below the main
dungeons — a cell hewn in the basic, Archean gneiss at a profound depth, with no entrance other than a hole through which
he was lowered and drawn up by means of a long rope and
windlass. This hole was lidded with a huge block and was
guarded day and night by a dozen men-at-arms. However,
there was no attempt at escape on the part of Knygathin
Zhaum: indeed, he seemed unnaturally resigned to his prospec-

tive doom. To me, who have always been possessed of a strain
of prophetic intuition, there was something overtly ominous in
this unlooked-for resignation. Also, I did not like the demeanor
of the prisoner during his trial. The silence which he had preserved at all times following his capture and incarceration was
still maintained before his judges. Though interpreters who
knew the harsh, sibilant Eiglophian dialect were provided, he
would make no answer to questions; and he offered no defense.
Least of all did I like the unabashed and unblinking manner in
which he received the final pronouncement of death which was
uttered in the high court of Commoriom by eight judges in
turn and solemnly re-affirmed at the end by King
Loquamethros. After that, I looked well to the sharpening of
my sword, and promised myself that I would concentrate all
the resources of a brawny arm and a flawless manual artistry
upon the forthcoming execution.

My task was not long deferred, for the usual interval of a
fortnight between condemnation and decapitation had been
shortened to three days in view of the suspicious pecularities of
Knygathin Zhaum and the heinous magnitude of his proven
crimes.

On the morning appointed, after a night that had been rendered dismal by a long-drawn succession of the most abominable dreams, I went with my unfailing punctuality to the
block of *eighon*-wood, which was situated with geometrical
exactness in the center of the main square. Here a huge crowd
had already gathered; and the clear amber sun blazed royally
down on the silver and nacarat of court dignitaries, the hodden
of merchants and artisans, and the rough pelts that were worn
by outland people.

With a like punctuality, Knygathin Zhaum soon appeared
amid his entourage of guards, who surrounded him with a
bristling hedge of bill-hooks and lances and tridents. At the
same time, all the outer avenues of the city, as well as the
entrances to the square, were guarded by massed soldiery, for it

was feared that the uncaught members of the desperate outlaw band might make an effort to rescue their infamous chief at the last moment.

Amid the unremitting vigilance of his warders, Knygathin Zhaum came forward, fixing upon me the intent but inexpressive gaze of his lidless, ochre-yellow eyes, in which a face-to-face scrutiny could discern no pupils. He knelt down beside the block, presenting his mottled nape without a tremor. As I looked upon him with a calculating eye, and made ready for the lethal stroke, I was impressed more powerfully and more disagreeably than ever by the feeling of a loathsome, underlying plasticity, an invertebrate structure, nauseous and non-terrestrial, beneath his impious mockery of human form. And I could not help perceiving also the air of abnormal coolness, of abstract, impenetrable cynicism, that was maintained by all his parts and members. He was like a torpid snake, or some huge liana of the jungle, that is wholly unconscious of the shearing axe. I was well aware that I might be dealing with things which were beyond the ordinary province of a public headsman; but nathless I lifted the great sword in a clean, symmetrically flashing arc, and brought it down on the piebald nape with all of my customary force and address.

Necks differ in the sensations which they afford to one's hand beneath the penetrating blade. In this case, I can only say that the sensation was not such as I have grown to associate with the cleaving of any known animal substance. But I saw with relief that the blow had been successful: the head of Knygathin Zhaum lay cleanly severed on the porous block, and his body sprawled on the pavement without even a single quiver of departing animation. As I had expected, there was no blood — only a black, tarry, fetid exudation, far from copious, which ceased in a few minutes and vanished utterly from my sword and from the *eighon*-wood. Also, the inner anatomy which the blade had revealed was devoid of all legitimate vertebration. But to all appearance Knygathin Zhaum had yielded up his obscene life; and the sentence of King Loquamethros and the eight judges of Commoriorn had been fulfilled with a legal precision.

Proudly but modestly I received the applause of the waiting multitudes, who bore willing witness to the consummation of my official task and were loudly jubilant over the dead scourge. After seeing that the remains of Knygathin Zhaum were given into the hands of the public grave-diggers, who always disposed of such offal, I left the square and returned to my home, since no other decapitations had been set for that day. My conscience was serene, and I felt that I had acquitted myself worthily in the performance of a far from pleasant duty.

Knygathin Zhaum, as was the custom in dealing with the bodies of the most nefarious criminals, was interred with contumelious haste in a barren field outside the city where people cast their orts and rubbish. He was left in an unmarked and unmounded grave between two middens. The power of the law had now been amply vindicated; and everyone was satisfied, from Loquamethros himself to the villagers that had suffered from the depredations of the deceased outlaw.

I retired that night, after a bounteous meal of *suvana*-fruit and *djongua*-beans, well-irrigated with *foum*-wine. From a moral standpoint, I had every reason to sleep the sleep of the virtuous; but, even as on the preceding night, I was made the victim of one cacodemoniacal dream after another. Of these dreams, I recall only their pervading, unifying consciousness of insufferable suspense, of monotonously cumulative horror without shape or name; and the ever-torturing sentiment of vain repetition and dark, hopeless toil and frustration. Also, there is a half-memory, which refuses to assume any approach to visual form, of things that were never intended for human perception or human cogitation; and the aforesaid sentiment, and all the horror, were dimly but indissolubly bound up with these. Awaking unrefreshed and weary from what seemed an aeon of thankless endeavor, of treadmill bafflement, I could only impute my nocturnal sufferings to the *djongua*-beans; and decided that I must have eaten all too liberally of these nutritious viands. Mercifully, I did not suspect in my dreams the dark, portentous symbolism that was soon to declare itself.

Now must I write the things that are formidable unto Earth and the dwellers of Earth; the things that exceed all human or terrene regimen; that subvert reason; that mock the dimensions and defy biology. Dire is the tale; and, after seven lustrums, the tremor of an olden fear still agitates my hand as I write.

But of such things I was still oblivious when I sallied forth that morning to the place of execution, where three criminals of a quite average sort, whose very cephalic contours I have forgotten along with their offenses, were to meet their well-deserved doom beneath my capable arm. Howbeit, I had not gone far when I heard an unconscionable uproar that was spreading swiftly from street to street, from alley to alley throughout Commoriom. I distinguished a myriad cries of rage, horror, fear and lamentation that were seemingly caught up and repeated by everyone who chanced to be abroad at that hour. Meeting some of the citizenry, who were plainly in a state of the most excessive agitation and were still continuing their outcries, I inquired the reason of all this clamor. And thereupon I learned from them that Knygathin Zhaum, whose illicit career was presumably at an end, had now re-appeared and had signalized the unholy miracle of his return by the commission of a most appalling act on the main avenue before the very eyes of early passers! He had seized a respectable seller of *djongua*-beans, and had proceeded instantly to devour his victim alive without heeding the blows, bricks, arrows, javelins, cobblestones and curses that were rained upon him by the gathering throng and by the police. It was only when he had satisfied his atrocious appetite, that he suffered the police to lead him away, leaving little more than the bones and raiment of the *djongua*-seller to mark the spot of this outrageous hap-

pening. Since the case was without legal parallel, Knygathin
Zhaum had been thrown once more into the oubliette below
the city dungeons, to await the will of Loquamethros and the
eight judges.

The exceeding discomfiture, the profound embarrassment
felt by myself, as well as by the people and the magistracy of
Commoriom, can well be imagined. As everyone bore witness,
Knygathin Zhaum had been efficiently beheaded and buried
according to the customary ritual; and his resurrection was not
only against nature but involved a most contumelious and
highly mystifying breach of the law. In fact, the legal aspects of
the case were such as to render necessary the immediate passing of a special statute, calling for re-judgement, and allowing
re-execution, of such malefactors as might thus-wise return
from their lawful graves. Apart from all this, there was general
consternation; and even at that early date, the more ignorant
and more religious among the townsfolk were prone to regard
the matter as an omen of some impending civic calamity.

As for me, my scientific turn of mind, which repudiated the
supernatural, led me to seek an explanation of the problem in
the non-terrestrial side of Knygathin Zhaum's ancestry. I felt
sure that the forces of an alien biology, the properties of a
transtellar lifesubstance, were somehow involved.

With the spirit of the true investigator, I summoned the
gravediggers who had interred Knygathin Zhaum and bade
them lead me to his place of sepulture in the refuse-grounds.
Here a most singular condition disclosed itself. The earth had
not been disturbed, apart from a deep hole at one end of the
grave, such as might have been made by a large rodent. No
body of human size, or, at least, of human form, could possibly
have emerged from this hole. At my command, the diggers
removed all the loose soil, mingled with potsherds and other
rubbish, which they had heaped upon the beheaded outlaw.
When they reached the bottom, nothing was found but a slight
stickiness where the corpse had lain; and this, along with an

odor of ineffable foulness which was its concomitant, soon dissipated itself in the open air.

Baffled, and more mystified than ever, but still sure that
the enigma would permit of some natural solution, I awaited
the new trial. This time, the course of justice was even quicker
and less given to quibbling than before. The prisoner was again
condemned, and the time of decapitation was delayed only till
the following morn. A proviso concerning burial was added to
the sentence: the remains were to be sealed in a strong wooden
sarcophagus, the sarcophagus was to be inhumed in a deep pit
in the solid stone, and the pit filled with massy boulders. These
measures, it was felt, should serve amply to restrain the
unwholesome and irregular inclinations of this obnoxious
miscreant.

When Knygathin Zhaum was again brought before me,
amid a redoubled guard and a throng that overflowed the
square and all of the outlying avenues, I viewed him with profound concern and with more than my former repulsion.
Having a good memory for anatomic details, I noticed some
odd changes in his physique. The huge splotches of dull black
and sickly yellow that had covered him from head to heel were
now somewhat differently distributed. The shifting of the facial
blotches, around the eyes and mouth, had given him an expression that was both grim and sardonic to an unbearable degree.
Also, there was a perceptible shortening of his neck, though the
place of cleavage and re-union, midway between head and
shoulders, had left no mark whatever. And looking at his limbs,
I discerned other and more subtle changes. Despite my acumen
in physical matters, I found myself unwilling to speculate
regarding the processes that might underlie these alterations;
and still less did I wish to surmise the problematic results of
their continuation, if such should ensue. Hoping fervently that
Knygathin Zhaum and the vile, flagitious properties of his
unhallowed carcass would now be brought to a permanent end,

I raised the sword of justice high in air and smote with heroic might.

Once again, as far as mortal eye was able to determine, the effects of the shearing blow were all that could be desired. The head rolled forward on the *eighon*-wood, and the torso and its members fell and lay supinely on the maculated flags. From a legal view-point, this doubly nefandous malefactor was now twice-dead.

Howbeit, this time I superintended in person the disposal of the remains, and saw to the bolting of the fine sarcophagus of *apha*-wood in which they were laid, and the filling with chosen boulders of the ten-foot pit into which the sarcophagus was lowered. It required three men to lift even the least of these boulders. We all felt that the irrepressible Knygathin Zhaum was due for a quietus.

Alas! for the vanity of earthly hopes and labors! The morrow came with its unspeakable, incredible tale of renewed outrage: once more the weird, semi-human offender was abroad, once more his anthropophagic lust had taken toll from among the honorable denizens of Commoriom. He had eaten no less a personage than one of the eight judges; and, not satisfied with picking the bones of this rather obese individual, had devoured by way of dessert the more outstanding facial features of one of the police who had tried to deter him from finishing his main course. All this, as before, was done amid the frantic protests of a great throng. After a final nibbling at the scant vestiges of the unfortunate constable's left ear, Knygathin Zhaum had seemed to experience a feeling of repletion and had suffered himself to be led docilely away once more by the jailers.

I, and the others who had helped me in the arduous toils of entombment, were more than astounded when we heard the news. And the effect on the general public was indeed deplorable. The more superstitious and timid began leaving the city forthwith; and there was much revival of forgotten prophecies; and much talk among the various priesthoods anent the necessity of placating with liberal sacrifice their mystically angered gods and eidolons. Such nonsense I was wholly able to disregard; but, under the circumstances, the persistent return of Knygathin Zhaum was no less alarming to science than to religion.

We examined the tomb, if only as a matter of form; and found that certain of the superincumbent boulders had been displaced in such a manner as to admit the outward passage of a body with the lateral dimensions of some large snake or musk-rat. The sarcophagus, with its metal bolts, was bursten at one end; and we shuddered to think of the immeasurable force that must have been employed in its disruption.

Because of the way in which the case overpassed all known biologic laws, the formalities of civil law were now waived; and I, Athammaus, was called upon that same day before the sun had reached its meridian, and was solemnly charged with the office of re-beheading Knygathin Zhaurn at once. The interment or other disposal of the remains was left to my discretion; and the local soldiery and constabulary were all placed at my command, if I should require them.

Deeply conscious of the honor thus implied, and sorely perplexed but undaunted, I went forth to the scene of my labors. When the criminal re-appeared, it was obvious not only to me but to everyone that his physical personality, in achieving this new recrudescence, had undergone a most salient change. His mottling had developed more than a suggestion of some startling and repulsive pattern; and his human characteristics had yielded to the inroads of an unearthly distortion. The head was joined to the shoulders almost without the intermediation of a neck; the eyes were set diagonally in a face with oblique bulgings and flattenings; the nose and mouth were showing a tendency to displace each other; and there were still further alterations which I shall not specify, since they involved an abhorrent degradation of man's noblest and most distinctive corporeal members. I shall, however, mention the strange, pendulous formations, like annulated dew-laps or wattles, into which his knee-caps had evolved. Nathless, it was Knygathin Zhaum himself who stood (if one could dignify the fashion of his carriage by that word) before the block of justice.

Because of the virtual non-existence of a nape, the third beheading called for a precision of eye and a nicety of hand which, in all likelihood, no other headsman than myself could have shown. I rejoice to say that my skill was adequate to the demand thus made upon it; and once again the culprit was shorn of his vile cephaloid appendage. But if the blade had gone even a little to either side, the dismemberment entailed would have been technically of another sort than decapitation.

The laborious care with which I and my assistants conducted the third inhumation was indeed deserving of success. We laid the body in a strong sarcophagus of bronze, and the head in a second but smaller sarcophagus of the same material. The lids were then soldered down with molten metal; and after this the two sarcophagi were conveyed to opposite parts of Commoriom. The one containing the body was buried at a great depth beneath monumental masses of stone; but that which enclosed the head I left uninterred, proposing to watch over it all night in company with a guard of armed men. I also appointed a numerous guard to keep vigil above the burial-place of the body.

Night came; and with seven trusty trident-bearers I went forth to the place where we had left the smaller of the two sarcophagi. This was in the courtyard of a deserted mansion amid the suburbs, far from the haunts of the populace. For weapons, I myself wore a short falchion and carried a great bill. We took along a plentiful supply of torches, so that we might not lack for light in our gruesome vigil; and we lit several of them at once and stuck them in crevices between the flag-stones of the court, in such wise that they formed a circle of lurid flames about the sarcophagus.

We had also brought with us an abundance of the crimson *foum*-wine in leathern bottles, and dice of mammoth-ivory with which to beguile the black nocturnal hours; and eyeing our charge with a casual but careful vigilance, we applied ourselves discreetly to the wine and began to play for small sums of no more than five *pazoors*, as is the wont of good gamblers till they have taken their opponents' measure.

The darkness deepened apace; and in the square of sapphire overhead, to which the illumination of our torches had given a jetty tinge, we saw Polaris and the red planets that looked down for the last time on Commoriom in her glory. But we dreamed not of the nearness of disaster, but jested bravely and drank in ribald mockery to the monstrous head that was now so securely coffined and so remotely sundered from its odious body. The wine passed and re-passed among us; and its rosy spirit mounted in our brains; and we played for bolder stakes; and the game quickened to a goodly frenzy.

I know not how many stars had gone over us in the smoky heavens, nor how many times I had availed myself of the ever-circling bottles. But I remember well that I had won no less than ninety *pazoors* from the trident-bearers, who were all swearing lustily and loudly as they strove in vain to stem the tide of my victory. I, as well as the others, had wholly forgotten the object of our vigil.

The sarcophagus containing the head was one that had been primarily designed for the reception of a small child. Its present use, one might have argued, was a sinful and sacrilegious waste of fine bronze; but nothing else of proper size and adequate strength was available at the time. In the mounting fervor of the game, as I have hinted, we had all ceased to watch this receptacle; and I shudder to think how long there may have been something visibly or even audibly amiss before the unwonted and terrifying behavior of the sarcophagus was forced upon our attention. It was the sudden, loud, metallic clangor, like that of a smitten gong or shield, which made us

realize that all things were not as they should have been; and
turning unanimously in the direction of the sound, we saw that
the sarcophaghus was heaving and pitching in a most unseemly
fashion amid its ring of flaring torches. First on one end or corner, then on another, it danced and pirouetted, clanging reso-
nantly all the while on the granite pavement.

The true horror of the situation had scarcely seeped into
our brains, ere a new and even more ghastly development
occurred. We saw that the casket was bulging ominously at top
and sides and bottom, and was rapidly losing all similitude to
its rightful form. Its rectangular outlines swelled and curved
and were horribly erased as in the changes of a nightmare, till
the thing became a slightly oblong sphere; and then, with a
most appalling noise, it began to split at the welded edges of
the lid, and burst violently asunder. Through the long, ragged
rift there poured in hellish ebullition a dark, ever-swelling mass
of incognizable matter, frothing as with the venomous foam of
a million serpents, hissing as with the yeast of fermenting wine,
and putting forth here and there great sooty-looking bubbles
that were large as pig-bladders. Overturning several of the
torches, it rolled in an inundating wave across the flagstones
and we all sprang back in the most abominable fright and stu-
pefaction to avoid it.

Cowering against the rear wall of the courtyard, while the
overthrown torches flickered wildly and smokily, we watched
the remarkable actions of the mass, which had paused as if to
collect itself, and was now subsiding like a sort of infernal
dough. It shrank, it fell in, till after awhile its dimensions began
to re-approach those of the encoffined head, though they still
lacked any true semblance of its shape. The thing became a
round, blackish ball, on whose palpitating surface the nascent
outlines of random features were limned with the flatness of a
drawing. There was one lidless eye, tawny, pupilless and phos-
phoric, that stared upon us from the center of the ball while the
thing appeared to be making up its mind. It lay still for more

than a minute; then, with a catapulting bound, it sprang past us toward the open entrance of the courtyard, and disappeared from our ken on the midnight streets.

Despite our amazement and disconcertion, we were able to note the general direction in which it had gone. This, to our further terror and confoundment, was toward the portion of Commoriom in which the body of Knygathin Zhaum had been intombed. We dared not conjecture the meaning of it all, and the probable outcome. But, though there were a million fears and apprehensions to deter us, we seized our weapons and followed on the path of that unholy head with all the immediacy and all the forthrightness of motion which a goodly cargo of *foum*-wine would permit.

No one other than ourselves was abroad at an hour when even the most dissolute revellers had either gone home or had succumbed to their potations under tavern tables. The streets were dark, and were somehow drear and cheerless; and the stars above them were half-stifled as by the invading mist of a pestilential miasma. We went on, following a main street, and the pavements echoed to our tread in the stillness with a hollow sound, as if the solid stone beneath them had been honeycombed with mausolean vaults in the interim of our weird vigil.

In all our wanderings, we found no sign of that supremely noxious and execrable thing which had issued from the riven sarcophagus. Nor, to our relief, and contrary to all our fears, did we encounter anything of an allied or analogous nature, such as might be abroad if our surmises were correct. But, near the central square of Commoriom, we met with a number of men, carrying bills and tridents and torches, who proved to be the guards I had posted that evening above the tomb of Knygathin Zhaum's body. These men were in a state of pitiable agitation; and they told us a fearsome tale, of how the deep-hewn tomb and the monumental blocks of stone that were piled within it had heaved as with the throes of earthquake; and of how a python-shapen mass of frothing and hissing matter had poured

forth from amid the blocks and had vanished into the darkness
toward Commoriom. In return, we told them of that which had
happened during our vigil in the courtyard; and we all agreed
that a great foulness, a thing more baneful than beast or serpent, was again loose and ravening in the night. And we spoke
only in shocked whispers of what the morrow might declare.

Uniting our forces, we searched the city, combing cautiously its alleys and its thoroughfares and dreading with the
dread of brave men the dark, iniquitous spawn on which the
light of our torches might fall at any turn or in any nook or portal. But the search was vain; and the stars grew faint above us
in a livid sky; and the dawn came in among the marble spires
with a glimmering of ghostly silver; and a thin, phantasmal
amber was sifted on walls and pavements.

Soon there were footsteps other than ours that echoed
through the town; and one by one the familiar clangors and
clamors of life awoke. Early passers appeared; and the sellers of
fruits and milk and legumes came in from the country-side. But
of that which we sought there was still no trace.

We went on, while the city continued to resume its matuti-
nal activities around us. Then, abruptly, with no warning, and
under circumstances that would have startled the most robust
and affrayed the most valorous, we came upon our quarry. We
were entering the square in which was the *eighon*-block
whereon so many thousand miscreants had laid their piacular
necks, when we heard an outcry of mortal dread and agony
such as only one thing in the world could have occasioned.
Hurrying on, we saw that two wayfarers, who had been crossing the square near the block of justice, were struggling and
writhing in the clutch of an unequalled monster which both
natural history and fable would have repudiated.

In spite of the baffling, ambiguous oddities which the thing
displayed, we identified it as Knygathin Zhaum when we drew
closer the head, in its third re-union with that detestable torso,
had attached itself in a semi-flattened manner to the region of

the lower chest and diaphragm; and during the process of this
novel coalescence, one eye had slipped away from all relation
with its fellow on the head and was now occupying the navel,
just below the embossment of the chin. Other and even more
shocking alterations had occurred: the arms had lengthened
into tentacles, with fingers that were like knots of writhing
vipers; and where the head would normally have been, the
shoulders had reared themselves to a cone-shaped eminence
that ended in a cup-like mouth. Most fabulous and impossible
of all, however, were the changes in the nether limbs: at each
knee and hip, they had re-bifurcated into long, lithe pro-
boscides that were lined with throated suckers. By making a
combined use of its various mouths and members, the abnormality was devouring both of the hapless persons whom it had
seized.

Drawn by the outcries, a crowd gathered behind us as we
neared this atrocious tableau. The whole city seemed to fill with
a wellnigh instantaneous clamor, an ever-swelling hubbub, in
which the dominant note was one of supreme, all-devastating
terror.

I shall not speak of our feelings as officers and men. It was
plain to us that the ultra-mundane factors in Knygathin
Zhaum's ancestry had asserted themselves with a hideously
accelerative ratio, following his latest resurrection. But, despite
this, and the wholly stupendous enormity of the miscreation
before us, we were still prepared to fulfill our duty and defend
as best we could the helpless populace. I boast not of the hero-
ism required: we were simple men, and should have done only
that which we were visibly called upon to do.

We surrounded the monster, and would have assailed it
immediately with our bills and tridents. But here an embarrassing difficulty disclosed itself: the creature before us had
entwined itself so tortuously and inextricably with its prey, and
the whole group was writhing and tossing so violently, that we
could not use our weapons without grave danger of impaling or

otherwise injuring our two fellow-citizens. At length, however,
the strugglings and heavings grew less vehement, as the substance and life-blood of the men consumed; and the loathsome
mass of devourer and devoured became gradually quiescent.

Now, if ever, was our opportunity; and I am sure we should
all have rallied to the attack, useless and vain as it would certainly have been. But plainly the monster had grown weary of
all such trifling and would no longer submit himself to the
petty annoyance of human molestation. As we raised our
weapons and made ready to strike, the thing drew back, still
carrying its vein-drawn, flaccid victims, and climbed upon the
eighon-block. Here, before the eyes of all assembled, it began to
swell in every part, in every member, as if it were inflating itself
with a superhuman rancor and malignity. The rate at which the
swelling progressed, and the proportions which the thing
attained as it covered the block from sight and lapsed down on
every side with undulating, inundating folds, would have been
enough to daunt the heroes of remotest myth. The bloating of
the main torso, I might add, was more lateral than vertical.
When the abnormality began to present dimensions that were
beyond those of any creature of this world, and to bulge aggres-
sively toward us with a slow, interminable stretching of
boa-like arms, my valiant and redoubtable companions were
scarcely to be censured for retreating. And even less can I
blame the general population, who were now evacuating
Commoriom in torrential multitudes, with shrill cries and wail-
ings. Their flight was no doubt accelerated by the vocal sounds,
which, for the first time during our observation, were being
emitted by the monster. These sounds partook of the character
of hissings more than anything else; but their volume was overpowering, their timbre was a torment and a nausea to the ear;
and, worst of all, they were issuing not only from the diaphrag-
mic mouth but from each of the various other oral openings or
suckers which the horror had developed. Even I, Athammaus,

drew back from those hissings and stood well beyond reach of the coiling serpentine fingers.

I am proud to say, however, that I lingered on the edge of the empty square for some time, with more than one backward and regretful glance. The thing that had been Knygathin Zhaum was seemingly content with its triumph; and it brooded supine and mountainous above the vanquished *eighon*-block. Its myriad hisses sank to a slow, minor sibilation such as might issue from a family of somnolent pythons; and it made no overt attempt to assail or even approach me. But seeing at last that the professional problem which it offered was quite insoluble; and divining moreover that Commoriom was by now entirely without a king, a judicial system, a constabulary or a people, I finally abandoned the doomed city and followed the others. 🕸

About "The Tale of Satampra Zeiros"

Smith completed this story on November 16, 1929, and professed to be quite pleased with it, calling it "one of my best." Lovecraft agreed; only three weeks after Smith finished writing it, Lovecraft commented:

> I must not delay expressing my well-nigh delirious delight at "The Tale of Satampra Zeiros" — which has veritably given me the one arch-kick of 1929! Yug! n'gha k'yun bth-gth R'lyeh gllur ph'ngui Cthulhu yzkaa . . . what an atmosphere! I can see & feel & smell the jungle around immemorial Commoriom, which I am sure must lie buried today in glacial ice near Olathoë, in the land of Lomar! It is of this crux of elder horror, I am certain, that the mad Arab Abdul Alhazred was thinking when he — even he — left something unmention'd & signify'd by a row of stars in the surviving codex of his accursed & forbidden Necronomicon! You have achieved in its fullest glamour the exact Dunsanian touch which I find it almost impossible to duplicate, & I am sure that even the incomparable Nuth would have been glad to own Satampra Zeiros as his master. Altogether, I think this comes close to being your high spot in prose fiction to date — for Zothar's sake keep it up . . . my anticipations assume fantastic proportions! (December 3, 1929).

The Dunsanian influences upon the tale are clear, not solely on the lyrical, antique style, but also thematically. The abrupt desertion of Commoriom at the prophetic word of the White Sybil recalls Dunsany's "Bethmoora," while Lovecraft's reference to Dunsany's tale of ill-advised thievery "How Nuth Would Have Practised His Art upon the Gnoles" shows another likely model.

The mention of the White Sybil is one of several vestiges of the origin of Hyperborea in the Greek myths of Apollo, who was worshipped there. The Sybils were ancient oracles of Apollo, god of prophecy. Another hint of the Greek background of Smith's Hyperborea is to be found in many of his coined names, which often have a Greek ring to them (*e.g.*, Zeiros). The name Ompallios is no doubt based on the Greek *omphalos*, bellybutton, Apollo's oracular shrine at Delphi was built around the *omphalos*-stone, beleived to be the world's center.

"The Tale of Satampra Zeiros" appeared almost exactly two years after Smith wrote it, in the November 1931 issue of *Weird Tales*.

The Tale of Satampra Zeiros

by Clark Ashton Smith

I Satampra Zeiros of Uzuldaroum, shall write with my left hand, since I have no longer any other, the tale of everything that befell Tirouv Ompallios and myself in the shrine of the god Tsathoggua, which lies neglected by the worship of man in the jungle-taken suburbs of Commoriom, that long-deserted capital of the Hyperborean rulers. I shall write it with the violet juice of the *suvana*-palm, which turns to a blood-red rubric with the passage of years, on a strong vellum that is made from the skin of the mastodon, as a warning to all good thieves and adventurers who may hear some lying legend of the lost treasures of Commoriom and be tempted thereby.

Now, Tirouv Ompallios was my life-long friend and my trustworthy companion in all such enterprises as require deft fingers and a habit of mind both agile and adroit. I can say without flattering myself, or Tirouv Ompallios either, that we carried to an incomparable success more than one undertaking from which fellow-craftsmen of a much wider renown than ourselves might well have recoiled in dismay. To be more explicit, I refer to the theft of the jewels of Queen Cunambria, which were kept in a room where two-score venomous reptiles wandered at will; and the breaking of the adamantine box of Acromi, in which were all the medallions of an early dynasty of Hyperborean kings. It is true that these medallions were difficult and perilous to dispose of, and that we sold them at a dire

sacrifice to the captain of a barbarian vessel from remote
Lemuria: but nevertheless, the breaking of that box was a glorious feat, for it had to be done in absolute silence, on account
of the proximity of a dozen guards who were all armed with tridents. We made use of a rare and mordant acid . . . but I must
not linger too long and too garrulously by the way, however
great the temptation to ramble on amid heroic memories and
the high glamor of valiant or sleightful deeds.

In our occupation, as in all others, the vicissitudes of fortune are oftentimes to be reckoned with; and the goddess
Chance is not always prodigal of her favors. So it was that
Tirouv Ompallios and I, at the time of which I write, had found
ourselves in a condition of pecuniary depletion, which, though
temporary, was nevertheless extreme, and was quite inconve-
nient and annoying, coming as it did on the heel of more prosperous days, of more profitable midnights. People had become
accursedly chary of their jewels and other valuables, windows
and doors were double-barred, new and perplexing locks were
in use, guards had grown more vigilant or less somnolent — in
short, all the natural difficulties of our profession had multiplied themselves. At one time we were reduced to the stealing
of more bulky and less precious merchandise than that in which
we customarily dealt; and even this had its dangers. Even now,
it humiliates me to remember the night when we were nearly
caught with a sack of red yams; and I mention all this that I
may not seem in any wise vainglorious.

One evening, in an alley of the more humble quarter of
Uzuldaroum, we stopped to count our available resources, and
found that we had between us exactly three *pazoors* — enough
to buy a large bottle of pomegranate wine or two loaves of
bread. We debated the problem of expenditure.

"The bread," contended Tirouv Ompallios, "will nurture
our bodies, will lend a new and more expeditious force to our
spent limbs, and our toilworn fingers."

"The pomegranate wine," said I, "will ennoble our thoughts, will inspire and illuminate our minds, and perchance will reveal to us a mode of escape from our present difficulties."

Tirouv Ompallios yielded without undue argument to my superior reasoning, and we sought the doors of an adjacent tavern. The wine was not of the best, in regard to flavor, but the quantity and strength were all that could be desired. We sat in the crowded tavern, and sipped it at leisure, till all the fire of the bright red liquor had transferred itself to our brains. The darkness and dubiety of our future ways became illumined as by the light of rosy cressets, and the harsh aspect of the world was marvellously softened. Anon, there came to me an inspiration.

"Tirouv Ompallios," I said, "is there any reason why you and I, who are brave men and nowise subject to the fears and superstitions of the multitude, should not avail ourselves of the kingly treasures of Commoriom? A day's journey from this tiresome town, a pleasant sojourn in the country, an afternoon or forenoon of archaeological research — and who knows what we should find?"

"You speak wisely and valiantly, my dear friend," rejoined Tirouv Ompallios. "Indeed, there is no reason why we should not replenish our deflated finances at the expense of a few dead kings or gods."

Now Commoriom, as all the world knows, was deserted many hundred years ago because of the prophecy of the White Sybil of Polarion, who foretold an undescribed and abominable doom for all mortal beings who should dare to tarry within its environs. Some say that this doom was a pestilence that would have come from the northern waste by the paths of the jungle tribes; others, that it was a form of madness; at any rate, no one, neither king nor priest nor merchant nor laborer nor thief, remained in Commoriom to abide its arrival, but all departed in a single migration to found at the distance of a day's journey the new capital, Uzuldaroum. And strange tales are told, of

horrors and terrors not to be faced or overcome by man, that
haunt forevermore the shrines and mausoleums and palaces of
Commoriom. And still it stands, a luster of marble, a magnifi-
cence of granite, all a-throng with spires and cupolas and
obelisks that the mighty trees of the jungle have not yet over-
towered, in a fertile inland valley of Hyperborea. And men say
that in its unbroken vaults there lies entire and undespoiled as
of yore the rich treasure of olden monarchs; that the high-built
tombs retain the gems and electrum that were buried with
their mummies; that the fanes have still their golden altar-ves-
sels and furnishings, the idols their precious stones in ear and
mouth and nostril and navel.

I think that we should have set out that very night, if we
had only had the encouragement and inspiration of a second
bottle of pomegranate wine. As it was, we decided to start at
early dawn: the fact that we had no funds for our journey was
of small moment, for, unless our former dexterity had altogether failed us, we could levy a modicum of involuntary tribute from the guileless folk of the country-side. In the mean-
while, we repaired to our lodgings, where the landlord met us
with a grudging welcome and a most ungracious demand for
his money. But the golden promise of the morrow had armed
us against all such trivial annoyances, and we waved the fellow
aside with a disdain that appeared to astonish if not to subdue
him.

We slept late, and the sun had ascended far upon the azure
acclivity of the heavens when we left the gates of Uzuldaroum
and took the northern road that leads toward Commoriom. We
breakfasted well on some amber melons, and a stolen fowl that
we cooked in the woods, and then resumed our wayfaring. In
spite of a fatigue that increased upon us toward the end of the
day, our trip was a pleasurable one, and we found much to
divert us in the varying landscapes through which we passed,
and in their people. Some of these people, I am sure, must still

remember us with regret, for we did not deny ourselves anything procurable that tempted our fancy or our appetites.

It was an agreeable country, full of farms and orchards and running waters and green, flowery woods. At last, somewhile in the course of the afternoon, we came to the ancient road, long disused and well-nigh overgrown, which runs from the highway through the elder jungle to Commoriom.

No one saw us enter this road, and thenceforward we met no one. At a single step, we passed from all human ken; and it seemed that the silence of the forest around us had lain unstirred by mortal footfall ever since the departure of the legendary king and his people so many centuries before. The trees were vaster than any we had ever seen; they were interwoven by the endless labyrinthine volumes, the eternal web-like convolutions of creepers almost as old as they themselves. The flowers were unwholesomely large, and their petals bore a lethal pallor or a sanguinary scarlet; and their perfumes were overpoweringly sweet or fetid. The fruits along our way were of great size, with purple and orange and russet colors, but somehow we did not dare to eat them.

The woods grew thicker and more rampant as we went on, and the road, though paved with granite slabs, was more and more overgrown, for trees had rooted themselves in the interstices, often forcing the wide blocks apart. Though the sun had not yet neared the horizon, the shades that were cast upon us from gigantic boles and branches became ever denser, and we moved in a dark-green twilight fraught with oppressive odors of lush growth and of vegetable corruption. There were no birds nor animals, such as one would think to find in any wholesome forest, but at rare intervals a stealthy viper with pale and heavy coils glided away from our feet among the rank leaves of the roadside, or some enormous moth with baroque and evil-colored mottlings flew before us and disappeared in the dimness of the jungle. Abroad already in the half-light, huge purpureal bats with eyes like tiny rubies arose at our approach from the poisonous-looking fruits on which they feasted, and watched us with malign attention as they hovered noiselessly in the air above. And we felt, somehow, that we were being watched by other and invisible presences; and a sort of awe fell upon us, and a vague fear of the monstrous jungle; and we no longer spoke aloud, or frequently, but only in rare whispers.

Among other things, we had contrived to procure along our way a large leathern bottle full of palm-spirit. A few sips of the ardent liquor had already served to lighten more than once the tedium of our journey; and now it was to stand us in good stead. Each of us drank a liberal draught, and presently the jungle became less awesome; and we wondered why we had allowed the silence and the gloom, the watchful bats and the brooding immensity, to weigh upon our spirits even for a brief while; and I think that after a second draught we began to sing.

When twilight came, and a waxing moon shone high in the heavens after the hidden daystar had gone down, we were so imbued with the fervor of adventure that we decided to push on and reach Commoriom that very night. We supped on food that we had levied from the country-people, and the leathern bottle passed between us several times. Then, considerably fortified, and replete with hardihood and the valor of a lofty enterprise, we resumed our journeying.

Indeed, we had not much farther to go. Even as we were debating between ourselves, with an ardor that made us oblivious of our long wayfaring, what costly loot we would first choose from among all the mythical treasures of Commoriom, we saw in the moonlight the gleam of marble cupolas above the tree-tops, and then between the boughs and boles the wan pillars of shadowy porticoes. A few more steps, and we trod upon paven streets that ran transversely from the high-road we were following, into the tall, luxuriant woods on either side, where the fronds of mighty palmferns overtopped the roofs of ancient houses.

We paused, and again the silence of an elder desolation claimed our lips. For the houses were white and still as sepulchers, and the deep shadows that lay around and upon them were chill and sinister and mysterious as the very shadow of death. It seemed that the sun could not have shone for ages in this place — that nothing warmer than the spectral beams of the cadaverous moon had touched the marble and granite ever since that universal migration prompted by the prophecy of the White Sybil of Polarion.

"I wish it were daylight," murmured Tirouv Ompallios. His low tones were oddly sibilant, were unnaturally audible in the dead stillness.

"Tirouv Ompallios," I replied, "I trust that you are not growing superstitious. I should be loth to think that you are succumbing to the infantile fancies of the multitude. Howbeit, let us have another drink."

We lightened the leathern bottle appreciably by the demand we now made upon its contents, and were marvellously cheered thereby — so much so, indeed, that we forthwith started to explore a left-hand avenue, which, though it had been laid out with mathematical directness, vanished at no great distance among the fronded trees. Here, somewhat apart from the other buildings, in a sort of square that the jungle had not yet wholly usurped, we found a small temple of antique architecture which gave the impression of being far older even than the adjoining edifices. It also differed from these in its material, for it was builded of a dark basaltic stone heavily encrusted with lichens that seemed of a coeval antiquity. It was square in form, and had no domes nor spires, no facade of pillars, and only a few narrow windows high above the ground. Such temples are rare in Hyperborea now-a-days; but we knew it for a shrine of Tsathoggua, one of the elder gods, who receives no longer any worship from men, but before whose ashen altars, people say, the furtive and ferocious beasts of the jungle, the ape, the giant sloth and the long-toothed tiger, have sometimes been seen to make obeisance and have been heard to howl or whine their inarticulate prayers.

The temple, like the other buildings, was in a state of well-nigh perfect preservation: the only signs of decay were in the carven lintel of the door, which had crumbled and splintered away in several places. The door itself, wrought of a swarthy bronze all overgreened by time, stood slightly a-jar. Knowing that there should be a jewelled idol within, not to mention the various altar-pieces of valuable metals, we felt the urge of temptation.

Surmising that strength might be required to force open the verdigris-covered door, we drank deeply, and then applied ourselves to the task. Of course, the hinges were rusted; and only by dint of mighty and muscular heavings did the door at last begin to move. As we renewed our efforts, it swung slowly inward with a hideous grating and grinding that mounted to an almost vocal screech, in which we seemed to hear the tones of some unhuman entity. The black interior of the temple yawned before us, and from it there surged an odor of long-imprisoned mustiness combined with a queer and unfamiliar fetidity. To this, however, we gave little heed in the natural excitement of the moment.

With my usual foresight, I had provided myself with a piece of resinous wood earlier in the day, thinking that it might serve as a torch in case of any nocturnal explorations of Commoriom. I lit this torch, and we entered the shrine.

The place was paven with immense quinquangular flags of the same material from which its walls were built. It was quite bare, except for the image of the god enthroned at the further end, the two-tiered altar of obscenely-figured metal before the image, and a large and curious-looking basin of bronze supported on three legs, which occupied the middle of the floor. Giving this basin hardly a glance, we ran forward, and I thrust my torch into the face of the idol.

I had never seen an image of Tsathoggua before, but I recognized him without difficulty from the descriptions I had heard. He was very squat and pot-bellied, his head was more like that of a monstrous toad than a deity, and his whole body was covered with an imitation of short fur, giving somehow a vague suggestion of both the bat and the sloth. His sleepy lids were half-lowered over his globular eyes; and the tip of a queer tongue issued from his fat mouth. In truth, he was not a comely or personable sort of god, and I did not wonder at the cessation of his worship, which could only have appealed to very brutal and aboriginal men at any time.

Tirouv Ompallios and I began to swear simultaneously by the names of more urbane and civilized deities, when we saw that not even the commonest of semi-precious gems was visible anywhere, either upon or within any feature or member of this execrable image. With a niggardliness beyond parallel, even the eyes had been carven from the same dull stone as the rest of the abominable thing, and mouth, nose, ears and all other orifices were unadorned. We could only wonder at the avarice or poverty of the beings who had wrought this unique bestiality.

Now that our minds were no longer enthralled by the hope of immediate riches, we became more keenly aware of our surroundings in general; and in particular we noticed the unfamiliar fetor I have spoken of previously, which had now increased uncomfortably in strength. We found that it came from the bronze basin, which we proceeded to examine, though without any idea that the examination would be profitable or even pleasant.

The basin, I have said, was very large; indeed, it was no less than six feet in diameter by three in depth, and its brim was the height of a tall man's shoulder from the floor. The three legs that bore it were curved and massive and terminated in feline paws displaying their talons. When we approached and peered over the brim, we saw that the bowl was filled with a sort of viscous and semi-liquescent substance, quite opaque and of a sooty color. It was from this that the odor came — an odor which, though unsurpassably foul, was nevertheless not an odor of putrefaction, but resembled rather the smell of some vile and unclean creature of the marshes. The odor was almost beyond endurance, and we were about to turn away when we perceived a slight ebullition of the surface, as if the sooty liquid were being agitated from within by some submerged animal or other entity. This ebullition increased rapidly, the center swelled as if with the action of some powerful yeast, and we watched in utter horror, while an uncouth amorphous head with dull and bulging eyes arose gradually on an ever-lengthening neck, and stared us in the face with primordial malignity. Then two arms — if one could call them arms — likewise arose inch by inch, and we saw that the thing was not, as we had thought, a creature immersed in the liquid, but that the liquid itself had put forth this hideous neck and head, and was now forming these damnable arms, that groped toward us with tentacle-like appendages in lieu of claws or hands!

A fear which we had never experienced even in dreams, of which we had found no hint in our most perilous nocturnal excursions, deprived us of the faculty of speech, but not of movement. We recoiled a few paces from the bowl, and co-incidentally with our steps, the horrible neck and arms continued to lengthen. Then the whole mass of the dark fluid began to rise, and far more quickly than the *suvana*-juice runs from my pen, it poured over the rim of the basin like a torrent of black quicksilver, taking as it reached the floor an undulant ophidian form which immediately developed more than a dozen short legs.

What unimaginable horror of protoplastic life, what loathly spawn of the primordial slime had come forth to confront us, we did not pause to consider or conjecture. The monstrosity was too awful to permit of even a brief contemplation; also, its intentions were too plainly hostile, and it gave evidence of anthropophagic inclinations; for it slithered toward us with an unbelievable speed and celerity of motion, opening as it came a toothless mouth of amazing capacity. As it gaped upon us, revealing a tongue that uncoiled like a long serpent, its jaws widened with the same extreme elasticity that accompanied all its other movements. We saw that our departure from the fane of Tsathoggua had become most imperative, and turning our backs to all the abominations of that unhallowed shrine, we crossed the sill with a single leap, and ran headlong in the moonlight through the suburbs of Commoriom. We rounded every convenient corner, we doubled upon our tracks behind the palaces of time-forgotten nobles and the ware-houses of unrecorded merchants, we chose preferably the places where the incursive jungle trees were highest and thickest; and at last, on a by-road where the outlying houses were no longer visible, we paused and dared to look back.

Our lungs were intolerably strained, were ready to burst with their heroic effort, and the various fatigues of the day had told upon us all too grievously; but when we saw at our heels the black monster, following us with a serpentine and undulating ease, like a torrent that descends a long declivity, our flagging limbs were miraculously re-animated, and we plunged from the betraying light of the by-road into the pathless jungle, hoping to evade our pursuer in the labyrinth of boles and vines and gigantic leaves. We stumbled over roots and fallen trees, we tore our raiment and lacerated our skins on the savage brambles, we collided in the gloom with huge trunks and limber saplings that bent before us, we heard the hissing of tree-snakes that spat their venom at us from the boughs above, and the grunting or howling of unseen animals when we trod upon them in our precipitate flight. But we no longer dared to stop or look behind.

We must have continued our headlong peregrinations for hours. The moon, which had given us little light at best through the heavy leafage, fell lower and lower among the

enormous-fronded palms and intricate creepers. But its final
rays, when it sank, were all that saved us from a noisome marsh
with mounds and hassocks of bog-concealing grass, amid
whose perilous environs and along whose mephitic rim we were
compelled to run without pause or hesitation or time to choose
our footing, with our damnable pursuer dogging every step.

Now, when the moon had gone down, our flight became
wilder and more hazardous — a veritable delirium of terror,
exhaustion, confusion, and desperate difficult progression
among obstacles to which we gave no longer any distinct heed
or comprehension, through a night that clung to us and
clogged us like an evil load, like the toils of a monstrous web.
It would seem that the creature behind us, with its unbelievable facilities of motion and self-elongation, could have overtaken us at any time; but apparently it desired to prolong the
game. And so, in a semi-eternal protraction of inconclusive horrors, the night wore on. . . . But we never dared to stop or look
back.

Far-off and wan, a glimmering twilight grew among the
trees — a foreomening of the hidden morn. Wearier than the
dead, and longing for any repose, any security, even that of
some indiscernible tomb, we ran toward the light, and stumbled forth from the jungle upon a paven street among marble
and granite buildings. Dimly, dully, beneath the crushing of our
fatigue, we realized that we had wandered in a circle and had
come back to the suburbs of Commoriom. Before us, no farther
away than the toss of a javelin, was the dark temple of
Tsathoggua.

Again we ventured to look back, and saw the elastic monster, whose legs had now lengthened till it towered above us,
and whose maw was wide enough to have swallowed us both at
a mouthful. It followed us with an effortless glide, with a surety
of motion and intention too horrible, too cynical to be borne.
We ran into the temple of Tsathoggua, whose door was still
open just as we had left it, and closing the door behind us with

a fearful immediacy, we contrived, in the superhuman strength of our desperation, to shoot one of the rusty bolts.

Now, while the chill drearness of the dawn fell down in narrow shafts through the windows high in the wall, we tried with a truly heroic resignation to compose ourselves, and waited for whatever our destiny should bring. And while we waited, the god Tsathoggua peered upon us with an even more imbecile squatness and vileness and bestiality than he had shown in the torchlight.

I think I have said that the lintel of the door had crumbled and splintered away in several places. In fact, the beginning process of ruin had made three apertures, through which the daylight now filtered, and which were large enough to have permitted the passage of small animals or sizable serpents. For some reason, our eyes were drawn to these apertures.

We had not gazed long, when the light was suddenly intercepted in all three openings, and then a black material began to pour through them and ran down the door in a triple stream to the flagstones, where it re-united and resumed the form of the thing that had followed us.

"Farewell, Tirouv Ompallios," I cried, with such remaining breath as I could summon. Then I ran and concealed myself behind the image of Tsathoggua, which was large enough to screen me from view, but, unfortunately, was too small to serve this purpose for more than one person. Tirouv Ompallios would have preceded me with the same laudable idea of self-preservation, but I was the quicker. And seeing that there was not room for both of us to the rearward of Tsathoggua, he returned my valediction and climbed into the great bronze basin, which alone could now afford a moment's concealment in the bareness of the fane.

Peering from behind that execrable god, whose one merit was the width of his abdomen and his haunches, I observed the actions of the monster. No sooner had Tirouv Ompallios crouched down in the three-legged bowl, when the nameless enormity reared itself up like a sooty pillar and approached the basin. The head had now changed in form and position, till it was no more than a vague imprint of features on the middle of a body without arms, legs or neck. The thing loomed above the brim for an instant, gathering all its bulk in an imminent mass on a sort of tapering tail, and then like a lapsing wave it fell into the bowl upon Tirouv Ompallios. Its whole body seemed to open and form an immense mouth as it sank down from sight.

Hardly able to breathe in my horror, I waited, but no sound and no movement came from the basin — not even a groan from Tirouv Ompallios. Finally, with infinite slowness and trepidation and caution, I ventured to emerge from behind Tsathoggua, and passing the bowl on tip-toe, I managed to reach the door.

Now, in order to win my freedom, it would be necessary to draw back the bolt and open the door. And this I greatly feared to do because of the inevitable noise. I felt that it would be highly injudicious to disturb the entity in the bowl while it was digesting Tirouv Ompallios; but there seemed to be no other way if I was ever to leave that abominable fane.

Even as I shot back the bolt, a single tentacle sprang out with infernal rapidity from the basin, and elongating itself across the whole room, it caught my right wrist in a lethal clutch. It was unlike anything I have ever touched, it was indescribably viscid and slimy and cold, it was loathsomely soft like the foul mire of a bog and mordantly sharp as an edged metal, with an agonizing suction and constriction that made me scream aloud as the clutch tightened upon my flesh, cutting into me like a vise of knife-blades. In my struggles to free myself, I drew the door open, and fell forward on the sill. A moment of awful pain, and then I became aware that I had broken away from my captor. But looking down, I saw that my hand was gone, leaving a strangely withered stump from which little blood issued. Then, gazing behind me into the shrine, I saw the tentacle recoil and shorten till it passed from view behind the rim of the basin, bearing my lost hand to join whatever now remained of Tirouv Ompallios. 🕷

About "The Theft of the Thirty-Nine Girdles"

Smith's master-thief Satampra Zeiros made a comeback, this time as a Hyperborean Robin Hood, in this tale, written long after the original "Tale of Satampra Zeiros." Smith started work on "The Theft of the Thirty-Nine Girdles" in October 1952 and finished it in April 1957; it saw print first (under the title "The Powder of Hyperborea," which cannot have been Smith's idea) in *Saturn Science Fiction and Fantasy*, March 1958. Series characters are pretty rare in Smith's fiction, and one only regrets he did not follow this story up with a series of adventures of Satampra Zeiros, who might even have become his Conan or Jirel.

Smith can be viewed as the Voltaire of weird fiction, and his droll dismissal of religion as hypocritical priestcraft comes through loud and clear in this story of a primeval panty raid. His penchant for exotic names which one only later recognizes as puns provides us with the wonderful coinage of "Vixeela," which the scribe rendereth "Foxy Lady."

I have restored the poem "Lament for Vixeela," which Smith had originally placed at the head of an earlier version of the tale.

The Theft of the Thirty-Nine Girdles

by Clark Ashton Smith

LAMENT FOR VIXEELA

Thy name, an invocation, calls to light
Dead moons, and draws from overdated night
The rosy-bosomed spectre of delight.
Like some delaying sunset, brave with gold,
The glamors and the perils shared of old
Outsoar the shrunken empire of the mould.

L et it be said as a foreword to this tale that I have robbed no man who was not in some way a robber of others. In my entire long and arduous career, I, Satampra Zeiros of Uzuldaroum, sometimes known as the master-thief, have endeavored to serve merely as an agent in the rightful redistribution of wealth. The adventure I have now to relate was no exception: though, as it happened in the outcome, my own pecuniary profits were indeed meager, not to say trifling.

Age is upon me now. And sitting at that leisure which I have earned through many hazards, I drink the wines that are heartening to age. To me, as I sip, return memories of splendid loot and brave nefarious enterprise. Before me shine the out-poured sackfuls of *djals* or *pazoors*, removed so dexterously from the coffers of iniquitous merchants and money-lenders. I dream of rubies redder than the blood that was shed for them; of sapphires bluer than depths of glacial ice; of emeralds greener than the jungle in spring. I recall the escalade of pronged balconies; the climbing terraces and towers guarded by monsters; the sacking of altars beneath the eyes of malign idols or sentinel serpents.

Often I think of Vixeela, my one true love and the most adroit and courageous of my companions in burglary. She has long since gone to the bourn of all good thieves and comrades; and I have mourned her sincerely these many years. But still dear is the memory of our amorous or adventurous nights and the feats we performed together. Of such feats, perhaps the most signal and audacious was the theft of the thirty-nine girdles.

These were the golden and jeweled chastity girdles, worn by the virgins vowed to the moon god Leniqua, whose temple had stood from immemorial time in the suburbs of Uzuldaroum, capital of Hyperborea. The virgins were always thirty-nine in number. They were chosen for their youth and beauty, and retired from service to the god at the age of thirty-one.

The girdles were padlocked with the toughest bronze and their keys retained by the high priest who, on certain nights, rented them at a high price to the richer gallants of the city. It will thus be seen that the virginity of the priestesses was nominal; but its frequent and repeated sale was regarded as a meritorious act of sacrifice to the god.

Vixeela herself had at one time been numbered among the virgins but had fled from the temple and from Uzuldaroum several years before the sacerdotal age of release from her bondage. She would tell me little of her life in the temple, and I surmised that she had found small pleasure in the religious prostitution and had chafed at the confinement entailed by it.

After her flight she had suffered many hardships in the cities of the south. Of these too, she spoke but sparingly, as one who dreads the reviving of painful recollections.

She had returned to Uzuldaroum a few months prior to our first meeting. Being now a little over age, and having dyed her russet-blonde hair to a raven black, she had no great fear of recognition by Leniqua's priests. As was their custom, they had promptly replaced her loss with another and younger virgin, and would have small interest now in one so long delinquent.

At the time of our foregathering, Vixeela had already committed various petty larcenies. But, being unskilled, she had failed to finish any but the easier and simpler ones, and had grown quite thin from starvation. She was still attractive and her keenness of wit and quickness in learning soon endeared her to me. She was small and agile and could climb like a lemur. I soon found her help invaluable, since she could climb through windows and other apertures impassable to my greater bulk.

We had consummated several lucrative burglaries, when the idea of entering Leniqua's temple and making away with the costly girdles occurred to me. The problems offered, and the difficulties to be overcome, appeared at first sight little less than fantastic. But such obstacles have always challenged my acumen and have never daunted me.

Firstly, there was the problem of entrance without detection and serious mayhem at the hands of the sickle-armed priests who guarded Leniqua's fane with baleful and incorruptible vigilance. Luckily, during her term of temple service, Vixeela had learned of a subterranean adit, long disused but, she believed, still passable. This entrance was through a tunnel, the continuation of a natural cavern located somewhere in the woods behind Uzuldaroum. It had been used almost universally by the virgin's visitors in former ages. But the visitors now entered openly by the temple's main doors or by posterns little less public: a sign, perhaps, that religious sentiment had deepened or that modesty had declined. Vixeela had never seen the cavern herself but she knew its approximate location. The temple's inner adit was closed only by a flagstone, easily levitated from below or above, behind the image of Leniqua in the great nave.

Secondly, there was the selection of a proper time, when the women's girdles had been unlocked and laid aside. Here again Vixeela was invaluable, since she knew the nights on which the rented keys were most in demand. These were known as nights of sacrifice, greater or lesser, the chief one being at the moon's full. All the women were then in repeated request.

Since, however, the fane on such occasions would be crowded with people, the priests, the virgins and their clients, a seemingly insurmountable difficulty remained. How were we to collect and make away with the girdles in the presence of so many persons? This, I must admit, baffled me.

Plainly, we must find some way in which the temple could be evacuated, or its occupants rendered unconscious or otherwise incapable during the period needed for our operations.

I thought of a certain soporific drug, easily and quickly vaporized, which I had used on more than one occasion to put the inmates of a house asleep. Unfortunately the drug was limited in its range and would not penetrate to all the chambers and alcoves of a large edifice like the temple. Moreover it was necessary to wait for a full half hour, with doors or windows opened, till the fumes were dissipated: otherwise the robbers would be overcome together with their victims.

There was also the pollen of a rare jungle lily, which, if cast in a man's face, would induce a temporary paralysis. This too I rejected: there were too many persons to be dealt with, and the pollen could hardly be obtained in sufficient quantities.

At last I decided to consult the magician and alchemist, Veezi Phenquor, who, possessing furnaces and melting-pots, had often served me by converting stolen gold and silver into ingots or other safely unrecognizable forms. Though skeptical of his powers as a magician, I regarded Veezi Phenquor as a

skilled pharmacist and toxicologist. Having always on hand a
supply of strange and deadly medicaments, he might well be
able to provide something that would facilitate our project.

We found Veezi Phenquor decanting one of his more noisome concoctions from a still bubbling and steaming kettle
into vials of stout stoneware. By the smell I judged that it must
be something of special potency: the exudations of a pole-cat
would have been innocuous in comparison. In his absorption he
did not notice our presence until the entire contents of the kettle had been decanted and the vials tightly stoppered and
sealed with a blackish gum.

"That," he observed with unctuous complacency, "is a love-
philter that would inflame a nursing infant or resurrect the
powers of a dying nonagenarian. Do you — ?"

"No," I said emphatically. "We require nothing of the sort.
What we need at the moment is something quite different." In
a few terse words I went on to outline the problem, adding:

"If you can help us, I am sure you will find the
melting-down of the golden girdles a congenial task. As usual,
you will receive a third of the profits."

Veezi Phenquor creased his bearded face into a half-lubri-
cious, half-sardonic smile.

"The proposition is a pleasant one from all angles. We will
free the temple-girls from incumbrances which they must find
uncomfortable, not to say burdensome; and will turn the irk-
some gems and metal to a worthier purpose — notably, our
own enrichment." As if by way of afterthought, he added:

"It happens that I can supply you with a most unusual
preparation, warranted to empty the temple of all its occupants
in a very short time."

Going to a cobwebbed corner, he took down from a high
shelf an abdominous jar of uncolored glass filled with a fine
grey powder and brought it to the light.

"I will now," he said, "explain to you the singular properties of this powder and the way in which it must be used. It is

truly a triumph of chemistry, and more devastating than a plague."

We were astounded by what he told us. Then we began to laugh.

"It is to be hoped," I said, "that none of your spells and cantrips are involved."

Veezi Phenquor assumed the expression of one whose feelings have been deeply injured.

"I assure you," he protested, "that the effects of the powder, though extraordinary, are not beyond nature."

After a moment's meditation he continued: "I believe that I can further your plan in other ways. After the abstraction of the girdles, there will be the problem of transporting undetected such heavy merchandise across a city which, by that time, may well have been aroused by the horrendous crime and busily patrolled by constabulary. I have a plan . . . ."

We hailed with approval the ingenious scheme outlined by Veezi Phenquor. After we had discussed and settled to our satisfaction the various details, the alchemist brought out certain liquors that proved more palatable than anything of his we had yet sampled. We then returned to our lodgings, I carrying in my cloak the jar of powder, for which Veezi Phenquor generously refused to accept payment. We were filled with the rosiest anticipations of success, together with a modicum of distilled palm-wine.

Discreetly, we refrained from our usual activities during the nights that intervened before the next full moon. And we kept closely to our lodgings, hoping that the police, who had long suspected us of numerous peccadilloes, would believe that we had either quitted the city or retired from burglary.

A little before midnight, on the evening of the full moon, Veezi Phenquor knocked discreetly at our door — a triple knock as had been agreed.

Like ourselves, he was heavily cloaked in peasant's homespun.

"I have procured the cart of a vegetable seller from the country," he said. "It is loaded with seasonable produce and drawn by two small asses. I have concealed it in the woods, as near to the cave-adit of Leniqua's temple as the overgrown road will permit. Also, I have reconnoitered the cave itself.

"Our success will depend on the utter confusion created. If we are not seen to enter or depart by the rear adit, in all likelihood no one will remember its existence. The priests will be searching elsewhere.

"Having removed the girdles and concealed them under our load of farm produce, we will then wait till the hour before dawn when, with other vegetable and fruit dealers, we will enter the city."

Keeping as far as we could from the public places, where most of the police were gathered around taverns and the cheaper lupanars, we circled across Uzuldaroum and found, at some distance from Leniqua's fane, a road that ran countryward. The jungle soon grew denser and the houses fewer. No one saw us when we turned into a side-road overhung with leaning palms and closed in by thickening brush. After many devious turnings, we came to the ass-drawn cart, so cleverly screened from view that even I could detect its presence only by the pungent aroma of certain root-vegetables and the smell of fresh-fallen dung. Those asses were well-trained for the use of thieves: there was no braying to betray their presence.

We groped on, over hunching roots and between clustered boles that made the rest of the way impassable for a cart. I should have missed the cave; but Veezi Phenquor, pausing, stooped before a low hillock to part the matted creepers, showing a black and bouldered aperture large enough to admit a man on hands and knees.

Lighting the torches we had brought along, we crawled into the cave, Veezi going first. Luckily, due to the rainless season, the cave was dry and our clothing suffered only earth-stains such as would be proper to agricultural workers.

The cave narrowed where piles of debris had fallen from the roof. I, with my width and girth, was hard put to squeeze through in places. We had gone an undetermined distance when Veezi stopped and stood erect before a wall of smooth masonry in which shadowy steps mounted.

Vixeela slipped past him and went up the steps. I followed. The fingers of her free hand were gliding over a large flat flagstone that filled the stair-head. The stone began to tilt noiselessly upward. Vixeela blew out her torch and laid it on the top step while the gap widened, permitting a dim, flickering light to pour down from beyond. She peered cautiously over the top of the flag, which became fully uptilted by its hidden mechanism, and then climbed through motioning us to follow.

We stood in the shadow of a broad pillar at one side of the back part of Leniqua's temple. No priest, woman or visitor was in sight but we heard a confused humming of voices at some vague remove. Leniqua's image, presenting its reverend rear, sat on a high dais in the center of the nave. Altar-fires, golden, blue and green, flamed spasmodically before the god, making his shadow writhe on the floor and against the rear wall like a delirious giant in a dance of copulation with an unseen partner.

Vixeela found and manipulated the spring that caused the flagstone to sink back as part of a level floor. Then the three of us stole forward, keeping in the god's wavering shadow. The nave was still vacant but noise came more audibly from open doorways at one side, resolving itself into gay cries and hysterical laughters.

"Now," whispered Veezi Phenquor.

I drew from a side-pocket the vial he had given us and pried away the wax with a sharp knife. The cork, half-rotten with age, was easily removed. I poured the vial's contents on the back bottom step of Leniqua's dais — a pale stream that quivered and undulated with uncanny life and luster as it fell in the god's shadow. When the vial was empty I ignited the heap of powder.

It burned instantly with a clear, high-leaping flame. Immediately, it seemed, the air was full of surging phantoms — a soundless, multitudinous explosion, beating upon us, blasting our nostrils with charnel fetors till we reeled before it, choking and strangling. There was, however, no sense of material impact from the hideous forms that seemed to melt over and through us, rushing in all directions, as if every atom of the burning powder had released a separate ghost.

Hastily we covered our noses with squares of thick cloth that Veezi had warned us to bring for this purpose. Something of our usual aplomb returned and we moved forward through the seething rout. Lascivious blue cadavers intertwined around us. Miscegenations of women and tigers arched over us. Monsters double-headed and triple-tailed, goblins and ghouls rose obliquely to the far ceiling or rolled and melted to other and more nameless apparitions in lower air. Green sea-things, like unions of drowned men and octopi, coiled and dribbled with dank slime along the floor.

Then we heard the cries of fright from the temple's inmates and visitors and began to meet naked men and women who rushed frantically through that army of beleaguering phantoms toward the exits. Those who encountered us face to face recoiled as if we too were shapes of intolerable horror.

The naked men were mostly young. After them came middle aged merchants and aldermen, bald and pot-bellied, some clad in under-garments, some in snatched-up cloaks too short to cover them below the hips. Women, lean, fat or buxom, tumbled screaming for the outer doors. None of them, we saw with approbation, had retained her chastity girdle.

Lastly came the temple-guards and priests, with mouths like gaping squares of terror, emitting shrill cries. All of the guards had dropped their sickles. They passed us, blindly disregarding our presence, and ran after the rest. The host of powder-born specters soon shrouded them from view.

Satisfied that the temple was now empty of its inmates and clients, we turned our attention to the first corridor. The doors of the separate rooms were all open. We divided our labors, taking each a room, and removing from disordered beds and garment-littered floors the cast-off girdles of gold and gems. We met at the corridor's end, where our collected loot was thrust into the strong thin sack I had carried under my cloak. Many of the phantoms still lingered, achieving new and ghastlier fusions, dropping their members upon us as they began to diswreathe.

Soon we had searched all the rooms apportioned to the women. My sack was full, and I had counted thirty-eight girdles at the end of the third corridor. One girdle was still missing; but Vixeela's sharp eyes caught the gleam of an emerald-studded buckle protruding from under the dissolving legs of a hairy satyr-like ghost on a pile of male garments in the corner. She snatched up the girdle and carried it in her hand henceforward.

We hurried back to Leniqua's nave, believing it to be vacant of all human occupants by now. To our disconcertion the High Priest, whose name Vixeela knew as Marquanos, was standing before the altar, striking blows with a long phallic rod of bronze, his insignia of office, at certain apparitions that remained floating in the air.

Marquanos rushed toward us with a harsh cry as we neared him, dealing a blow at Vixeela that would have brained her if she had not slipped agilely to one side. The High Priest staggered, nearly losing his balance. Before he could turn upon her again, Vixeela brought down on his tonsured head the heavy chastity girdle she bore in her right hand. Marquanos toppled like a slaughtered ox beneath the pole-ax of the butcher, and lay prostrate, writhing a little. Blood ran in rills from the serrated imprint of the great jewels on his scalp. Whether he was dead or still living, we did not pause to ascertain.

We made our exit without delay. After the fright they had received, there was small likelihood that any of the temple's denizens would venture to return for some hours. The movable slab fell smoothly back into place behind us. We hurried along the underground passage, I carrying the sack and the others preceding me in order to drag it through straitened places and over piles of rubble when I was forced to set it down. We reached the creeper-hung entrance without incident. There we paused awhile before emerging into the moon-streaked woods, and listened cautiously to cries that diminished with distance. Apparently no one had thought of the rear adit or had even realized that there was any such human motive as robbery behind the invasion of terrifying specters.

Reassured, we came forth from the cavern and found our way back to the hidden cart and its drowsing asses. We threw enough of the fruits and vegetables into the brush to make a deep cavity in the cart's center, in which our sackful of loot was then deposited and covered over from sight. Then, settling ourselves on the grassy ground, we waited for the hour before dawn. Around us, after awhile, we heard the furtive slithering and scampering of small animals that devoured the comestibles we had cast away.

If any of us slept, it was, so to speak, with one eye and one ear. We rose in the horizontal sifting of the last moonbeams and long eastward-running shadows of early twilight.

Leading our asses, we approached the highway and stopped behind the brush while an early cart creaked by. Silence ensued, and we broke from the wood and resumed our journey cityward before other carts came in sight.

In our return through outlying streets we met only a few early passers, who gave us no second glance. Reaching the neighborhood of Veezi Phenquor's house, we consigned the cart to his care and watched him turn into the courtyard unchallenged and seemingly unobserved by others than ourselves. He was, I reflected, well supplied with roots and fruits. . . .

We kept closely to our lodgings for two days. It seemed unwise to remind the police of our presence in Uzuldaroum by any public appearance. On the evening of the second day our food supply ran short and we sallied out in our rural costumes to a nearby market which we had never before patronized.

Returning, we found evidence that Veezi Phenquor had paid us a visit during our absence, in spite of the fact that all the doors and windows had been, and still were, carefully locked. A small cube of gold reposed on the table, serving as paper-weight for a scribbled note.

The note read:

My esteemed friends and companions: After removing the various gems, I have melted down all the gold into ingots, and am leaving one of them as a token of my great regard. Unfortunately, I have learned that I am being watched by the police, and am leaving Uzuldaroum under circumstances of haste and secrecy, taking the other ingots and all the jewels in the ass-drawn cart, covered up by the vegetables I have providentially kept, even though they are slightly stale by now. I expect to make a long journey, in a direction which I cannot specify — a journey well beyond the jurisdiction of our local police, and one on which I trust you will not be perspicacious enough to follow me. I shall need the remainder of our loot for my expenses, et cetera. Good luck in all your future ventures.

Respectfully,

Veezi Phenquor

POSTSCRIPT: You too are being watched, and I advise you to quit the city with all feasible expedition. Marquanos, in spite of a well-cracked mazzard from Vixeela's blow, recovered full consciousness late yesterday. He recognized in Vixeela a former temple-girl through the trained dexterity of her movements. He has not been able to identify her; but a thorough and secret search is being made, and other girls have already been put to the thumb-screw and toe-screw by Leniqua's priests.

You and I, my dear Satampra, have already been listed, though not yet identi-fied, as possible accomplices of the girl. A man of your conspicuous height and bulk is being sought. The Powder of the Fetid Apparitions, some traces of which were found on Leniqua's dais, has already been analyzed. Unluckily, it has been used before, both by myself and other alchemists.

I hope you will escape — on other paths than the one I am planning to follow."

About "Shadow of the Sleeping God"

If Smith neglected to carry on the adventures of Satampra Zeiros, that doesn't mean others can't retrieve the fallen banner. Ambuehl's "Shadow of the Sleeping God," which first appeared in *Cthulhu Codex* # 14, Hallowmas 1999, offers a new installment in the saga of the king of thieves, one built solidly upon Smith's two tales of Satampra Zeiros.

The hasty reader may think to spot an apparent contradiction between Ambuehl's tale and Smith's "The Theft of the Thirty-Nine Girdles," namely that Vixeela's death is already known to Satampra Zeiros in Smith's story, whereas our hero discovers the fact the hard way in Ambuehl's, though "Shadow of the Sleeping God" takes place after "Theft of the Thirty-Nine Girdles." But the problem vanishes away like an icy mist when we realize that Vixeela's death is known only to the "narrating I" of Smith's first-person tale, not to the "narrated I," *i.e.*, not to Satampra Zeiros' younger self, the narrated protagonist. We are not told when he learned of her passing. And the first-person "Theft of the Thirty-Nine Girdles" must have been recounted by the aging Satampra Zeiros well after the occurence of the events of the third-person "Shadow of the Sleeping God."

Ambuehl depicts for us a torrent of Satampra Zeiros' grief at learning of Vixeela's fate. Here is a draft version of Smith's own lament, taken from Steve Behrends (ed.), *Strange Shadows: The Uncollected Fiction and Essays of Clark Ashton Smith* (Greenwood Press, 1989).

> *O dauntless child of beauty and of dross,*
>
> *My verdant love enzones thy lonely tomb*
>
> *With secret, proud fluorescence and perfume.*
>
> *Like some delaying sunset, brave with gold,*
>
> *The glamor and the perils shared of old*
>
> *Outsoar the shrunken empire of the mould.*
>
> — Elegy for Vixeela

The Shadow of the
Sleeping God

by James Ambuehl

I.

A lthough it had been many a month since Satampra Zeiros, master-thief of all Hyperborea had set eyes upon his latest in a long string of companions, fellow-adventurers and oftimes partners-in-crime, the youth called Alu Kuthos, their union was not a particularly joyous occasion. In fact, both rogues had once again met up with each other in the throne-room of Ruul-Vash, hierophant and high priest of the temple of the moon-god Leniqua — which stood untouched for centuries imemmorial in the suburbs of Uzuldaroum, capital since the fall of mighty Commoriom, of all Hyperborea — having each been dragged therin perforce by a company of sickle-armed temple guards.

It seems that the young Alu Kuthos had been discovered in the pre-dawn hours by way of a sneezing fit brought on by the inevitable cold he had come down with whilst earlier that eve clutching to the ramparts of the outer temple walls, all the while an over-eager Captain disciplined a platoon of temple guards within the hallways a mere few yards from the youth's long-intended ingress. At long last the Captain had finished his bellowing and gesturing, and the guards had moved on to their posts. Alu Kuthos had finally entered, but a while later even more alert temple guards, following the sound of this uncontrollable sneezing, found him secreted within the chambers of the daughter of Ruul-Vash, even Filhomeena. Now had it been her bed-chambers the youth had occupied the high priest would not have been so concerned, in fact would have been overjoyed at such a prospect as gaining a new son-in-law, the maiden Filhomeena having become rather insufferable of late. But it had been the maiden's treasure room, alas, in which the youth had been discovered, indeed buried nearly to the neck in a great pile of gold *pazoors.* One thing this Ruul-Vash certainly could not tolerate, being particulary greedy himself, was the chance that someone would have the audacity to steal from him or his, yet still did he offer the rash and impetuous Alu Kuthos an out from his current unfortunate predicament. All that would be required of him was that he merely wed the aforementioned Filhomeena, and even be given a fiefdom of his own to rule as he saw fit in the bargain. But Alu Kuthos gained one look at the maiden Filhomeena — who was neither fair nor willowy, but in fact rather squat and portly, with a face not too unlike that of the wild boar — and decided he'd do better to take his chances with Ruul-Vash.

Satampra Zeiros on the other hand, older and assuredly wiser, had been caught red-handed as they say, attempting merely to relieve a rather fat and jovial merchant of his likewise fat purse — whose bulging contents promised to make the thief decidedly jovial himself. But when he at last gained hold of it he was astonished to see it move as of a life all its own, full-a-squirm and setting the not-too-modest contents a-jingle! For he, master-thief of Hyperborea, found himself betrayed by a burglar alarm worthy of even his own cleverness and wit — a tiny live marmot, placed within the pouch of *pazoors!* And how was he, Satampra Zeiros, to know that the merchant was the high priest's own brother?

So it was that the two companions presently found themselves manacled and at sicklepoint at the foot of the dais of the
throne of Ruul-Vash.

"Ah, it seems that Leniqua shines his fortune down upon
me this very night!" exclaimed Ruul-Vash. "it is *you*, is it not,
my friend? Yes, long-sought Satampra Zeiros, before me in
chains at last!'

The high priest rose from his throne to his full, gaunt
height, and strode down the dais steps to stand before the
guard-encircled rogues. Reaching forth a thin, almost skeletal
hand, he seized a hank of Alu Kuthos' hair and brought the
youth's face up to his own.

"No . . . I don't know you. Still, you would have done well
to accept my offer of my daughter in wedlock, lad." The boy
stared at the high priest and said naught, merely sniffled, stifling a sneeze.

Ruul-Vash dropped the boy's head and crossed to Satampra
Zeiros. The masterthief stared at him defiantly.

"I hope you lived well on the loot gained you from the fenc-
ing of the thirty-nine girdles stolen from this temple of
Leniqua, lo so many years gone, Satampra Zeiros." The high
priest paused. Sensing rather than seeing the masterthief's look
of surprise, RuulVash went on. "Actually, I am rather indebted
to you, O Satampra Zeiros. For had you not committed so rash
and bold a robbery as the girdles of Leniqua the former high
priest of Leniqua, Marquanos, would not have been deposed,
and I'd still be a mere acolyte of the moongod. But deposed
Marquanos was, for his failure to bring you to justice as I have
finally done — and your fellow in the girdles affair," the high
priest added as an afterthought

Satampra Zeiros started at this last. He quickly regained
his composure, but not before the high priest noted his surprise.

"Yes, Satampra Zeiros, I know it was you who took part in
the theft of the thirty-nine girdles. Your part in the affair was
long suspect, but it was finally confirmed by the confession I

extracted personally from your companion in the affair and once true love. A confession extracted under torture, of course." The high priest fairly gloated.

"You damned buzzard!" Satampra Zeiros strained at his chains. "What did you do to her?" he cried.

"The beauteous Vixeela?" asked the high priest, clearly unconcerned. "Why, I simply took from her what I desired and put her to death," he replied offhandedly.

The form of the master thief slumped forward and shook with mighty sobs.

"All right, you've *ah, ah*, caught us," challenged Alu Kuthos. "Now wha — what do you in — *ah, ah*, intend to do with us, you *dadachoo!* damned priest? *Sniffle.*"

Ruul-Vash turned again to the youth and began to lean closer to him, as if to impart an obscene and mocking secret, and Alu Kuthos couldn't help himself but to at that moment give forth a particular virulent and wet sneeze directly into the face of the high priest. Startled, Ruul-Vash quickly drew himself to his full height and slapped the youth a hard backhand across the face. "You snivelling snot! I shall have you drawn and quartered for this!" Ruul-Vash wiped his face on his tunic sleeve.

Then a sardonic look stole across the features of the high priest and he began to cackle like a rabid hyena.

"Wait, I have a better fate in store for you. Aye, and your stoic partner as well!" He stole a look at the now recovered Satampra Zeiros, then began pacing purposefully before the two prisoners, hands rubbing together behind his back pensively.

"It is a task I would have of you, one I wouldn't wish even upon my worst enemy," he began. "But then," he cackled softly, "I have never heretofore set eyes upon you two ere fate, or perhaps Leniqua himself, thought to bring you to my very door. And perhaps, if you should fail in this quest, I shall never have the fortune to do so again!" he intoned sarcastically. "Aye, I think you two shall do quite nicely indeed."

Here Ruul-Vash paused, to gather his thoughts before continuing.

"Has either of you two heard aught of the fabulous and noxious *Voormish Tablets*? I thought not. Well, they are a fabulously rare collection of sigils set in ancient stone, the written records of the half-legendary furry and prehuman Voormis, who ruled Hyperborea long ages ere man ever set foot upon her glorious shores.

Now as the *Voormish Tablets* have it, at the height of the Voormish reign there did sit a mighty citadel, Ta-Shon, on an unnamed isle in the Cinartrel Sea, which was itself the main stronghold of the Voormis ere it sank beneath the waves long ages past."

Satampra Zeiros, his chains biting uncomfortably into his wrists, who was sorely irascible and vexed with anger at the high priest's rambling monologue, suddenly felt compelled to express his perturbance quite vociferously.

"Cease this prattle, priest!" he bellowed. "My companion and I care naught for sunken lands nor near-extinct furry savages! Please release us, O Ruul-Vash, from these chains, or mercifully put us to death, or at least hack off our ears that we may be spared this interminable chatter!" the master thief waxed sarcastically.

For a moment the high priest was stunned into silence, whitefaced and livid with anger. His wormthin lips compressed into a narrow line, and he sputtered and choked furiously.

Alu Kuthos rattled his chains mightily, protesting to his companion, as well as Ruul-Vash: "No, Ruul-Vash! Please spare us! *Ah-choo*. Do not put us to death!" The youth was fairly trembling with fear.

"Silence, whelp!" commanded Ruul-Vash, his composure once again fully regained. " . . . No, I'll not put you to death." He again seized a hank of the lad's hair and gave it a savage twist, eliciting a yelp of pain from Alu Kuthos' lips but ensuring his undivided attention. "But you'll wish I had, boy!" He twisted his wrist again, savagely

He turned again to the master thief a look of unholy glee crossing his nigh-skeletal features, lips drawing back to bare teeth like those of a rabid canines.

"It is not of Ta-Shon, nor even of the Voormis that I wish ultimately to discuss, Satampra Zeiros, but rather the dark and noisome god of that prehuman civilization, even black and plastic Tsathoggua, who himself sleeps beneath Mount Voormithadreth!"

At the utterance of that black and accursed name even he, Satampra Zeiros, could not stifle a sudden chill. Indeed, the foetid air in that dank chamber seemed to grow a few degrees colder as if the icy breath of a star-born god suddenly had been exhaled from voids unknown. For Tsathogqua was himself one of that race of ancient and terrible gods come down to Earth from the stars in ages long past, one of the very Great Old Ones themselves!

Too, at the sound of that alien name the fight went out of the master thief, and he slumped uselessly in his chains, his mind wandering unbidden upon sundry dim horrors. The wolfish countenance of the high priest of the moongod, Leniqua, picked up on this at once.

"Ah, yes, it seems I've heard that you yourself had a little adventure with the Spawn of this selfsame Tsathoggua a few years aback." The high priest gestured to the stump of Satampra Zeiros' right hand pointedly. He chuckled. " It was a frightening tale indeed," he continued. "But let me assure you, Satampra Zeiros, that this adventure I plan to set you on promises to be even more harrowing, even for one such as you!" Ruul-Vash's mocking face gloated nearly into his own. "But let me at last continue before I digress further .

"You see, as the *Voormish Tablets* state, a hierophant and shaman of these furry Voormis, one Hurun, was himself the high priest of this selfsame Tsathoggua in this citadel of Ta-Shon. Many and dark were Hurun's magicks, doubtless gained him by his monstrous beneficiary, and nearly all Hyperborea bent itself under his rule. But, alas, Hurun was not imparted his sponsor's immortality, and with the Curse of Rhan-Tegoth he at last succumbed to his death.

"How he came to bear the Curse of Rhan-Tegoth and thereby succumb, or even just what this Curse entails, is of no matter to me, as it is all recorded in the *Voormish Tablets*, of which I myself own a set, albeit a fragmentary one, should I ever wish to peruse such matters. But what is of import to me, aye, of even greater import than my own post here as high priest to Lenigua the moongod, is, quite simply, Hurun's magicks." He paused for effect.

"And my simple task, dear gentlemen," continued the high priest, "is for the pair of you to acquire for me those magickal relics and artefacts said to be buried within the earthen mound-tomb of Hurun, just within the gates of the citadel of Ta-Shon sunken in the Cinartrel Sea."

II.

For Ruul-Vash, high priest of Leniqua the moongod and sorcerer seldom surpassed in his own right, it was no great matter to use his magickal potions and charms to transport Satampra Zeiros and his youthful companion Alu Kuthos to the wavepressured realm beneath the Cinartrel Sea of the sunken citadel of Ta-Shon, within whose fabulous gates lay the mound-tomb of Hurun. And it was likewise no great feat to administer to the two rogues the wondrous properties bequeathed them by use of the Breath of Dagon, to be found hidden within the text of the *Black Tablets of R' lyeh* which, many centuries later, would come to be known as the *R'lyeh Text*. This spell benefited the pair the ability to breathe in water, aye, even unto the very bottom of the sea, as if they were themselves denizens of the deep.

Great indeed was the two thieves' surprise by this method of transformation and transportation, so that it were several moments before they had at last sufficiently regained their faculties to unroll the map enscribed on pterosaur-hide given them by Ruul-Vash and directing them to the location of Hurun's tomb. This done, they pressed onward through the very gates of the wondrous citadel that loomed before them. The pair had, too, the benefits of a fantastic ring the high priest had given unto Satampra Zeiros, which itself had the ability to cast forth at will a veritable cone of light which spread out before the pair and lit all in their path, aye, even in the murky green depths of the Cinartrel Sea!

Drawing their daggers, the pair made their way forward, peering all about them in awe. Aye, of a certainty it was Ta-Shon a wondrous city in its day, for though it lay submerged in the aqueous murk of silt and slime it virtually lay untouched by time. Very little of the citadel lay in ruin, but stood almost whole and silent as if awaiting its reemergence into the light of the Hyperborean sun. Here rose great pillars of basaltic black stone, and there stood towering arches of soapy green stone, and white marbled columns and smooth gray flagstones spread out before them in every direction.

Too, the citadel teemed with life — albeit life of an aquatic and submarine nature. Fish swam, crabs scuttled, sea-snakes slithered, and things less nameable flopped and humped their way across the slimy flags.

Shadows loomed before them in the cone of light given off by the ring worn by the older master thief, and more than once Alu Kuthos felt sure he espied trident-bearing merfolk swimming amidst the alien masonry, following them curiously yet cautiously. But Satampra Zeiros and Alu Kuthos found themselves thankfully unmolested on their *outre* trek, and at last they reached the earthen mound-tomb of the Voormish shaman Hurun.

Before them lay a low, humped hill of black mud, bearing a rough cavelike entranceway choked with a great boulder of scintillant crystal. At once the two rogues put their shoulders to the task of rolling away the boulder, relishing an end at last to this subaqueous realm of horror.

It was as the boulder began to move, slowly but surely, when the youth spotted something in the distance swimming wierdly toward them. It rather *rolled* at them, and as it came into the light the two were alarmed to see a monstrous disc-shaped thing with tentacles radiating from it in a spokelike fashion leering malevolently at them from a score of spiderlike red eyes. Its circular maw stood agape and was ringed with a number of gnashing teeth like those of the shark. The two rogues prepared for the worst. But even as it moved to attack the Hyperboreans at the last it turned aside and swam off of a sudden, almost as if signaled to do.

Catching their breaths again, the two thieves heave-hoed a final time, and at last the boulder rolled aside and they entered the tomb. They made their way up a gently sloping passage-way, which must have formed an air pocket, for as they neared the top of the tunnel they emerged into the air once again. Miraculously, the Breath of Dagon suspended its effects even as Ruul-Vash warned it might should they encounter dry air. Nonplussed, they made their way into the main burial chamber.

In the direct center of the circular vault, on a low pedestal stood the stone sarcophagus of the archancient Hurun. Satampra Zeiros made haste to extract from his pack the mallet and iron spikes, with which to break the ancient seal of the sarcophagus. But ere the hammer-blow fell the master thief paused and shuddered.

"What is it, Satampra Zeiros? Why do you pause?" asked the frightened youth.

"Look you, Alu Kuthos," answered the master thief, "atop this stone-carven lid" — he pointed with one of the iron spikes

— "and look ye upon the unholy carven Seal of Tsathoggua! And be damned in the doing!"

For there, carven into the surface of the lid, stood something monstrous: something not altogether bat, nor toad, nor sloth, nor ape, but instead something suggesting a soul-shattering composite of all four!

Alu Kuthos stifled a shriek, then buried his head in his hands and sobbed. The older thief put a reassuring hand on his shoulder. "Aye, Alu Kuthos, I truly wish to all the gods, divine and demoniacal alike, of Hyperborea, I had not involved you in this affair." The master thief's heart weighed heavy.

"Nay, Satampra Zeiros," protested the youth, gazing up at his mentor in admiration. "You are not at fault! I am the one who dared to rob that sow-daughter of Ruul-Vash!"

"Aye, lad, so you did. Still, your association with me has earned you much more punishment indeed than you would have else received. Aye, I am to blame; just as I myself brought on the death of my beloved Vixeela, to say nothing of the awful and doubtless total dissolution of my lifelong companion from my dim-remembered youth, Tirouv Ompallios in the digestive acids and stomach enzymes of the formless hellspawn of that   . . that *Thing*!" He gestured contemptuously at the pictoglyph of the Sleeping God Tsathoggua. "Of a certain, young Alu Kuthos, have I, Satampra Zeiros been the death and doom of *all* — and there have been many — who have befriended me!"

"Not so, friend Satampra!" shouted Alu Kuthos. "You, my dear old friend, have been the greatest boon to my budding nimble-fingered career, and aye, my comrade since first we met in the spectre-haunted ruins of Yongras. Remember you the plundering of the Lord Vester! And how about the affair of the Jewel of Deb'rshen and our adventure on Gar Hill? Gods, we made a haul that night!" He clapped the elder thief on the shoulder. "Nay, I'll not have you down in the doldrums whilst I break my strong young back on this damned sarcophagus lid, my not-so-aged friend. Now break you the seal, and let us begin our plunder!"

His spirits lifted by his companion's reminiscences, Satampra Zeiros proceded to do just that, and the two adventurers heave-hoed again. Not long after, the lid fell with a crash to the floor.

The pair could not believe their eyes, for instead of coins or gems, wands or books or any relics of sorcerous power, instead of swords or daggers or even *bones* (nor the dust therefrom) of the long-dead Hurun, the sarcophagus *held nothing!* Indeed it contained naught but a fine black powder or dust, certainly not the dust of the remains of the Voormish shaman! Moreover, this powder had of itself a noxious stench, so that Alu Kuthos' cold-sensitized nose got to sneezing once again. And as he sneezed he half-stumbled, half-fell into the open stone box, thereby smudging his fine gray cloak with the noxious sooty powder. The youth tried to rub it out, but it was of a certainty ground into the very grain of the fibers, and the noisome stench clung cloyingly to the hapless Alu Kuthos.

Stunned and shaken, there was naught for the pair to do but intone the words given them by Ruul-Vash to return them to the temple of Leniqua the moongod.

III.

Of course, Ruul-Vash did not believe the sarcophagus of the Voormish Hurun had been empty, and charged Satampra Zeiros and Alu Kuthos with having secreted away the doubtless many sorcerous relics and artefacts found therein. Moreover, so convinced of this trickery on the part of the thieves was Ruul-Vash that no entreaty to the contrary would be recognized. As a result, Ruul-Vash had the two thieves conducted to his dungeon, and there stripped of their garments and tortured mercilessly. Satampra Zeiros had been forced to undergo the pain of the rack whilst being forced to watch the painful ordeal that Alu Kuthos had to endure. Even now the youth's face was battered and bruised, blood flowing from crushed lips as Ruul-Vash's head torturer stood over his weeping form.

"So, Satampra Zeiros, are you now ready to tell me what I wish to hear?" taunted Ruul-Vash. Behind him the high priest's head torturer, Dobros, chuckled, Alu Kuthos' blood dripping freely from his mailed and hooked gloves. "Tell me, master thief, the veracity, that you and the lad conspired against me." Satampra Zeiros watched the bald giant Dobros wipe his bloody metaled fists on Alu Kuthos' previously fine gray, now smudged cloak and contemptuously throw the garment into the corner behind him.

"Tell me, thief, else I shall have Dobros fetch the irons awarming in the forge, and set them to your hapless companion."

Even through his pain Satampra Zeiros sensed movement in the corner where Alu Kuthos' cloak lay. Focussing his mind on the cloak, he tried to block out the high priest's taunts. What did he see there?

"Look, Dobros, he fights us still. Very well, get you the irons."

It was a crawling, slithering motion. Shadowy, yet semi-solid. He watched in fascination.

Dobros lifted the irons from the fire and returned to his spot behind RuulVash, the rods glowing incandescently in the gloom of the dungeon.

Now it was a floating, swirling motion — something was coalescing. . . .

Alu Kuthos' shriek pierced the air, as the redhot iron met his skin. The acrid reek of burning flesh filled the room. Mercifully, the youth passed out.

The spinning mass grew in the corner as it spilled forth inky black pseudopods. One of these lashed out at Dobros. As it touched him he screamed. His giant body began to instantly blacken and crumble like charcoal, then fell to fine black powder.

Ruul-Vash turned, eyes wide with fear.

It had ceased its whirling now, its coalescence complete. For a moment it bulked in the shadow, then it hopped into the light on its massive splayed feet.

It was a monstrous conglomeration of bat, toad, sloth and ape, the thing from the carving on the lid of the sarcophagus of Hurun, but no carving could do it justice! Its greasy, furred body was grossly swollen like an obscene fat toad, and yet there was a noisome plasticity to its bulk, a suggestion of its being capable of fluid movement. There was also that which suggested it could change its shape at will. Its half-closed eyes regarded them sleepily, and its cavernous maw smiled evilly.

"Tsathoggua " breathed Ruul-Vash.

An impossibly long, snaky tongue protruded from the great fanged maw, coiled itself about the body of the high priest Ruul-Vash, and drew him, screaming and kicking, within. The great lips of the Sleeping God smacked monstrously.

At once the Tsathoggua shadow thing, the simulacrum of the Sleeping God, whose actual body yet slumbered beneath Mount Voormithadreth, and whose indomitable will made manifest this psychic projection for its unholy purpose as guardian of the tomb of Hurun — brought here in the smudge on the Hyperborean youth's cloak, of course — hopped horribly on those massive splayed feet over to the bound form of Satampra Zeiros. Its sleepy eyes glared down at his helpless body, regarded him hungrily. The master thief's eyes nearly burned from their sockets, his skin acrawl. A cold, emotionless yet powerful voice reverberated in the master thief's mind.

"*TWICE* NOW HAVE OUR PATHS CROSSED, O SATAMPRA ZEIROS. AND YET YOU LIVE. FEW ARE SO FORTUNATE. BUT I WARN YOU, TAKE CARE THAT

WE DO NOT MEET AGAIN, HUMAN . . . ELSE I SHALL
DEVOUR YOU, TOO . . . *UTTERLY!*"

With that the Sleeping God stretched forth a great splayed
claw and touched the masterthief's bonds, and at Tsathoggua's
touch the chains rusted and fell away instantly! The shadow-
entity did the same for the still unconscious form of Alu
Kuthos; then the god turned and hopped again into the gloom
and shadows of the dungeon of the temple of the moon-god.

When Alu Kuthos regained consciousness, he and
Satampra Zeiros made haste to quit that noxious place and
return once again to the haunts of civilized man, truly shaken
yet wiser in a cosmic way for their experiences. And evermore
the dreams of Satampra Zeiros were singularly haunted by the
form of that cyclopean thing from far Cykranosh, black and
plastic and furry Tsathoggua, the Sleeping God.

About "The Curse of the Toad"

In Lovecraft's "Winged Death," ghost-written (or, rather, fly-written) for Hazel Heald, he makes a fleeting reference to an ancient Ugandan cult of Tulu and Tsadogua. Hall and Dale have cultivated this far-flung seed and raised up a suitably eldritch African Strangler from it.

An earlier version of this story appeared in 1979 in Loay Hall's fanzine *On Wings of Darkness* # 2, produced for the Esoteric Order of Dagon Amateur Press Association. That version was one big in-joke in which the explorer Burkes was named "William Fulwiller," actually the moniker of a friendly and erudite Lovecraftian researcher who is in every way the opposite of the villain Burkes! Hall later decided to shape the tale up a bit and omit the in-joke element, and this is the first publication of that version.

There does remain, however, one tip of the hat to a fellow E.O.D. member: among the esoteric books on the shelf in the taxidermy shop is something called *The T'sman Manuscript*. This is an arcane repository of blasphemous secrets invented by stalwart fan (and leading expert on Robert Bloch) Randall G. Larson. The hellish volume appears in Larsonian opii including "The Gunfight Against Nyarlathotep" (*Eldritch Tales* # 5, April 1979, and # 6, Fall 1979) and "The Horror in the Garden" (*Eldritch Tales* # 9, April 1983). I have edited a collection of Larson's Mythos tales called *The Thing That Collected Larson* for Mythos Books , due to appear one of these days.

The Curse of the Toad

by Loay Hall and Terry Dale

I had not seen Jason Giles since our graduation from high school in 1954. We had at the time been the closest of friends, although our desired careers were as different as night from day: Jason sought a career in Taxidermy — his father's trade — while I prepared for a career in writing. Hence, after graduation, we went our separate ways; Jason to a college of taxidermy in Texas, and later to one in Los Angeles, where he finally opened his own shop, while I moved to New England, settling in a secluded cottage outside Eddyville, Rhode Island. And twenty years passed before I again saw Jason Giles. Then one afternoon in July of 1974 1 found myself called to L. A. on business — legal business regarding my latest book . . . *Shades of Cthulhu* and, curious to see how Jason had fared over the years, I decided to visit him again . . . GOD WOULD THAT I HAD NEVER DONE SO!

I started to call Jason to let him know I was coming, but on a whim I decided to surprise him instead. Obtaining his address from a telephone directory, I took a cab to the location. But it was I who received the surprise. The shop, a dilapidated redbrick affair, was located in the most squalid district of town, where drunks, panderers and pickpockets begged, solicited, and plied their illbegotten trades on all who came their way.

As I paid the cabbie and walked toward the shop, I noted the sign swinging over his door: *Jason Giles, Taxidermist*. The capital 'T' on taxidermist was missing, while the other letters were almost faded to the point of being unreadable. I stopped at the display window before entering the shop to see a few of Jason's wares on exhibit: stuffed birds, toads, rabbits, fishes, skunks, etc. Of all of the exhibits, however, only one caught my eye: a big toad with a series of white specks on its warty back. The price tag attached to it read $7.00. It seemed reasonable enough. . . .

I entered the cluttered shop and began browsing: stopping here and there, looking at this animal and that, awed at the workmanship of all. Jason had indeed learned his trade well! Yet, regardless how I tried, I could not but shiver at the intensity with which one of Jason's employee's stared at me. He was short and fat and balding; his clothes were faded and stained; while his face — with its beady eyes, flat nose and unusually wide mouth in a perpetual smile — brought to mind the term batrachian!

I shuddered and looked away. He was horrible!

I browsed a full fifteen minutes, I suppose, before I found the courage to approach him and ask about the toad in the window.

"May I help you, sir?" he asked as I walked up to the counter.

"Ah, yes . . ." I stammered. "I'd like to look at one of the toads in your window, if I may."

"Certainly. Which one . . . ?" he asked, coming out from behind the great walnut counter.

"The one with the specks on its back. . . . "

He smiled hideously. "Oh yes, that one. . . . A most unusual toad. . . . "

He handed it to me with the utmost of care. It was the biggest toad I had ever seen; certainly no American species. As I followed him back to the counter, where he boxed and wrapped it for me, I inquired if Mr. Giles, the proprietor, might be available.

His smile widened. "For you, Teddy Roberts — yes. I'm Jason Giles. . . . "

I looked at him stunned. Why, it was impossible! The last time I had seen Jason — at the postgraduation celebration at Burkes Manor — he was short and thin, and could easily have passed as the handsomest boy in school. Twenty years, of course, can bring great changes in a man's physical appearance. But could this be the Jason Giles I knew? It seemed impossible, and yet . . .

"My God, Jason," I gaped. "Y-you've changed. . . . "

The smile vanished from his wide mouth. He nodded his head and sighed.

"I suppose I have changed since we last saw each other, Teddy. But I've experienced things over the years that could change the heartiest man. . . . However, you haven't changed much," he said, perking up. "Just got a little gray. I recognized you the instant you walked into the shop. That's why I was staring so. And I don't have to ask how your writing has been progressing" he said, motioning to a bookshelf on the wall behind the counter.

It was labelled Edward Roberts and I saw copies of many of the books I'd written during the past twenty years — most of them my more erudite works: such as *The T'Sman Manuscript*, *Tcho-Tcho: Fact or Fiction?*, *Cthaat Aquadingen: A Translation*, *The Blood Countess: The Life and Times of Elizabeth Bathory*.

"Yes . . . Well, I've been lucky, Jason, mighty lucky." Then I looked at my friend and asked: "Jason, what happened? What caused this — this — transformation?"

The shop grew silent as he looked at me thoughtfully, as if he was trying to decide if he should confide in me or not, and then he sighed wearily, nodding his head.

"All right, Teddy," he said, "I'll tell you what happened. Yes, I've changed; drastically so. But I didn't look like this until that damned Gordon Burkes took me to Africa on his blasted expedition and messed with that goddamned Congolose bitch!

If he hadn't killed Old Ghanta . . . Aka, the witch doctor, wouldn't have uttered his damnable curse . . . !"

I started. "Gordon Burkes? Witch doctor? Curse? Jason, what the hell are you talking about?" I demanded.

Gordon Burkes, the famous explorer and archaeologist, had been a classmate of Jason's and mine in school; he had helped me gather material for my book *Y'ha-nthlei in the Deep*. And, although in school we had never been close friends, by the time I returned to Eddyville to write the book, an intimate friendship was beginning to develop. Hence I was naturally surprised, and concerned, to hear Jason, who knew Burkes better than I, curse his very name!

Jason sighed and shifted nervously. "Five years ago, when my shop was located in a better district of town, Gordon came to see me on a rather sad but exciting note: his parents had been tragically killed in a plane crash in Southern Vermont. . . ."

"Yes, I remember well. He had just finished helping me with my book, and when I learned of their deaths they had already been buried."

"But the exciting news was that he had inherited his father's wealth, which was considerable — and he was planning to outfit an expedition to Africa in search of a lost tribe. A friend of his father's, Sir John Parker, had learned of the supposed discovery of a tribe of natives believed to be an offshoot of the fabled Tcho-Tcho of Burma, and. . . . "

"But that's absurd, " I interrupted again. "The Tcho-Tcho were slaughtered, in toto, in 1932."

Jason nodded his head slowly. "So I read in your book. But Burkes — you know how persuasive he can be when excited — disagreed with your premise; he felt that some of the Tcho-Tcho had escaped and fled to other parts of the world, and had been absorbed by the natives. . . . Well, he invited me to go along — told me it would give me a chance to bag unusual specimens for my shop — and I agreed. Also — and most importantly

— I admit it, Teddy, I figured that should by chance you be wrong, anyone connected with such a monumental find would surely get rich. . . . But I should never have gone!" his voice shrilled.

"We flew to Johannesburg, where Burkes consulted with Sir John Parker, and then traveled on to Leopoldville. From there we went up the Congo river to Mbandaka, and then into the very heart of the Congo itself. The tribe, we soon discovered, had moved since the last report had reached Parker, and we spent several weeks in locating them again. But the trip had been in vain: for although the natives were certainly smaller than normal and definitely unique in appearance, they possessed none of the marks of the Tcho-Tcho — the beady eyes, bald heads or stunted growth.

"Burkes was crushed with disappointment. The trip had cost him thousands of dollars — and for nothing. He began drinking heavily and became sullen and testy. More than once one of our carriers crossed him — and nearly lost his life! I tried to reason with him; to persuade him to return to America . . . All I got for my trouble was a sound cursing . . .

"It readily became evident that the only way to get along with Gordon was to keep out of his way. So for this reason I became friendly with Aka, the village witch doctor, from whom I learned a bit of their native tongue, and began visiting the 'temple' of their god, Gua. The 'temple' was a great circular hut at one end of the village. Here the natives prayed to Gua, Lord of the Earth, for better crops and more prosperous hunts. The image, which sat on a baked earth dais, was about three feet in height, with a potbelly; its head resembled a toad with sleepy eyes. . . . "

My eyes must have bulged in surprise. For Jason, a smile on his lips, paused long enough for me to utter one spinechilling word: "Tsathoggua!"

He nodded. "As the weeks passed, Burkes began to ease up on his drinking and was easier to get along with. I took this as a sign that he was returning to his senses and was preparing to return home. But I was wrong. I soon learned why the sudden change. One night he slipped out of our hut around midnight and vanished into the jungle, which crouched nearby. Fearing that he might meet the old lion which was feeding on the native's cattle (as he had forgotten his rifle), I grabbed my gun and followed him. He met no lion — just Sadas, wife of Ghanta, the village chief . . .

"Well, when he returned hours later, I told him I knew of his affair with Sadas and demanded that he lead the expedition back to civilization with the first light of dawn or else. . . . My threats, however, only enraged him, and he tried his best to choke me to death! And he would have succeeded too if Ghanta hadn't been awakened by our struggles and stopped him at spearpoint! Never before was I so happy to see anyone in all my days! He was a kind man and I liked him greatly. Burkes, however, swore he'd kill Ghanta if he ever interfered in his business again.

"The next day the hunters, led by a sullen Ghanta, left the village for two days of hunting. A half dozen or so men remained behind to protect the women and children from ranging animals. I noticed Burkes glaring at me as I watched the hunters leaving the village, so I went with Aka to the temple of Gua. Several hours later, as Aka was explaining to me how Gua first descended from the heavens, we heard several gunshots, apparently coming from Burkes's and my hut. We rushed there and discovered a horrible scene of death: Ghanta, a vicious-looking knife in one hand, lay on the dirt floor in a pool of his own blood, half his face blown away; standing over him, his revolver in one hand, stood a grim-faced Gordon Burkes. Behind him, holding her dress in front of her to hide her nakedness, crouched Sadas, her eyes wide with terror!

"Before I could stop him, Aka grabbed the knife in his belt and rushed upon Burkes, who sent two bullets into the old man's guts before he had gone a half-dozen steps. He collapsed to his knees. Before he died, as blood rushed from his mouth and stomach, he mouthed the 'Curse of the Toad.' And Sadas fainted with a shriek. Then Aka fell beside his chief, dead.

" . . . Well, Burkes picked up Sadas and we fled the village, perforce killing several of the natives. The survivors ran in the direction the hunters had gone. It was then that I realized that to demand Burkes leave her behind would mean her death. Hate her as I did, however, I could not leave her to certain death.

"Two days passed and nothing happened. We saw no sign of the hunters and Aka's curse, if indeed one existed, was ineffective. Burkes and I began to laugh and mock at the very idea. But Sadas would only sit in silence and terror, only rarely speaking to herself, murmuring 'the curse' over and over again. Finally her carrying on got under Burkes's nerves and he beat her within an inch of her life, threatening that if she didn't shut up he'd kill her. That evening we camped along the bank of the Congo River. Gordon and I had gone in search of firewood when we heard Sadas scream a blood-chilling scream. We found her just in time to see her disappear beneath the surface of a pool of quicksand near the campsite. At the edge of the pit, its eyes bulging and mouth open as if in mocking laughter, was a big toad. . . .

"Then nothing further untoward occurred. We arrived back in the United States and were just beginning to think the curse had been aimed at Sadas, when it happened!" Jason said mournfully.

"My God, Jason," I gasped. "You mean that's how you came to be like this?" It seemed almost too incredible for belief.

"Oh no, Teddy!" He laughed horribly, patting his bloated belly. "I got this from gluttonous eating! No, you see it wasn't Sadas or me whom the curse was intended for — it was Burkes!"

I looked at him in confusion.

"Then what happened to Gordon Burkes?" I asked.

"Why, you just bought him, of course. . . . "

With a scream of terror I fled the shop, leaving the door open behind me. As I ran, I heard Jason's voice:

"Hey, you forgot your package!"

And then he burst into insane laughter.

About "Dark Swamp"

What follows is James Anderson's ingenious attempt to solve the mystery of Dark Swamp, a legendary Rhode Island miasma Lovecraft and C.M. Eddy sought in vain to visit one day in 1923. The tale told was that the thickets of the swamp were so dense and over-grown that there were parts of it where the sun never shone. Lovecraft used the idea in "The Colour out of Space": "West of Arkham the hills rise wild, and there are valleys with deep woods that no axe has ever cut. There are dark narrow glens where the trees slope fantastically, and where thin brooklets trickle without ever having caught the glint of sunlight." Derleth liked this evocative description so much that he decided it couldn't hurt to recycle it in "Wentworth's Day": "There are areas of woodland in which no axe has ever fallen, as well as dark, vine-grown glens, where brooks trickle in a darkness unbroken by sunlight even on the brightest day." Of Dark Swamp itself, however, neither man ever wrote.

But, even as Anderson notes, C.M. Eddy, who accompanied Lovecraft on the search for Dark Swamp, much as Randolph Carter accompanied Harley Warren on a similar mission, did essay to write up the adventure that might have been. Ominously, though, he did not live to finish it. Here is the account of Muriel E. Eddy, Clifford Eddy's wife and also Lovecraft's good friend. "In 1967 Cliff started *BLACK NOON*, an imaginative fictionalized parallelism of his adventures with Howard, but he was unable to complete it due to illness. He passed away later that year. August Derleth was intending to finish this work, and perhaps expand it into a full-length novel. But it remained unfinished due to August's death in 1971" (Introduction to C.M. Eddy, *Exit into Eternity: Tales of the Bizarre and Supernatural*, Providence: Oxford Press, Inc., 1973, p. v.).

Eddy did complete 24 pages, and I have included this draft in a Fedogan & Bremer anthology called *Acolytes of Cthulhu*. One hates to joke about such things (or at least to be caught joking about them), but one can hardly resist wondering if there was some terrible revelation at Dark Swamp which Lovecraft knew better than to record, and which caught up with two intrepid men who did try to reveal it, Eddy and Derleth! If I were James Anderson, I'd be watching my back! But, as far as I know, he's been relatively safe since the original publication of "Dark Swamp" in a classic issue of *Eldritch Tales* (# 9 from April 1983) which also featured Peter Cannon's "The Madness out of Space," Donald R. Burleson's "The Shape in the Room," and Thomas Ligotti's "Dream of a Mannikin."

Dark Swamp

by James Anderson

I will begin to write despite my trembling hands, and despite the fact that I cannot possibly submit the manuscript once it is completed. *The Rhode Island Review* is a respected magazine dealing with factual articles and well-researched journalism. They could never publish the story I am about to relate.

Sometimes when I look back on the incidents surrounding the tale, I question my own mind. I suppose I would consider myself quite mad were it not for the photograph that is my proof, but how could I possibly ask anyone else to believe my story if I doubt it myself? Submitting the article is out of the question — that I realize — yet I must write the story, to preserve my own sanity if nothing more.

I still find it hard to believe that it all began just one short week ago. I phoned Roy, the editor of the *Review*, and suggested doing an article on H.P. Lovecraft, the famous Rhode Island author. I proposed to revisit some of the places that Lovecraft frequented, and write about how these places affected his work. Roy liked the idea and told me to begin it immediately; if I finished before August ninth it would make the next issue. So I took my camera and spent the rest of the week on Benefit Street, photographing the "Shunned House" and the homes where Lovecraft had lived. On Saturday I drove to Newport and photographed the old tower, where Viking seamen are believed to have landed years before Columbus.

Then I remembered hearing of a place in Chepachet, Rhode Island called the "Dark Swamp". According to legend it is located somewhere along Putnam Pike. As far as I knew the swamp existed only in local mythology and is supposed to be a place of impenetrable darkness where even the sun never shines. I recalled that Lovecraft had unsuccessfully tried to find the swamp, and had given up after spending most of a day in the August sun.

The idea of the Dark Swamp took hold of me and I was unable to dislodge it. I thought it might be interesting to follow Lovecraft's route and find out if the swamp existed at all. Perhaps there was some truth to the myth, I thought. Now that would make a story!

I packed my camera and equipment, prepared a thermos of iced tea, and put a few sandwiches in the cooler. It would probably be a long day, I thought as I left early that Sunday morning.

The traffic was light on route 95 — everyone was headed south for the beaches while I went north — and I made good time. I turned off at route 44 near the Statehouse, and I followed the road for a half hour as it wound its way through Providence and then through the towns of North Providence and Smithfield. I suffered in the early morning heat, wishing the air conditioner hadn't been broken as usual. I could imagine how Lovecraft must have felt, coming all this distance on a trolley and then walking for the rest of the day.

I passed through the town of Chepachet and followed the two lane road until it blended into the woodlands and rolling farms. I realized that, though much of route 44 had been built up and industrialized since Lovecraft's time, this section of Putnam Pike had remained virtually unchanged since 1923. There was no traffic to speak of and I drove slowly, taking a good look at my surroundings.

I drove by a farm and noticed a farmer setting up irrigation pipes in the cornfield. I stopped the car by the side of the road and walked through the rows of plants, savoring the sweet smell of the corn.

"Sorry," the farmer said. "I don't sell retail. The corn's for the markets. There's a stand 'bout four miles down the road though."

"No," I said. "I'm not looking for corn. Just information."

"Oh," he said, raising his eyebrows.

"Have you ever heard of the Dark Swamp?"

The farmer frowned and seemed to withdraw. "Hmmm. Dark Swamp? No. Never heard of it. There's Great Swamp out in Narragansett. Big Indian battle there, years ago."

"No, I've been to Great Swamp. I'm looking for Dark Swamp. It's supposed to be between Chepachet and Putnam."

"Sorry," he said, turning away rather quickly. "I never heard of it."

Somehow I was left with the distinct impression that the farmer was holding back whatever he knew.

I returned to the car and continued along the road, knowing that the swamp was nearby. I kept my eye out for another farmer or a house where I might try again for information, but all I passed was a narrow dirt driveway with a chain stretched across and a "No Trespassing" sign attached.

The scenery remained unchanged for several miles, thick deciduous forests broken only by an occasional clearing. I had not realized how far I'd come until I passed another large cornfield and then saw the vegetable stand ahead.

I slowed the car and pulled into the turnout. It was an old wooden stand, the paint peeling and the sides weatherbeaten by too many New England winters. A young girl, about twelve years old, busily unpacked crates of corn and lined the ears on the shelves while an old woman sat in a rocking chair and read a romance novel.

I entered the shade of the stand and could not help notice the fine assortment of native produce. Thinking I might have better luck if I made a purchase, I picked out a half-dozen ears of corn and a few tomatoes.

The old woman carefully marked her place in the book, then bagged my purchase.

"That'll be two dollars," she said.

I handed her a five and watched as she pocketed the bill and made change, her bony fingers sure of themselves.

"Do you know where I might find the Dark Swamp?"

The old woman shuddered as she regarded me through steady eyes.

"Why do you want to know?"

"I'm . . . I'm a writer. I'm doing an article on the swamp."

"Hmm. A writer. There was another, a writer, who came looking for the swamp many years ago. I was just a girl then."

"Lovecraft!" I exclaimed. "He was here! Did you meet him?"

"His name was Howard. Yes, I met him. Actually, I was quite struck with him. He looked so helpless — so sensitive. As I said, I was a girl and very impressionable."

"My God! You've met Lovecraft."

"Was that his name?"

"Yes. Yes, that man was Howard Phillips Lovecraft, one of the greatest writers who ever lived."

The woman stared into the distance for a moment, lost in thought.

"He was a most gentle man," she said. "He asked me where the Dark Swamp was."

"And did you tell him?"

"Yes. He said he'd been looking the week before with another man and that he'd come back alone this time. I should never have told him. But I could not say no."

"Why shouldn't you have told him?"

"Why," she asked. "Then you don't know? I guess Howard never wrote about the Dark Swamp then."

"Well, no. He never did."

"Young man. The Dark Swamp is an evil place, better left alone. Evil beings dwell there, trapped by their own wickedness. These demons are just waiting to be let out, just waiting to escape and invade the world of men.

"Once I told the secret of Dark Swamp and I have lived in fear since that day, almost sixty years of fear. I will not tell the secret again."

"Well, thank you anyway," I said. "May I take your picture?"

"Why not," she said.

I took a couple of photographs before walking back toward the car, elated yet disappointed. Then, standing beside the stand was the girl I'd noticed earlier.

"Meet me in the cornfield," she whispered as I left the stand.

I nodded, then returned to the car and drove off. After travelling a little way down the road I stopped beside the cornfield. I waited a few minutes and the girl appeared from between the rows of corn.

"I overheard you talking to Grandma," she said with a youthful smile. "I know where Dark Swamp is."

"Will you tell me?"

"Yes. "

"Aren't you afraid?"

"No," she said gravely, "Grandma is old and superstitious. I don't believe any of those stories. Dark Swamp is just that — a dark swamp."

"Have you been there?"

"No," she admitted. "I'm not that brave. But I'll tell you; then you can tell me all about it."

"It's a deal," I said. "I'll even send you a copy of my article."

"Would you! I've never met a writer before! Would you autograph it?'

"Sure." I said, "What's your name?"

"Chris."

"I'm Jim," I said.

She gave me the address to send the article and then she gave me directions to Dark Swamp.

"Go back down the road a couple of miles," she said. "On your right you'll see a small dirt road with a chain going across."

"Yes. I remember passing the spot."

"Good. You'll have to park your car and walk from there. Just follow the dirt path. I think it goes on for about a mile, then it narrows to a trail and finally disappears altogether. Keep going straight through the woods. You'll find Dark Swamp."

"Thank you. I'll send you the article."

"And Jim," she said. "You don't believe Grandma's tales, do you?"

"Of course not," I said.

She smiled and waved as I drove away.

I found the dirt road with no trouble and I parked the car. Before setting off on foot I gulped a sandwich and drank a cup of iced tea; after all, I had no idea of how long this excursion might take. Then, trying to control my excitement, I took out my camera and snapped a couple of pictures of the road itself before going on.

Half expecting a farmer to appear with a loaded shotgun, I stepped over the chain and began my walk down the deserted road. Although I'd left early, it was almost noon now and the sun was hotter than ever.

I followed the dirt road for about fifteen minutes, entranced with the idea that the Dark Swamp really did exist after all. I noticed the abundance of wildlife: squirrels, rabbits, and chipmunks. As I walked on I thought that perhaps no one had traveled this route since 1923 when Lovecraft himself had come to Dark Swamp.

It was strange, I thought, that Lovecraft had never written of the place, either in his journals or letters. C.M. Eddy had written of the first unsuccessful trip, when he had accompanied Lovecraft, but aside from that the Dark Swamp was never mentioned.

I supposed it would remain a mystery, unless the swamp turned out to be not even worth writing about.

The road ended abruptly and turned into a small trail. Although no vegetation grew on the footpath, it looked as if it had not been trodden in years. As I walked along I also noticed the sudden absence of birds or other wildlife. The trees grew thicker and the ground became moist, dotted with small mushrooms and fungi. The sunlight became more faint; but the heat intensified as the forest thickened and the path narrowed.

Finally the trail disappeared altogether and I found myself walking through thick mud. I continued on, glad that I'd worn my old sneakers, and stopped occasionally to adjust my flash unit and take a photograph.

The mud deepened with each step and the sunlight dimmed. I cursed myself for not bringing a flashlight, but I admitted to myself that I'd never expected the tales of the Dark Swamp to be so accurate — at least as far as the darkness was concerned.

Suddenly all trace of light ended with a single step. Although I could not see into the blackness, my senses warned me of a swamp just ahead. There was an eerie stillness and not even a mosquito disturbed the calm. The odor was of death and decay, as if some huge creature had been rotting away in the humidity for the last two thousand years.

So this was the Dark Swamp, I thought, still wishing I'd brought along a flashlight. At least I had a powerful flash unit on my camera. I'd take a couple of pictures to use with the article and I'd be in business. Excitedly I fumbled with the camera,

adjusting the florescent dials in the darkness. I decided to take
several pictures, just to make sure. The swamp was frightening
enough and I had no desire to return if the pictures failed to
come out.

As I lifted the camera I became aware of the overpowering
odor; it was the same smell of death and decay magnified a
hundred times. What was strange was the fact that there was
not even the slightest hint of a breeze to stir the air; there was
no wind to fan the disgusting smell toward me.

Ignoring the smell as best I could, I lifted the camera and
snapped the shutter. The brilliant light of the flash illuminated
the swamp for a brief fraction of a second.

I will never forget that instant. The image will remain
welded to my brain for as long as I may live. I will remember
each and every vivid detail, each shadow, each tiny reflection of
light. I will relive the moment each night, in terrible dreams,
and I will live each day in fear.

The swamp itself seemed black, even under the unnatural
light. There were no trees, merely the empty blackness of the
swamp. Yet somehow, though there was no shade, sunlight
could not enter or pierce the darkness.

But it was more than this violation of all physical laws that
caused me to turn and flee from the Dark Swamp, that made
me run the entire distance back through the woods and into my
car, that made me speed and not slow down until I had reached
the familiar surroundings of Providence. Indeed, it was more
than this. For in the swamp I saw a figure wading through the
murky waters, wading toward the shore, its yellow eyes blazing
with hatred and evil and its fangs dripping with blood. What I
saw in the terrible brackish waters was one of the Old Ones
themselves, awakened from the deepest reaches of the swamp.

As I said, I fled and did not slow down until I reached
Providence. I drove more slowly then and my nerves had
almost returned to normal when I reached my home in the suburbs. I began to doubt what I'd seen. I decided it must have

been the eerie setting coupled with a strange reflection of light that caused the apparition. I tried to calm myself and almost succeeded. Then I remembered the camera. Surely this was proof that nothing existed in the Dark Swamp.

Feeling much better, I hurried to my darkroom and removed the film. Slowly, painstakingly, I developed the pictures, one by one, calming myself with my work. Not until I had finished exposing the photographs of the dirt road, the forest and the old woman, did I reach the picture of the Dark Swamp. Tensely I waited for the image to appear on the paper. Nervously I watched as it formed, the dark waters, the absence of any tree — and the figure of the Old One, bloated and toad-like as it walked from the swamp.

I screamed, alone in the darkroom, and I opened the door and ran into the sunlight of the room.

It was almost an hour before I had the courage to return. Not until I had made three prints was I sure that the thing was real.

It's evening now. The darkness has descended much too quickly, and my hands tremble even as I write. The thing from the swamp needs darkness and Chepachet is not so far from here. And I cannot help but remember the words of the old woman who sold vegetables by the side of the road. I remember what she said about the swamp and about the evil that lives there: "These demons are just waiting to be let out, just waiting to escape and invade the world of man."

I shudder whenever I think about it. And I wonder if I am the one who set them free.

About "The Old One"

Whence the Great Glasby's notion of Tsathoggua seeing out of a single Cyclopean eye? In a March 28, 1934 letter to James Ferdinand Morton (the prototype of the Paterson, New Jersey museum curator in whose office narrator Thurston finds the newspaper story about Johansen in "The Call of Cthulhu"), Lovecraft unleashes a stream of mineralogical jokes, including this one: "Then there are the hellish stony secrets filtering down from the forgotten elder world - think of the Eye of Tsathoggua, hinted at in the Livre d'Eibon." In context, of course, this would refer to a gem, not unlike, we may suppose, the Shining Trapezohedron in form and function.

Indeed, in view of the fact that the whole notion of the avatar of Nyarlathotep being prisoned in the steeple of a church seems to have been derived from Lovecraft's frivolous reference to the "scratching within the sealed spire" of "the abandoned Church of St. Toad in the crumbling slums of ancient Yothby" (to Smith, September 11, 1933), it may not be too much to suggest that the Eye of Tsathoggua was the prototype for the Shining Trapezohedron in "The Haunter of the Dark," written the year after this letter to Morton. In fact, I am convinced that Lovecraft first wrote the story with the monster identified as an "avatar of Tsathoggua" (a phrase occurring in an April 24, 1935 letter to Robert Bloch), not of Nyarlathotep. See my article "Who Was the Avatar of Darkness?" in *Crypt of Cthulhu* # 95.

"The Old One" first appeared in *Crypt of Cthulhu* # 67, Michaelmas 1989.

The Old One

by John S. Glasby

That there are still many mysteries associated with this planet and, in particular how and when life first came into existence is something no self-respecting scientist will deny. Geologists accept that the Earth is some four billion years old while archaeologists maintain that thinking Man evolved only ten or fifteen thousand years ago. But suggest to them that Man is only the latest in a long line of intelligent races to have inhabited this planet and they either turn a deaf ear to such theories or verbally attack the proposer of such ideas, labeling him a crank or a fanciful dreamer.

They state categorically that there is not a single shred of concrete evidence for such wild propositions; that no archaeological expedition has yet uncovered the ruins of such civilisations and if questioned about the ancient myths and legends of the old gods and the days when giants lived in the earth, they claim these are nothing more than superstitious tales and old religions perpetrated by the priestly cults to gain power for themselves.

But it is the scientists who are blinkered by their ignorance and refusal to believe in anything they cannot measure and weigh with their instruments. They utterly fail to comprehend that all which is not visible need not necessarily have no existence.

In my post as associate professor of archaeology at a small American university I had come up against this brick wall of strict scientific agnosticism from many of my colleagues, in particular Professor Dorman, my immediate superior. Where matters of a bizarre or highly controversial nature were concerned, he absolutely refused to discuss them, insisting that his students must be taught only conventional theories and if I held any other ideas it would be best if I kept them to myself.

Being only a relatively obscure figure in archaeolog,. I did as I was bid during working hours. But after the lectures were finished, and during my weekends away from university work, I actively pursued my own ideas, haunting the various bookshops and libraries in my search for any reference to these most ancient of civilisations. My main purpose at that time was to extend my knowledge of these distant cultures as far back into Earth's prehistoric history as possible.

I read avidly of the religious beliefs of the early Egyptian dynasties and those of neighbouring Ur and of the British archaeologist Sir Arthur Evans's discoveries on Crete, which resulted in rescuing the Minoan civilisation from mythological fiction and putting it before the scientific world as fact.

Yet in spite of all my researches, I seemed doomed to go so far back in time and no further. There were, of course, the numerous references to fabled Atlantis, but these were so varied and placed this civilisation in so many different locations, they were virtually useless.

Then, one October evening, I came across a bookshop I had not previously visited. It was in a narrow street well removed from any of the major thoroughfares and the dim-fit window did little to attract attention. I entered it with a curious sense of precognitive excitement, noticing that it appeared far more spacious than I would have expected, viewing it from outside. There were a few late-night customers browsing among the shelves but most appeared interested in the shelves devoted to modern novels and I soon found myself at the rear of the shop where the dusty appearance of the books was indicative both of their age and infrequent sale.

The majority dealt with mundane subjects such as geography and travel. There were one or two containing experiments in alchemy with vague references to the search for the Philosopher's Stone and the Elixir of Life. These I glanced through and then replaced; I was beginning to despair of finding anything worthwhile when I spotted a slim volume tucked away, almost out of sight, behind a large treatise on the life of Samuel Pepys.

What initially caught my attention was the curious nature of the covers and binding. The covers had a smooth, slippery touch, more like metal than cloth or board, and the pages were bound by incredibly thin strips of a dull grey metal. It looked like a fake made by some modern process cunningly treated to give it the appearance of great age. Yet even in the dim light, I would have sworn that the pages were of some kind of papyrus, yellowed and brittle. Many of them were oddly stained as if by sea water and in places they were stuck together.

The text was handwritten and this, coupled with the fact that the ink had faded, made it singularly difficult to read. It was in Latin but that, in itself, presented no problem for I was well versed in this dead language. Almost at once my eye fell upon a curious passage:

It is written in the Book of K'yog that long eons before the first men came there was a great city built where the rivers Karnodir and Deb ran together at the head of a delta which vanished in fire and cataclysm more than thirty thousand years ago. It is further told that the beings which erected the grey-hued pillars and columns of Yuth migrated from a dark planet on the outer edge of the solar system, drifting sunward on huge leathery wings and bearing with them an amorphous entity they called Tsathoggua which they enshrined within a central temple and worshipped with abominable ceremonies each night when the moon was full.

To say that my excitement and curiosity reached fever pitch on reading this extraordinary passage would be an understatement. This volume promised to provide me with such revelations into the distant past of our planet as I had never before encountered. There remained of course the possibility the book was a deliberate fake. Yet, somehow, I did not think so. There was something about it, some strange aura which spoke of a long forgotten age. That the text had been copied from some much earlier volume, I did not doubt.

But if it provided me with but a single clue to further reading, it would be well worth whatever price the owner asked. I took it back to the front of the shop and handed it over the counter, asking him the price. He quoted a ridiculously low figure which I accepted at once and before leaving with my prize I inquired of him where he had obtained it.

I had noticed his curious expression the moment he had glanced at it and, although he had raised no objection to my purchasing it, he seemed singularly evasive as to its origin. Finally, however, he consulted a large ledger, running his finger down the pages until he found the entry he sought.

The volume, he informed me, was part of a small lot he had bought some seven years earlier from a house in Winson Street when the owner, a recluse well into his nineties, had died leaving the house and contents to his grandson, a wealthy industrialist, who had not the slightest interest in such fantastic literature. On further questioning, he gave me, albeit reluctantly, the name and present address of this grandson.

The hour was now growing late and I hurried back to my rooms at the university, clutching my find under my coat for it had begun to rain and I did not wish any further damage to befall the book which, from my brief perusal, I felt certain was more than a thousand years old. I had already resolved to get in touch with Simon Howarth, the grandson, as soon as possible to see if he could possibly throw any light upon where his grandfather had obtained the volume.

That very evening, I sat until the early hours of the morning, reading through the book. Strangely, it bore no title, nor was there any indication of the identity of the author which was highly unusual. The only conclusion I could reach was that the writer, whoever he was, had penned these pages anonymously for fear of persecution. Down through the ages, those who had delved into such forbidden writings were considered warlocks and witches and had suffered a harsh fate at the hands of the church.

Despite the numerous portions which had faded beyond legibility where I could make out only disjointed sentences, there was much in the book to convince me of its authenticity. There were, of course, no dates given which I could use to correlate with known historical facts and events for it told of an era long before the primitive nomadic tribes of the Egyptian delta had come together after the war between North and South under the double crown of a united Egypt.

Briefly, it was a compilation of historical events covering a period, if I could read the text correctly, of more than fifty thousand years and ending some twenty thousand years ago, between the coming of this alien race to Earth from the Dark Planet on the rim of the solar system — which I assumed to be Pluto — to the destruction of their capital city of Yuth.

There were also veiled, and necessarily vague, references which went back in time much further than this, possibly millions of years, detailing a great war between two races fought far out in space among the stars. For the first time I had come across evidence which went far beyond even my ideas upon this subject, alluding to beings far different from humans in their ability to move through space and time quite freely, employing weapons beyond all imagining, able to produce living creatures from inanimate matter and energy, keeping them as slaves to perform all manner of menial tasks requiring only brute strength and little intelligence.

The outcome of this great interstellar war was defeat for the race which the unknown writer called the Old Ones and they had been hurled down onto the young, evolving planets of a number of suns, including our own. Here, they had been held in check throughout the ages by powerful spells and sigils of immense potency.

It made fascinating reading. But it ended on a chilling and menacing note which sent a shudder of nameless dread through me as I sat at my table; for it suggested that with the passage of untold eons, the potency of these ancient spells might weaken sufficiently for the Old Ones to throw off their shackles and rise again with terrible consequences for the inhabitants of those planets where they had been held in bondage.

I considered showing the volume to Professor Dorman but knowing his deep aversion to such bizarre ideas I decided against such a course, at least for the present. He would undoubtedly have judged the book a very clever fake and ridiculed me for even thinking it could be genuine.

The following day was a Saturday and, having no lectures, I had plenty of time to check the town map for the address, before ringing Simon Howarth and arranging an appointment to see him on a matter which I described as particularly urgent.

He was a tall, bearded man in his late forties who received me cordially and evinced some surprise to learn that I had purchased one of the old books which had belonged to his grandfather. He himself had considered them to be worthless and had been glad to get rid of them when his grandfather's house had been emptied some ten years earlier.

I explained who I was and my interest in what had been written in the book; that the main purpose of my visit was to inquire if he could give me any information at all on where his grandfather had obtained the book in question.

"Well, now, Professor Sheldon," he said, shaking his head slowly, "I'm afraid there's very little I can tell you. My grandfather was a strange man with more than a passing interest in this incredible mythos of alien races which existed on Earth long before man."

"The volume speaks of the *Book of K'yog*," I said. "Obviously this was the original source from which this book was copied."

Howarth's face showed he had never heard of the *Book of K'yog*, a fact which did not surprise me. But his next statement roused my curiosity.

"I do recall he had some correspondence with several people who had similar ideas to his own many years ago. Much of it came from abroad, remote parts of Asia and Africa."

I sat up straight in my chair. "I don't suppose any of these letters are still in existence?"

Howarth pursed his lips. "I'm not certain." He got to his feet. "There is an old casket of his containing some letters which I brought with me from his house."

"May I see it?" I asked.

Howarth hesitated for a moment, then went out of the room and I heard him going upstairs. He came back a few minutes later carrying an antique oak box which he placed on the table in front of him. The lid, which was delicately carved with scrolls and minute figures, was evidently locked but neither of us were able to find any keyhole.

Howarth gave a shaky laugh. "It doesn't seem as though he meant it to be opened," he muttered, turning it over and over in his hands. "Unless there's a concealed spring catch somewhere."

He moved his fingers over the curious arabesques carved on the lid and sides, then uttered a sharp exclamation as his finger depressed one and the lid flew open with a sudden snap.

Inside, bound with a length of black ribbon, was a bundle of letters, yellow with age. With Howarth's permission, I removed them and glanced at the dates. All were more than fifty years old and had come from many parts of the world, some written in hasty scribbles which were difficult to decipher; others in more stylish hands with flowing letters.

Howarth readily agreed I could take them with me to examine at my leisure and, after promising to return them at the earliest opportunity, I left. Back at the university, I lost no

time in reading through the curious correspondence Jethro
Howarth had carried on more than fifty years before.

That he had believed implicitly in these fabulously ancient
myths and legends was immediately apparent and his interest
clearly stemmed from a very early age for two of the letters
dated from the early years of the century when he could have
barely entered his teens.

One, dated January 27, 1935, had been posted in Nairobi
and contained the following cryptic passage —

> Brenton claims we have now uncovered virtually all of the ruins which
> certainly cover a very large extent. We are all agreed that this previ-
> ously unsuspected city in the middle of the African continent is incred-
> ibly old. Allen maintains it to be contemporary with Ur while I am
> positive that not only is it far older but we have merely uncovered the
> topmost layers and will discover even more if we dig deeper. However,
> the buildings are too regular, too normal for it to be Yuth as men-
> tioned in the *Book of K'yog*.

Many of the other letters were in a similar vein giving
accounts of excavations in various regions of the world, but all
from places where no known civilisations were believed to have
existed in far-off days.

All mentioned Yuth, that grey city of this alien race which
had disappeared twenty thousand years ago, millennia before
the stones for the pyramids had been hewn from the earth.
That they were all searching for it was self-evident. But why
had nothing of this got into the newspapers or scientific journals of the time? While I would almost certainly have missed
the former, it was unlikely I would have overlooked any reference in the latter. It took planning and finances to embark
upon expeditions such as these to remote and generally inac-
cessible parts of the world.

The more I read of the letters, the more I became convinced
that there was something distinctly odd about these excavations which were widely spread in both space and time. It was
almost as if there existed a cult dedicated to the discovery of

Yuth and one which had gone to great pains to keep its activities well hidden from both the scientific community and the
world at large.

There was one mysterious and portentous letter which was
among the last Jethro Howarth had received before his death.
It bore neither address nor signature but it yielded a cryptic
clue to what I was seeking. Since it had a direct bearing upon
subsequent events, I feel I should give it in full:

Dear Howarth:

My physicians have told me I do not have much longer to live and I
am therefore sending you the book which I promised you several years
ago. Keep it well for, as I am aware, there is no other copy in existence and should it be lost or destroyed, no means of recopying its
contents.

As you are doubtless aware, all efforts to locate the eon-old city of
Yuth have been doomed to failure for the *Book of K'yog* has been lost for
countless millennia and the cataclysmic events which annihilated Yuth,
coupled with the geological upheavals which have altered the Earth's
surface since that time, means that it may never be found.

However, all may not necessarily be lost. I have recently read that certain underwater discoveries have been made off the Bimini Islands
which form part of the Bahamas. There is a road constructed of huge
stone blocks and my own reassessment of the various legends indicate
that it is just possible Yuth lies there, submerged beneath the ocean,
for there are a number of scientific facts to support one of two theories. Firstly, that a large meteor shower struck the region off the
Carolina coast some fifteen thousand years ago as witnessed by the
numerous craters which have been found there, and secondly, that the
rapid melting of the Laurentide ice-sheet twelve thousand years ago
utterly inundated the area around the Bahamas.

Your sincere friend,

Marcus Goravius

I replaced the mystic letters in the box and carefully closed
the lid. There the matter may have ended for there seemed no
other avenues of research I could explore regarding this fantastic race of long-forgotten eons. But events were soon to tran-

spire which were to lead me into a realm of cosmic horror that transcended anything I had ever imagined and result in the horrific death of Professor Dorman.

The sequence of events began some three weeks later when it was announced that the university had been chosen to mount a small-scale archaeological expedition, and of the three suggested sites, one was Bimini.

Of the other two, one was a site in the middle of the Brazilian jungle and the third among the foothills of the Andes. Dorman and I discussed the alternatives at great length and, although leaving him totally ignorant of my true motives, I was finally able to persuade him that the Bimini site was the most logical since it was readily accessible, still posed several unsolved questions of archaeological importance in spite of the work which had already been carried out there, and would require less financing than the other two.

Since we were not due to start out for another four months we were able to ensure that our preparations were extremely thorough. The team was to consist of Dorman, two senior members of the Archaeology Department, Conlon and Brown, and myself. Two ships were put at our disposal, one carrying a bathysphere with all its ancillary equipment. We also made arrangements for a light aircraft to be based on the island so that aerial photographs might be taken of the various submerged artifacts which were known to lie in the shallow water off the island. Any divers we might need could readily be hired for the purpose once we arrived.

We flew down to Miami at the beginning of April where we joined the ship which was to take us the fifty miles or so to North Bimini. The second vessel had gone ahead and was anchored in the lagoon on the opposite side of the island to Paradise Point, northwest of which was what had come to be known as the Bimini Road, an underwater structure of regular and polygonal stones.

We finally arrived after a pleasant and uneventful crossing and caught our first sight of the islands in brilliant sunshine, going ashore at the small settlement of Bailey Town.

In view of my unspoken knowledge concerning an alien race which had existed on Earth many thousands of years prior to the advent of man on this planet, I was anxious to begin work at once. But Dorman vetoed such a plan, insisting it was essential we did not waste our efforts by mistakenly repeating earlier work. It was not, he maintained, as if we had discovered a completely new archaeological site where we could literally excavate anywhere in the hope of making new and important finds.

With this I had to be content for I could see the wisdom in what he said. Accordingly, the first couple of days were spent in getting all of the gear ready and surveying the maps of the undersea discoveries already made. We knew that carbon dating had already been done on that plant and animal life found in the blocks of stone which made up the Bimini Road. These indicated these remains to be between six and twelve thousand years old although the age of the huge stones themselves was probably much older than this since they were being constantly recrystallized due to the high mineral content of the water itself.

It was finally agreed that we would begin our examination of the ocean bed considerably further from the island than had hitherto been possible, using the bathysphere. This was of the most modern design, capable of withstanding tremendous pressures and equipped, not only with a battery of powerful searchlights, but also scoops and grabs for retrieving objects from the floor of the sea, all manipulated from inside. The sphere was also large enough for two men to be seated in comfort and messages and instructions could be relayed to the surface by means of a radio-telephone link. Three exterior cameras, one using infrared film, completed the battery of scientific instruments.

On the morning of the third day we went out to the waiting vessel and headed north until we reached a point some
thirty miles from Bimini. It had already been agreed that
Conlon and I should make the first descent and it was with a
feeling of mounting excitement and trepidation that I followed
Conlon into the confined space of the bathysphere and seated
myself in front of the bank of instruments.

The hatch was closed and made secure before we were lifted
from the deck and lowered over the side. A few moments later
we hit the water and began the descent into the blue-green
world that gradually became darker as we went down. Of the
two of us, I must confess I was more nervous for I could not
help recalling that apocryphal letter addressed to Jethro
Howarth shortly before his death and I was oddly afraid of
what we might see in the beams of the searchlights once we
approached the bottom. Was it possible that the site of legendary Yuth lay directly below us? And if so, what alien won-
ders lay beneath the mud and ooze of the seabed, hidden from
sight for untold thousands of years?

The mere thought of finding this long-lost city filled me
with a chill which not even the warmth inside the bathysphere
could erase. I attempted to put the notion out of my mind by
concentrating on the task which lay ahead of us. Conlon
switched on the lights and we were both surprised by the sheer
clarity of the water. All around us were shoals of multi-coloured
fish and long green streamers of sea grass.

The ocean at this point was some forty feet in depth for we
were very close to the edge of the sandy shelf and Conlon was
the first to spot the bottom, a smoothly undulating plain covered with strange markings and long, waving strands of seaweed. We were then about ten feet above the bottom and I
called the ship to move very slowly ahead while my companion
began filming. Here and there, we noticed curious regularities
just visible in the sand-edges of almost perfect cubes poking up

from the ocean floor where the currents had swept away some of the clinging mud.

We were now progressing slowly northward and below us the shelf was falling away into greater depths. More of the oddly-shaped objects now became visible and it became clear that the surging currents had swept much of the overlying sand and silt away, depositing it over the lip of the shelf which we knew lay less than a quarter of a mile away. In my present state of mind, I seemed to see patterns and configurations in those half-concealed blocks which suggested an artificiality which grew more and more pronounced the further we went over that fantastic seabed.

I mentioned some of this to Conlon but he was far more cautious and conservative in his outlook, believing them to be nothing more than natural limestone blocks which had been split by nature into such seemingly regular features. That this could happen and, indeed, was a well-known phenomenon did little to lessen my growing apprehension.

A few minutes later, when the beam from one of the search-lights picked out a tall monolith thrusting from the sand, encrusted with shells and festooned with seaweed, I felt certain there were odd carvings visible on the surface but Conlon merely laughed at my suggestion, saying that my eyes were playing tricks with me and making me imagine things which were not there.

All this time, we had been in constant touch with the vessel and now we asked that we should continue northward until we reached the much deeper water so that we might glimpse whatever lay at much deeper levels. So far, we had come across nothing sufficiently interesting to attempt to bring to the surface.

Dorman was, at first, reluctant to agree but permission was eventually given and we began to drift more rapidly north-ward. Ahead of us, the ocean floor sloped downward at an increasing angle and the general topography of the undersea

terrain became more strange so that Conlon was forced to
admit there was something not quite right in the way odd pro-
trusions assumed domelike shapes with the hint of shattered
pillars and marble columns lying at all angles around them.
Curiously, I felt more at ease on seeing these artifacts which
spoke of them being manmade rather than natural fabrications
for if, as they suggested, they were of marble, gleaming whitely
in the light, they formed no part of the alien, grey city of Yuth.

Here and there were isolated time-shattered columns and
we decided that, once we had taken a look beyond the limestone shelf, we would pick up one of these objects and take it
to the surface where we could examine it at our leisure.

Less than five minutes later a long, almost straight line of
darkness appeared directly in front of us, stretching away in an
unbroken line in both directions. We knew immediately what
it was we were seeing — the edge of the shallows around the
islands. Beyond lay the dark abyss whose depths we did not
know.

I think we both held our breaths, sitting forward in our
seats, as we peered through the toughened glass of the porthole, straining our vision to make out details in the single beam
which shone downward. The light touched the end of the shelf
and then we had crossed over it and only an inky blackness con-
fronted us. There was now a much more powerful current tug-
ging at the bathysphere, pushing it forward on the cable and
for a while we found ourselves swinging helplessly like a pen-
dulum, unable to control our movements.

After a while the swinging ceased and with the motion of
the bathysphere stabilized we were able to give the signal for
the metal sphere to be lowered. To one side of us, the looming
rock wall ascended slowly with vague outcroppings which
showed eerily in the light. Despite the slowness of our descent
into the gloom, we were unable to discern much detail
although there was no doubt that at some time in the far past,
titanic convulsions had taken place here.

Below us, the blackness was absolute, the beam penetrating it for only a little way in stark contrast to the clarity of the water above the shallow shelf.

Then, almost before we were aware of it, we caught a fragmentary glimpse of something which rose from those benighted depths, clawing up from the unseen floor. My initial impression was of a jagged line of cones, spaced out at irregular intervals, thick, blunted needles of some curious rock formation which evidently covered a vast area.

To me, they held ineffable suggestions of a blasphemous structure and architecture utterly unlike anything I had ever seen. Conlon and I gazed in awe as we drifted slowly above them, striving to imbue them with some form of normality. How high they loomed above the ocean floor, it was impossible even to guess for the searchlight beam only touched their topmost regions. But even this was enough to show the sheer alienness of their general outlines. Had they been mere conical towers, it would not have offended our sense of perspective to such a degree. But there were bulbous appendages and truncated cones which intermeshed in angles bearing no relation to Euclidean geometry and I felt my eyes twist horribly as I tried vainly to take in everything I saw.

That Conlon was similarly affected I noticed at once. His hands were white-knuckled on the controls in front of him and his features bore an expression of mingled awe and surprise.

"What is it?" he asked finally. "Atlantis?"

I managed to shake my head. "Not Atlantis," I said. "Those ruins are far older and too alien to be Atlantis."

"Then what?"

"Yuth, perhaps," I said in a hushed voice although I could tell from the look on his face that he had never heard the name.

I did not elaborate because we were now too engrossed in checking the three cameras and watching the unfolding of the awesome scene below us. I could not help feeling there was something evil about those nightmarishly misshapen spires and pinnacles with their bizarre curves and planes; yet it was not an evil associated with Earth but rather with endless gulfs of space and time, with dimensions other than those we know.

The majority were smashed and broken with harsh, gaping orifices showing blackly against the sickly grey. What beings had once moved within these structures it was impossible to visualize. Certainly no hand of man had erected them and carved their cruel, hideous contours. Despite his sense of awe, Conlon wished to descend deeper, to determine the height of the buildings and what lay beneath but I hastily overruled him. The obscure quality of menace in their weird symbolism made me shudder and long for the sanity and safety of the ship.

Accordingly, I gave the order to raise the bathysphere and bring us back over the shelf where we soon succeeded in lifting one of the marble columns from the mud where it had lain for countless centuries.

Back on board the vessel we supervised the unloading of the pillar and the films from the cameras. While Brown developed the latter, Dorman, Conlon and I examined the remains of the pillar which bore curious resemblances to the classical early Greek style. Indeed, many of the fluted carvings were almost identical to those seen in the Athenian ruins. But the material from which it had been fashioned was a mystery. Certainly it was unlike any other form of marble known to us and as to the quarry from whence it had originally come, none of us could hazard a guess.

It was when we came to describe what we had seen in the much deeper water off the shelf, however, that Dorman evinced skepticism. While he was quite prepared to believe that some civilisation had existed at this spot perhaps four thousand years before, he could not accept that the curious structures we had seen later were anything but natural rock formations probably thrust up from the seabed by minor volcanic activity during some past geological age.

Even after the films had been developed and we watched them in a darkened room, he refused to alter his opinion. There was no doubt that seeing them as mere flickering shadows on a white screen in the relative comfort of the room, they lost some of their air of menace and mystery and it was possible to attach any explanation one wished to their nature and origin. Even Conlon appeared swayed by Dorman's persuasive arguments, agreeing that vulcanism could produce weird and wonderfully shaped forms, particularly when it occurred underwater when there were both pressure and cooling effects to be taken into account.

But I remained unconvinced for nothing could shake my conclusion that out there, only forty miles from where we lay at anchor, was that cyclopean city of grey stone, Yuth, built by artificially bred creatures that had come from the very rim of the solar system when the Earth was young, bearing a hideous, amorphous thing with them which they had worshipped as a god. Tsathoggua, one of that incredibly ancient race which had been flung down from the ethereal abysses onto the cooling magma of newly-formed planets.

That night, as I stood on deck, leaning against the rail and looking towards the north, I thought I saw vague, flickering lights on the distant horizon and a pallid gleam of glittering radiance, barely visible, which rose from the ocean towards the clear heavens. I drew the attention of one of the crew to it, but he maintained it was simply the glow of phosphorescence which one often saw at sea.

The following day, a sudden squall blew up with the wind gusting from the northwest and the sea became too choppy for any underwater exploration to be attempted. Driving sheets of rain forced us to remain undercover and I spent much of my time with Brown in the small cabin which had been fitted out as a darkroom. Here, we enlarged a number of the frames from the films, blowing them up as far as possible to bring out minute details of the grotesque spire. Two of these were of particular significance, for to me they clearly showed that no force of blind nature could have shaped such regular features.

There were also disturbing markings on one of the towers, less shattered and eroded than the others; markings which were oddly arranged in wide spirals which began at the top and descended into the unguessable depths of unplumbed blackness below. With the aid of a magnifying glass I was able to pick out curves and symbols, mostly incomplete, which tended to form such unnatural and terrifying patterns that I almost cried out aloud at the discovery and made Brown verify them.

When we showed them to Dorman he was forced to agree that, in spite of his initial skepticism, there was something pertaining to this region of monolithic spires which warranted further investigation although he still refused to commit himself to my way of thinking.

By the next day, the wind had abated and the skies had cleared and with a calm, unruffled sea, it was decided that a second descent of the bathysphere would be made, this time directly over the chasm. By now, my imagination had reached fever pitch and when the decision was made for Dorman and myself to make the descent, I was beset by odd, irrational fears in the face of Dorman's determination to proceed to the bottom of the deep trough which lay forty miles distant.

My sense of fearful expectancy as I clambered inside the bathysphere some two hours later can scarcely be described on paper for I knew that soon we would be touching a world that had been untrodden for close on thirty thousand years! Since we would be going deeper than before we made our preparations with undue care, checking and rechecking all of the apparatus. This time, we each carried a pair of powerful binoculars in order to make out more detail in that black world where slumbered the unknown secrets of an alien, elder race.

The first part of our descent was uneventful. There were two wide portholes facing in opposite directions and Dorman sat in front of one while I peered through the other, my gaze constantly fixed on what lay below us, taking little notice of the marine life which clustered abundantly all around us. As we went deeper, however, the number of fish I saw diminished rapidly until, when I judged we were below the level of the island shelf, they were curiously conspicuous by their complete absence.

Dorman had switched on the searchlights and I stared through the porthole, watching for the first indication of the vast grey-stone city. And then I saw them for the second time, rising out of the slime of the ocean floor, clawing upward for hundreds of feet; row upon seemingly endless row of fantastically symmetrical columns, the nearer ones blindingly clear in the harsh actinic light, with countless others stretching away into the black immensity. Dorman must have had some rational theory at the forefront of his mind. Yet, even so, he uttered a sudden exclamation of awed surprise and disbelief at what he saw.

For several seconds, he seemed stunned. Then he pulled himself together and gave rapid instructions for the bathysphere to be lowered very slowly. We were some fifty yards from the nearest spire but there seemed no doubt these buildings widened out towards the base and we did not wish to run the risk of striking one on our way down. We felt the unmistakable tug on the steel vessel almost at once as our rate of descent slowed appreciably.

The effect of that monstrous labyrinth which stretched away from us into inconceivable distances was indescribable for it was apparent at once that whatever stood on this undersea plateau had never been fashioned by nature, even in her wildest and most capricious moments. And it was equally obvious that whatever hands had erected these edifices had been far from human.

As we progressed downward, we saw there were other ruins, smaller than the towers, yet equally alien. Squat, flat-topped buildings with openings in them which were roughly semicircular in outline. If they were doors as I immediately assumed, I shuddered at the thought of the shape and size their occupants must have possessed.

After what seemed eons, but could only have been a few minutes, the bathysphere came to rest on the massive stone slabs of an enormous swathe, extending so far into the darkness on either side that we could not see its furthermost limits. Above us, the tops of the lofty towers were likewise lost. Now we were able to discern the prodigious size of these archaic stone piles. The cavernous openings gaped in a menacing and sinister fashion and I had the unshakable feeling that, at any moment, something monstrous would come wriggling out of them, huge beyond all our comprehension, intent upon our destruction.

I remember yelling at Dorman. "Now do you believe me?"

I saw him nod his head in stupefied acquiescence. "It's utterly fantastic. I'd never have believed it possible."

"It must be twenty or thirty thousand years old," I said. "There's no geological evidence for any inundation of this region later than that."

Many of the ruins were, of course, almost completely flattened by whatever titanic catastrophe had overtaken the city in that past age. But by switching off the interior lights, we were able to use the binoculars, sweeping the entire viewable scene with their enhanced vision.

There was no doubt now that the grey stonework was incised with the outlines of maddening cryptographs that made no sense to our purely terrestrial senses. Monstrous and suggestive of extraneous dimensions, they leered at us across a distance of a hundred feet and thousands of years as if mocking our futile efforts to unravel their secrets.

Many were representative of pre-human species neither of us could recognize but here and there were pictures of creatures which were familiar to us; terrestrial animals and marine life belonging to that bygone age.

How many miles in every direction the city stretched, it was impossible to estimate. Inwardly, I knew that our discovery totally verified everything that had been written in that book I had picked up and the letters which had belonged to Jethro Howarth. In spite of my sense of awe and bewilderment, I wondered what the old recluse's reactions would have been had he been there with Dorman and myself at that moment; sitting there in a tiny vessel which seemed miniscule and fragile in the face of the boundless metropolis which loomed all around us.

It was Dorman who drew my attention to a curious phenomenon in the distance. Far beyond the furthermost point the beam from the searchlight could reach, there appeared to be a faint glow, a curious reddish point of radiance that waxed and waned in a strangely hypnotic manner that was both puzzling and frightening. Leaving my seat, I crouched down beside him in the cramped space. It was impossible it had been here all the time but was so faint as to be invisible until we had switched off the lights inside the bathysphere. Almost simultaneously, we trained our binoculars on it. For a moment, I could make out nothing but a vague blur, but as I adjusted the focus, it suddenly sprang into breathtaking clarity.

We had previously believed this sunken city to be absolutely silent and dead. How could it have been otherwise when it had been destroyed long before man had evolved into a thinking, rational creature?

Yet all reason deserted me as I saw, through the lenses of the binoculars, the dark outlines of a great building with a single wide entrance through which poured that crimson effulgence that clearly had its ghastly origin somewhere far below the level of the ocean floor. We might have put it down to some volcanic activity still going on beneath the sea but for the obvious fact there was no indication whatsoever of any bubbling and seething of steam in the vicinity. The water was just as undisturbed there as it was in our immediate vicinity.

It was impossible for us to put forward any logical explanation for the phenomenon. Dorman's first instinctive reaction was to call up the ship to move us closer to the building but a single glance was enough to tell us there were far too many obstacles between it and us for that to be a feasible proposition. Reluctantly, he finally decided to return to the surface. We had been down for more than two hours and it soon became apparent that if we wished to examine this curious spectacle more closely we would have to resort to the more dangerous procedure of descending in diving suits which would allow us far more freedom of movement.

Once back on board the vessel, we communicated our findings to the other members of the team amid an atmosphere of mounting excitement and puzzlement. That we had made an outstanding discovery was beyond doubt, and before leaving the spot we dropped a marker buoy over the side to ensure our return to the exact spot.

That evening, we gathered in Dorman's cabin to discuss and plan our next moves. Brown and Conlon were of the opinion that news of our discovery should be telegraphed at once to the university, reporting a major archaeological find which went far beyond any others made in this area, but Dorman insisted on maintaining radio silence until further confirmatory evidence had been acquired.

We now knew the depth of water we would have to descend and since this was well within the safety limits of the diving suits we had on board, it was agreed that, the weather permitting, three of us should go down to explore the area around that enigmatic edifice we had sighted and, if possible, determine the cause of the peculiar radiance emanating from within it.

That night, I found it difficult to sleep. The nearness of things which properly belonged to an era far in the past, affected me strongly, intruding into my thoughts, forming odd and bizarre pictures in my mind. When I finally did fall into a restless doze I dreamed of the long-dead city under the sea. But before my dreaming gaze it now stood unbroken and untarnished by time on dry land and there was no sign of the ocean. On an incredibly ancient plateau, wreathed in clouds of steam and noxious vapours, the Cyclopean buildings stretched away in all directions as far as the eye could see and high into the lowering clouds where the topmost spires were lost to sight. There was something terribly unhuman about the geometry of its massive grey-stone walls, and the mind-wrenching alienness of its angles and intermeshing structures went against all reason, all known laws of mathematics, logic and architecture. I knew, by some weird instinct, I was seeing it as it had been perhaps several millions of years ago when it had been newly built by that race from the stars.

That it was a scene from all those eons ago was evident from the trees in the foreground which were huge cycads with monstrous ferns forming a thickly-tangled undergrowth around them. Fortunately for my sanity, the swirling columns of mist shrouded much of the city from full view. But where the vapours occasionally thinned I caught a glimpse of that central temple with its single entrance from the ruins of which that garish light had flared only a few waking hours before.

Yet there were now visible even more shocking exaggerations of nature than the city itself; for now I saw the inhabitants, those hideous and, if the *Book of K'yog* was to be believed — artificially — created abominations that had built it! I saw them as vague shapes in the vast avenues and squares, saw them clinging limpet-like to the sides of the buildings or, oozing jelly-like from grotesque apertures and doorways. What insane blasphemy had bred those *things* I could not conceive, but the mere sight of them woke me, yelling incoherently, from my dream.

I was sitting upright in my bunk, clutching nervously at the covers, when Brown burst into my cabin, roused by my unearthly scream. Shudderingly, I told him it had been nothing but a nightmare, probably brought on by what I had seen the previous day. He looked unconvinced but eventually accepted my explanation and left, obviously puzzled by my irrational behaviour. I remained awake for the rest of the night, sitting huddled on the bunk, waiting for the first light of dawn. Whether those abominable creatures were just images conjured up by my overwrought mind, or I had somehow seen things as they actually had been millions of years before, I could not tell. But the nightmare had been so clear in all its detail that I found it difficult to believe it had been only a fantasy born out of my mind.

If I had only recognized it for the premonition it was, I might well have opted out of going down with Dorman and Brown and I could, perhaps, sleep peacefully at night, instead of being plagued and assailed by recurrent dreams which now haunt my sleeping hours.

Our preparations for our third descent were even more thorough than the first two, for in that depth of water there were far more dangers associated with even the most modern diving equipment than going down in the bathysphere. We spotted the marker buoy a little after ten o'clock and the vessel came to a stop close beside it under a cloudless blue sky with scarcely any wind. The suits were all equipped with powerful underwater lamps, thereby leaving our hands free.

Half an hour later, we were ready. Cramped as conditions had been inside the bathysphere, inside the suits it was far worse. They did, however, possess one distinct advantage; on the ocean floor they would give us much greater freedom of movement. Then I was in the water and going down at what seemed a dangerous rate of descent. I could see no sign of my two companions. All around me was a dark-purple world which rapidly shaded into absolute blackness, pierced only by the light of my lamp which, although not as powerful as those on the bathysphere, was still able to pierce the gloom for a distance of several yards.

As I descended, I directed my whole attention downward
for I had no desire to become impaled upon one of those
uprearing pinnacles which dotted the vast plain below me in
such prodigious profusion.

After what seemed an age, but could only have been a few
minutes, I saw something huge looming up out of the stygian
darkness a little to my left. Almost before I was aware of it, I
was moving down past the side of one of those nightmare towers. The effect of seeing it so close at hand was indescribable,
for it was only then I realized its true dimensions. God alone
knew, or perhaps could ever know, the full extent of this long-
dead metropolis.

Once I stood on the massive pavings of the central swathe,
the horror of my dream returned a hundredfold for now I had
no normal ideas to fall back upon to enable me to fully maintain a hold on my toppling emotions. Had I remained alone in
that darkness of uncountable years I might have tugged frantically on the rope connecting me with the surface, demanding
to be pulled back up to the sanity and mundane surroundings
of the ship. But a few seconds later, I saw another shambling
figure, a second beam of light stabbing the gloom ahead of me.

Going forward, I recognised Brown's features behind the
transparent facepiece of the helmet and pointing along the
avenue, I urged him onward, keeping a safe distance between
us in order that our lines might not become entangled. Our
progress was not as rapid, nor as easy, as I had anticipated.
Now, for the first time, I was able to see the full extent of the
devastation that had struck this city all those thousands of
years before. The great stones which made up the avenue had
been twisted and buckled upward so they lay at crazy angles
with gaping holes between them We were forced to pick our
way forward with extreme care, working our way around the
individual stones, gingerly clambering over others, knowing
that the slightest tear in our suits would doom us to almost
instant death.

Curiously, although the light had not been in sight earlier, my sense of direction was not ill-founded. Working our way against the surging currents, often bent almost double as if against a gale, we soon sighted the dull-red glow which Dorman and I had witnessed before. I made to call Brown's attention to it, but he had already seen it and behind the transparent mask I saw his awestruck face staring at me questioningly. I nodded and pointed again, motioning him onward.

It was impossible to take in more than a miniscule part of the complete structure which, curiously, seemed to have suffered far less from the cataclysmic destruction of the other buildings we had seen.

As we approached it, we noticed two things which both filled us with a sense of shock and apprehension. Above the solitary portal, cut deep into the grey stone, we were just able to make out a vast, cryptic sign. Had it not been for the diffuse reddish glow, we might have missed it altogether. The second thing we saw was the diminutive figure already inside the massive building, moving steadily towards a gaping chasm deep within, from which poured the singular radiance.

That it was Dorman, we did not doubt. Yet why he had gone on ahead without waiting for us, we could not guess. Perhaps he wished to convince himself there was some natural explanation for the phenomenon, or, as I came later to believe, there was some outside compulsion which made him go forward against his will. Whatever the reason, I was suddenly so overcome by the feel of evil which radiated from that spot that I grasped Brown's arm as he made to follow and pulled him back.

The fact that we survived and made it back to the surface is proof enough that my instincts were right. Sheer luck and providence alone could not have saved us if we had gone any further into that blasphemous temple built by those long-dead alien creatures for the primeval entity they had brought with them from the dark planet on the rim of the solar system when the Earth was young.

Outlined against that hellish glare we saw Dorman reach the lip of the abyssal shaft which plummeted into unguessable deeps beneath the accursed cit, of Yuth, for such I now know it to be.

The old books from which occasional fragments come down to us over the ages speak wisdom to those who have eyes and ears to understand their message of warning. The spells and sigils which bind the grotesque and undying survivors of that war fought among the stars and in universes alien to our own untold millions of years ago, do indeed weaken in their potency with the passage of eons.

What happened next was born of horror and thankfully Brown and I witnessed only the smallest part of it. As it was, Brown was gibbering inarticulately to himself when we were eventually taken on board the waiting ship, and I am left with such wild nightmares I scarcely dare close my eyes at night. Neither Brown nor I returned to the university. Brown, because his mind snapped altogether under the impact of what we both saw, or thought we saw; and I, because I now know there are places and things on this Earth where eldritch, elder horrors still lurk, forgotten but not impotent, biding their time until the stars and spheres are right and they may once again walk the lands and undersea regions where Man believes himself to be supreme.

There are certain matters which, for the peace of mankind, should not be revealed and, furthermore, it is extremely doubtful if our story would be believed. We explained Dorman's death and the odd seismic disturbance which accompanied it as due to a small-scale volcanic eruption on the seabed and, in general, this was accepted by the scientific community and public at large. What really occurred was far different.

As I have said, Brown and I caught sight of Dorman's figure, bulky and ungainly in the heavy diving suit, silhouetted against that crimson coruscation. We saw him pause as he reached the edge, his body bent forward as he peered down into whatever depths lay beyond.

For what seemed an age, we stood there irresolutely, my grip on Brown's arm still tight as I strove to hold him back. Then, without warning, the ocean floor beneath our feet shuddered and heaved, hurling us both off balance. Brown clutched desperately at me for support. He was mouthing something behind his facepiece but I could not hear the words. The massive walls which had withstood endless years of cataclysm and decay cracked and huge lumps of masonry fell from the roof, crashing onto the buckling floor.

Only vaguely were we aware that for some unaccountable reason, the glare was fading, but for several moments we were too busy trying to keep our feet, so we paid little heed to it. Then, realizing that the entire structure was coming down about us, we somehow turned and fled; but only after throwing a quick glance in Dorman's direction to see if he, too, were attempting to escape the devastation. It was that glance which drove Brown over the bounds of sanity and left me as I am now, afraid of shadows and dark, lonely places.

It was no fiery force of nature that caused the unholy glow inside that infamous temple, nor the upheaval which almost cost us our lives. There was a shadow cast upon the scarlet glare, dimming it even as we watched. Even that ill-defined, leaping shadow was bad enough, but the reality which followed it, the lumbering, amorphous bulk that heaved itself from the depths below accursed Yuth and for one soul-searing moment came out into the open, was a million times worse.

The lost *Book of K'yog*, the merest fragments of which had been copied by some unknown hand thousands of years later, had not lied. Tsathoggua had not died when his ageless city had been destroyed, together with all his worshippers. The great glaring eye that stared at us across a hundred yards of grey stone held an evil malevolence that was infinitely more mind-destroying than anything of Earth.

Even in retrospect it is not possible to convey in words the nature of that monstrosity which squeezed its vast bulk through the gaping abyss. It held a hint of noxious plasticity, of writhing tentacles which changed their number and shape. But more than anything, I had the impression of gigantic size, that huge as that part of it looked where it almost completely blocked the opening, there was an infinitely greater bulk mercifully hidden from us.

Perhaps it was, as one or two of Brown's doctors have suggested, nothing more than an hallucination, something conjured from one of our minds and telepathically communicated to the other in that moment of supreme horror. Inwardly, I would like to believe that this is the truth and that vast sunken city of grey stone has been utterly dead and untenanted for thousands of years.

But I know there was nothing imaginary or hallucinatory about the black, coiling tentacle that seized Dorman around the waist and bore him, kicking and screaming frantically, into the gaping, beaked maw which appeared as if from nowhere beneath that single glaring red eye! 🕸

About "The Oracle of Sàdoqua"

This clever story (which first appeared in *Chronicles of the Cthulhu Codex #* 5, 1989) was inspired by the plot synopsis under the same title included in the *Black Book of Clark Ashton Smith*, which Lin Carter had considered writing up but never did. Hilger explains: "Rather than attempting an obvious pastiche, I attempted to elaborate or flesh out the story in a manner consistent with Smith's original conception, concentrating on plot rather than technique."

The story also recalls the hints vouchsafed by Lovecraft in a letter of February 11, 1934, where he speaks of "those reputedly immortal felines who guarded the shrine of Sadoqua, and whose regular disappearances at New Moon figure so largely in the folklore of medieval Averoigne. One recalls the disquieting suggestions in Jehan d'Arbois' *Roman des Sorciers* concerning the huge black cats captured at those very singular Sabbats on the rocky hill behind Vyones — the cats which could not be burned, but which escaped unhurt from the flames, uttering cries which, though not like any known human speech, were damnably close to the unknown syllables forming part of the Tsath-ritual in the *Livre d'Eibon*."

The business about the transforming vapors comes from the practice of Apollo's Delphic Oracle, who would bend over and breathe deep the gaseous fumes emitted from a crack in the cave floor and then, suitably entranced, speak forth the word of the god.

Finally, "The Oracle of Sàdoqua" presents us with the most perfectly balanced use known to me of what Fritz Leiber called the "confirmational" as opposed to the "revelational" ending: though the awful truth is blurted out fairly early on, the reader is then persuaded to share the incredulity of the protagonist ("No, that can't be . . . ") until it is too late. The strip-tease revelation in the beginning yields just enough of a portentous glimpse to strike the perfect gong-note of unease that reverberates through the remainder of the tale.

The Oracle of Sàdoqua

By Ron Hilger

"Black and unshap'd, as pestilant a Clod
As Dread Sàdoqua, Averonia's god."

"**B**y the beard of Jupiter! I'll not return to Rome until Galbius has been found or avenged," thundered Horatius as he strode forth from his military pavilion into the golden morning sunlight of the recently conquered province of Averonia, leaving a much-intimidated courier stammering in his wake.

"But — but my l — lord, what shall I tell the Senate?" The courier had been dispatched from the Roman Senate with written orders that Horatius, First Lieutenant under General Julius Caesar's forces in Gaul, return immediately to Rome under the dictum disbanding Caesar's army. Horatius wheeled about.

"The Senate will have to understand the importance of teaching these pagan savages the power and justice of Imperial Rome: I suspect Galbius has been captured or killed by the heathen Druids who infest this barbarous land. If the matter is not resolved, we invite open rebellion: I shall send half my men back under the command of Romulus, but I return with Galbius or with the blood of those responsible upon my sword. Tell that to the Senate."

Horatius signed the communiqué and dismissed the courier with an air of preoccupation, more concerned with his missing comrade than with the orders from Rome. After all, with luck

he would be returning long before any response from an irate
Senate could reach him. The disappearance of Galbius, however, concerned him greatly. Aside from tactical considerations
such as where Galbius could be and how to find him, Horatius
was deeply concerned about the welfare of his friend. The two
had been close as brothers ever since military training, when
drunken brawls had taught them each to respect the other's
fighting prowess. Together they had risen through the ranks to
become officers while battling their way across Gaul under the
ambitious General Caesar. Now it had been nearly two days
since Galbius had disappeared after leaving on a lone scouting
foray into the woods, and Horatius could not think of a more
disquieting place in which to lose a friend.

Werewolves, vampires, and lamias were reputed to haunt
this unfathomable forest, as well as the savage Druids who were
rumored to be tainted with a dark strain of Hyperborean ancestry. He shuddered involuntarily and wished again that Galbius
would return with some tale of amorous captivity in the
clutches of an insatiable Averonian maid.

Having decided at last to organize a search, Horatius
ordered a detachment of his cavalry to prepare their horses and
weapons to accompany him through the ancient forest to question anyone they encountered in the area of Galbius' disappearance. As they rode along a well-traveled road through sun-
lit meadows filled with the raucous cries of birds and the
colourful pageantry of myriad woodland flowers, Horatius felt
his spirits rise, as one who has been too long idle.

All too soon, the amaranthine meadows gave way to
higher, stonier ground, and the trees grew thicker until they
crowded out all but a few filtered rays of sunlight. They wound
their way beneath the cool umbrate of enormous moss and
mistletoe-encumbered oaks, and soon Horatius felt an ominous
unease settling down upon him like an invisible shroud. The
pagan Druids who dwelt here disgusted him, and their blasphemous sacrifices and heathen rituals filled him with horror

and righteous indignation. The road soon reduced to a narrow
footpath, and as a trailing vine of cobweb-covered mistletoe
brushed his face, Horatius reflected that in such a primordial,
god-forsaken place any number of pagan myths and monsters
were likely to be found.

As the trail rounded a large outcropping of rock the soldiers
unexpectedly came upon a scene which might well have been
taken from some ancient myth. Two savage-looking Druids sat
upon large boulders on either side of a low, dark aperture at the
base of a cliff, as if guarding it. The Druids appeared barbaric
to an extreme. They wore long coarse-looking robes of mottled
grey. Their dark hair was long and matted, as were their beards.
Gnarled hands clutched long cudgels of oak at the ends of
which long, wicked-looking pieces of obsidian were firmly
strapped at right angles, in the fashion of a scythe. But that
which caught and held the attention of the formidable horse-
men was a pair of the largest, most ferocious-looking felines the
Romans had ever beheld. The great cats sat immobile as statues, one beside each guard. The upper canine teeth of these
great beasts hung several inches below the lower jaw and their
hungry yellow eyes were fixed on the newcomers. Having
ordered weapons drawn, Horatius approached the larger of the
two savages.

"We seek word of Galbius, second lieutenant of the
Imperial Roman Army, last seen in this vicinity two days ago.
Some of your people must have seen or heard of him. Tell us
everything you know of this if you wish to live."

The brutes exchanged a series of low, gutteral remarks,
punctuated with vigorous gesticulations. Finally, they lowered
their weapons and the larger Druid spoke, his poor Latin
almost indecipherable beneath his heavy accent.

"The guardians of Sàdoqua are at your service. We know
nothing about this man you seek, but you stand at the doorway
of the Fane of Sàdoqua. The people of Averonia are wont to
consult the oracle within for answers to questions that defy the

wisest sage . . . for a small fee." The Druid added slyly, extending a crude wooden bowl in which rattled a few small coins and
nuggets of gold.

The Druid smiled malignly at the soldier's watchful wari-
ness of the great feline guardians.

"You have nothing to fear," the Druid said scornfully.
"These are here to guard against dangers far greater than your-
selves."

Horatius glared at the Druid, then suddenly knocked aside
the bowl with his blade, scattering the contents.

"Tullius, Florian, come with me," ordered Horatius, "the
rest of you watch these two heathens. If we return not after a
count of five hundred, kill these so-called guardians and come
to our assistance. . . ."He then turned and, with his sword
before him, disappeared into the dark opening followed closely
by his two picked men.

The three Romans shuffled forward slowly into the gloom,
letting their eyes adjust to the tenebrous interior of the cave.
Horatius distrusted the Druids, and suspected they might be
hiding something in the cave — perhaps Galbius, perhaps an
ambush. As they made their way through the musty tunnel,
the blackness slowly gave way to a dull, diffused light, and a
noisome odor now began to permeate the air. Horatius perceived that the light ahead appeared to be shifting about in an
eerie manner regarding which he did not feel entirely
comfortable.

He now recalled stories and rumors that circulated in Rome
and Greece about the barbarous northerners, that the Druids
were reported to make human sacrifice to the daemon Taranit
and to nurture the ancient cults of the Old Ones. The worship
of the toad-like Tsathoggua and the spider-god Atlach-Nacha
was confirmed by the Greek historian Hecataeus, who had
brought back and translated a copy of the notorious *Book of
Eibon* from northern lands. In his book, *Peri Hyperborean*,
Hecataeus described the evil effect of Hyperborean culture on

subsequent northern tribes. Horatius was compelled to mutter
a short prayer to Mars, god of war and soldiers, to grant him
victory over the many loathsome creatures he imagined while
moving cautiously towards the wavering light.

Soon they found themselves in a grotto riven from floor to
ceiling. Sunlight streamed through a great fissure in the roof,
but obscured by foul, cloudy vapors, which arose from the fathomless chasm before which they had halted. At the very brink
of the abyss, chained to an immense black altar-stone, was a
hideous being which appeared only vaguely human. The thing
was entirely covered with coarse black hair except on its pale
underside. Its head seemed to rest directly on its shoulders with
little or no neck. The facial features, also, were seemingly
nonexistent, save for its insanely staring eyes and toothless,
slavering maw.

Horatius' heart quailed at the abominable sight before him
and he grew somewhat unsteady from breathing the fetid
vapors. Yet the Roman summoned his courage and addressed
the fearsome oracle.

"The Druids have bidden me consult the oracle of Sàdoqua
concerning the fate of my lost friend Galbius. Answer then, if
you are the one of whom they speak." A cloud of roiling vapor
engulfed the oracle and as it cleared, the thing began to speak
in half-articulate Latin.

"The fate of Galbius is before you, as is your own. As yet
your friend lives, but it is decreed that he shall die before this
very altar before the setting of the next full moon."

Strangely disturbed by something about the creature's
voice, Horatius pressed the oracle for greater detail. Suddenly,
a shaft of sunlight pierced the reeking cloud and fell briefly on
the figure before him, and Horatius was shocked to imagine a
distorted, impossible resemblance to the lost Galbius.

"Galbius?" he whispered uncertainly. "Can it be you?"

The oracle cackled with laughter.

"Galbius is not here, and I have been the mouthpiece of Sàdoqua, who reposes in eternal slumber at the bottom of this abyss, for a thousand eternities."

Horatius and his subordinates glared uncomprehendingly at the squat obscenity, which now half crawled and half dragged itself into the dark recesses behind the altar-stone in apparent forgetfulness of their presence.

The Romans left the creature and soon emerged from the cavern, blinking in the strong light of noon as they mounted their steeds and prepared to depart. The great tawny cats still sat immobile. Horatius urged his mount forward and regarded them thoughtfully.

"I think perhaps these beasts permit all to pass within, yet stand ready to devour those whom you would not have escape. If I discover you have been less than completely honest with me, your heads shall be set on pikes down at the crossroads to proclaim your deceit and insolence before all the countryside." Without awaiting a reply, the commander wheeled his horse about and signaled for the company to ride on.

The soldiers continued their search through the forest. The trees crowded still closer together as if trying to choke the trail out of existence. As they rounded a bend, Horatius caught a fleeting glimpse of a shadowy form ducking behind a tree a short distance off the track to their left. Signaling a halt, he dismounted and plunged through the brush towards this mysterious apparition, several of his men close behind him. They soon found Horatius standing beside a huge, moss-covered oak with a young peasant girl struggling in his iron grasp. He studied his catch with undisguised delight. Shoulder-length chestnut colored hair surrounded a fair, blushing complexion, accented by her large hazel eyes. She wore a simple homespun dress that did little to conceal her youthful charms, though she had yet to achieve her fullest curves. Horatius waved away the men who had, understandably, begun to gather around her and reassured the girl in the Celtic dialect of the Gauls.

"Do not be afraid — we mean you no harm," he told her gently, releasing her wrist from his grip. "We only seek news of a missing comrade." He then described Galbius and asked if she had seen or heard of him. She shook her head slowly, glancing anxiously around her.

"I cannot say . . . Please let me go," she pleaded urgently. "The Druids must not see me talking with you."

"My friend Galbius," he repeated firmly. "Have you seen him?" She hesitated momentarily, then whispered close beside his ear.

"I have not . . . but I will ask my people. Meet me after moonrise in yonder meadow and I will tell you what I have learned." Without awaiting his reply she sprang lithely away through the trees. Two of his men leaped into pursuit, but held back at his command.

"Wait. Let her go. She may yet prove useful."

That evening Horatius set out alone to keep his woodland tryst. He had debated with himself the wisdom of going along. Indeed, he had thought of little else all afternoon, but something about the way she had clung to his arm while she whispered to him, some unspoken promise in her eyes, had decided the matter for him.

He made his way silently along the path, his sword and shield strapped to his back so he could walk unencumbered through the gloom of the nocturnal forest. He had left quite early so as to arrive first in case of a trap or ambush. He did not expect deceit, but such preparedness had saved his life on more than one occasion. The oaks closed around him, shutting out the stars and cutting off the breeze, making the air musty and stifling. He began hearing slight noises — twigs snapping and night-birds calling. He even thought he heard voices rising and falling in rhythm to drumbeats in the distance.

Suddenly he noticed a soft glimmering through the trees on his left and, making his way with great stealth, he crept through the brambles until he came upon a large, moonlit meadow. The full moon was just peering over the tops of the branches, filling the glade like a silver basin with soft pearly light and illuminating the great trees of the forest like giant granite cenotaphs or lofty snow covered peaks encircling the glade. The entire scene before him was bathed in soft moonlight, save only the pitch-black band of shadow under the trees, which even the noonday sun could never fully penetrate. Then, moving to a place providing optimal surveillance, he noticed with a start several shadows moving strangely about in the glade. Cursing, he reached over his shoulder and drew his sword. Crouching down behind a large oak, Horatius berated himself for his foolishness in coming alone and envisioned a grisly death upon some lichen-crusted altar of this vicious and degenerate people. But the shadows moved no closer. They seemed to be moving in circles, reversing directions and shifting patterns. He watched, enthralled by what he now perceived to be dancers, although he could make out none of their features.

A small noise close by brought him instantly to a defensive position, his sword and shield raised menacingly. He saw merely the peasant girl standing close beside him, and he marked the uncanny silence of her approach.

"Beautiful, aren't they?" she murmured as she knelt down next to him. Horatius regained his composure as he noticed the girl was, in fact, alone, but decided to keep his sword in hand for the present.

"What are they?" he returned, "and who are you, who managed to sneak so close without my hearing you?" She smiled, her teeth gleaming in the moonlight.

"My name is Selena, and they are the folk of the forest, whom you will likely frighten away with your boisterous whispering. As for my quiet passage, I have that skill in woodcraft shared by those who live within the shadow of the forest." She contemplated the Roman a moment before continuing.

"I hope you can forgive my mysterious behavior this morning, but I have good reason to fear the sorcerous Druids should they suspect me of helping you. I have heard they regularly sacrifice those whom they suspect of treachery in a most brutal and bloody manner."

"True — they are devils from the pit," interrupted Horatius, "but what of Galbius? Have you learned of his whereabouts?"

"I fear to answer that question, my lord," whispered the girl, avoiding his gaze with downcast eyes. "I will not lie and say I know nothing for I have learned that your comrade is already beyond all mortal assistance. You cannot help him." She quickly continued. "And I fear that once you discover what you wish to know, I will not see you ever again."

The Roman reached out his hand as if to caress her cheek, and gently tilted her face towards his searching eyes.

"And what if I promise to return to you once I have beheld the fate of Galbius with my own eyes?"

"Promise me instead an hour of your time. Escort me about this glade tonight as befits a lordly Roman officer, and tell me tales of Rome with its paved streets and marble statues. Tell me of your people and how they mingle and their manner of dress. Tell me of your armies that rule over half the world, let me feel the glory of this Rome of which I hear much splendid rumor, and make me not afraid of the cruel Druids you would have me betray. Do this for me and I will gladly tell you all I know of your friend."

Horatius decided her proposal was an attractive one, partly because of her considerable feminine charm, and chiefly because he had no alternative — the girl was his only hope thus far.

"And what of these strange folk who dance in the moonlight?" returned Horatius. "Surely they will resent our intrusion upon their festivities. Can you be sure of our safety amongst them?"

"We have nothing to fear from these shy and innocent creatures." Selena assured him. "It is more likely that they will flee if we approach them too directly. Therefore, let us stroll slowly along the edge of the glade, close to the shadow of the trees so we do not disturb them, for their dance is very beautiful to watch."

Horatius could think of no objection as she took his hand and led him along the perimeter of the moonlit meadow, plying him with questions about Rome, which he answered with great pride and enthusiasm. As they picked their way through the boulders and moss-covered branches strewn along their path, the Roman's eyes constantly returned to the weird ceremony. It seemed to stir within him a strange and blasphemous curiosity — almost a desire to join the pagan revel. The singing and chanting grew louder as their path drew nearer to the revelers, and Horatius began to notice strange abnormalities in the figures of the dancers; bizarre glimpses of horns and hooves, flapping wings and twitching tails, uncertain in the pale moonlight.

"Shades of Dis!" exclaimed the Roman. "I cannot tell if these beings are daemons on a dark errand from the netherworld, or only peasants in costume for some festival of Bacchantes."

"Nor can I tell you for certain, but I do not believe they are evil. One night I attempted to join in their dance, but although I approached slowly and spoke softly to them, they all fled silently into the forest."

Horatius paused and, taking the girl swiftly into his arms, he replied, "I do not know how any creature, man or beast, could be afraid of such a gentle and beautiful young maiden." He then bent his head and attempted a kiss, but she slipped away demurely and called teasingly from the protection of the wood.

"And I thought you were a gentleman. It seems I have more to fear from you than from yonder 'demons from Dis.'"

She then vanished between the trees, leaving only her silvery laughter lingering in the air.

Horatius plunged into the woods in pursuit and soon they were alone in a grassy moonlit bower, lying comfortably in each other's arms.

"I have heard that in your country the women do not work, but stay home and invent ways to please their men." Selena whispered. "Is this true?"

"Perhaps you would like to return to Rome with me to await my return in the evenings?" he replied. As the conversation ceased, Horatius could only assume that she would, indeed, like that very much.

Later, as the lovers walked about in the now empty glade, the full moon striding down from its zenith, Horatius explained his determination to find or avenge Galbius quickly before his return to Rome.

"For I grow weary of this savage land filled with pagan horrors, and long for the quiet groves of my villa." He kissed the back of her neck, and continued softly. "There you would be clothed in silk amid the luxury of Rome. Tell me, then, what do you know of Galbius?"

"First I must know if you questioned the Druids who guard the cavern of the oracle, and their answer."

"I did question the two savages," he admitted. "But they told me nothing. I even consulted their filthy oracle, but although I have a strange feeling the creature somehow knew the truth, the answer I received seemed little more than gibberish."

"But of course, you could not recognize the truth." Selena shook her head with pity. "I will explain, but you will not like the truth. The Druids worship the dread god Sàdoqua, whom they believe sleeps eternally at the bottom of the chasm atop which the oracle is chained to his black altar. It is held to be true by local shamans and sooth-sayers that the name of Sàdoqua is but a corrupt version of Tsathoggua, the god of

ancient Hyperborea. The legend tells how this evil one abandoned that country after it was overwhelmed by glaciers and
returned to the lightless abyss of N'Kai where he still abides.
Tsathoggua and others of the Old Ones first entered N'Kai
through a gate of foul sorcery, which connects N'Kai to a similar abyss located deep within the world you Romans call
Saturn. So say the dark legends of the Druid religion which is
founded largely on the writings of the great Hyperborean wizard Eibon. The Druids believe the vapors rising from the abyss
to be the actual breath of the slumbering Sàdoqua. Because of
the constant exposure to these noxious fumes the oracle is soon
reduced to a monstrous condition in which he receives and
relates the divinations of Sàdoqua, who is said to know all
things past, present, and future. This primal regression contin-
ues until the unfortunate creature dies, or is no longer useful as
a medium, having become too primitive to communicate.

"Because of the inevitably short life of the oracle, the
Druids must search constantly for new victims to serve
Sàdoqua. Usually they choose from amongst the criminals or
beggars who roam the countryside, but when these are scarce
they will often abduct strangers who happen to be travelling
through the forest. This undoubtedly was the fate of Galbius.
The men from my village say that your friend must have fought
well, for the remains of three Druids were found alongside the
forest trail. The great wounds and cloven limbs of the slain
Druids showed that a heavy short-sword, such as your own,
was wielded against them by one who knew well its use. That
foul thing you spoke with was indeed Galbius, but his mind
had long since succumbed to the lethal respiration of Sàdoqua."
Selena attempted to pull Horatius into the comfort of her arms.
"I am sorry for your friend, but can't you see there is nothing
you can do to help him?"

Upon hearing these words Horatius felt a black rage rising
within him. He shrugged off the girl's embrace, desiring only

the comfort of slaying the abhorrent Druids and dispatching the hideous oracle from the torture of its existence.

"If it is too late to save Galbius, then I shall at least honor our friendship by ending the misery of that witless ruin that was once my friend. Tell me the shortest route to the cavern," he demanded, his hand tightening on the hilt of his sword. Selena pointed the way and begged him to be careful.

"For if the Druids discover I have betrayed them they will carve my heart from my breast and devour it before my dying eyes. Such is their customary treatment of informers."

"Await me at my encampment and tomorrow we shall quit this barbarous land and return to Rome," cried Horatius as he set forth on his errand of mercy and vengeance. He quickly found the path, which showed up as a narrow, pale swath visible only a few feet into the gloom. The Roman slowed his pace and drew his sword as he realized his vulnerability. As a soldier, he had been trained to control his rage and use it effectively against his enemies. Now his tactician's mind began to assert itself and he realized that by storming unprepared into a stronghold of his enemies he might achieve little more than becoming a meal for the feline guardians of Sàdoqua. His wrath was too great to consider going back, but with caution and stealth, he might yet achieve his goal and possibly kill a great many of his foes.

When he reached the clearing which surrounded the entrance to the cave, the Roman peered cautiously around the base of a great rock until he noted with grim satisfaction a single Druid sitting in the wavering light of a torch which protruded from a notch in the cliff. The feline guardians were nowhere to be seen. The Roman attacked. The lone sentry had only enough time to bellow once before a dimly flashing blade cut off his scream and sent his head rolling across the ground, leaving a dark trail of gore in its wake. Horatius removed the torch from the cliff wall and, thrusting it before him, entered the cavern of the oracle.

The first thing he saw in the dim torchlight was an obsidian-bladed scythe moving downward in an arc toward his chest. In desperation he whipped his sword beneath the falling scythe and was rewarded by a dull thud as his sword encountered the firm resistance of bone. The scythe fell harmlessly over his shoulder, the still-gripping hand and arm dragging horribly after. Horatius felt little emotion as he drove his sword through the Druid who lay writhing in the dust — uttering only a mechanical grunt of satisfaction as another of his enemies died before him, leaving him yet alive to wreak further vengeance.

Hastening to the black altar, he found it engulfed by roiling mist and vapors which soon dissipated enough to reveal only an empty, slimy shackle lying in a pool of unmentionable filth.

The Roman cursed aloud, having been thwarted in his wish to render his friend the final service of releasing his tortured soul from the noxious will of Sàdoqua. Horatius held the torch aloft and searched about, hoping to find the miserable oracle hiding in some crevice when the rank, obscuring mist began to issue forth once more from the depths like some maleficent ethereal tide. He held his breath until the reeking cloud cleared once more, then he peered cautiously over the edge into the abyss. There, not a foot beneath the edge of the cliff, crawled a huge, hirsute, slug-like creature that could only be the transformed Galbius. Horatius recognized the insanely staring eyes, although they now protruded above the body on gently waving stalk-like appendages. The thing was sliding down the sheer wall along a well-slimed trail which ended, he imagined, in the batrachian jaws of Sàdoqua. In horror, he plunged his sword again and again into the quivering mass until it released its hold and fell silently into the yawning pit. As the Roman straightened from the grisly task, he was struck savagely on the head from behind. A hot, spreading numbness swept over him as he sank to the floor and into oblivion.

When Horatius regained consciousness, he was first aware of a sharp throbbing in his head and a burning asphyxiation in his throat and chest. He could see or hear nothing and his mind seemed strangely blank. He struggled to his knees and became aware of the heavy chains about his waist and ankles and noticed for the first time the abominable stench and the slime in which he knelt. Dimly he recalled the events which had led to his capture and he reached out in the darkness and felt the stone altar to confirm his fate. With dreadful irony he now recalled the prophecy of Sàdoqua: "The fate of Galbius is before you, as is your own." In this pitiable state he struggled against his bonds until he bethought him of Galbius, and with what fluid ease he must have escaped these very bonds. Horatius screamed and cursed his rage and frustration into the baleful abyss until, slowly, there arose from the stygian depths a vast chuckling, as one might utter during an amusing dream. Horatius continued to scream in fury and horror until, wearied from his exertion, he ceased and realized he no longer recalled why he screamed.

The following day, having waited the long night through in the encampment of the Romans, Selena slipped away and set her face toward that abominable cavern. Although filled with terror, she strove to appear at ease as she told the Druid guardians of her wish to consult the oracle regarding a matter of the heart. She thought she glimpsed a knowing leer in the expression of one as he stepped aside to permit her entry, but she refused to allow herself to be frightened away when close to learning the fate of her new love. Shuddering at the sight of great pools of congealed blood within the grotto's entrance, he fixed her gaze before her and continued until she came, at last, to the great black altar and its hideous oracle.

It squatted in semblance of an immense, boneless toad, tethered to the stone by massive, rusted chains. Its bulging eyes stared up at her uncomprehendingly, its slavering lips muttering soundlessly to itself in the dreams of its delirium. Stricken to her soul by a rushing horror, the girl yet found the strength to speak.

"Horatius, my lord . . ."she whispered, still fearful of the nearby Druids. "Is it truly you? Do you not remember me?" she sobbed.

The creature fixed its huge, unblinking eyes upon the girl and gave reply.

"Horatius is not here, and I have been the mouthpiece of Sàdoqua, who knows all things past, present and future, for a thousand eternities."

And then, in its madness, the oracle was seized by a fit of insane, tittering laughter which grew in volume until the cavern echoed with its mindless reverberations. Paralyzed in the extremity of her horror, Selena became as a statue as she heard, unmistakably, the addition of another hollow, rumbling laughter which seemed to rise up out of the black abyss on the surging clouds of foulness. At last she found refuge in shrieking flight, which ended abruptly in the waiting arms of the smiling Druids whom she had betrayed. 🕸

About "Horror Show"

Here is a brand new tale by the author Lin Carter deemed the most talented of the New Lovecraft Circle. It is one of a new series of Mythos tales set not, like Myers's earlier stories, in the Dunsanian dreamworld, but in the modern world, with a narrative style to match. And "Horror Show" jumps off (or given its Tsathogguan reference, perhaps "hops off" would be better) from a fascinating turn in religious evolution in the modern world. It has become increasingly evident that fandoms are in no wise different, sociologically, perhaps even psychologically, from religious sects or cults. Think of Elvis fandom (which has actually begun to mutate into a "Presleyterian Church"), or Star Trek fandom, or (blush) even Lovecraft fandom! Myers focuses on the Gothic movement, which has a distinctive sectarian uniform just as surely as the Amish, the Hasids, or Heaven's Gate. The sacred spaces of this "religion" are Goth clubs, where ritual behaviors abound. One important lesson to be learned from fan-religions is their understanding of a key point conventional religionists fail to grasp: that the sacred cosmos is a narrative universe, a symbolic universe. One need do no more than temporarily willingly suspend disbelief (Coleridge), live for a treasured hour in the "as if" mode. The liturgy (whether chanting the Nicene Creed or dancing to Skinny Puppy) will be just as cathartic, as transformative, as energizing either way. It is simply wasted effort to try and force oneself to believe in metaphysical paradoxes the rest of the week, and only fanatics really manage it anyway. In short, here is a religion that requires only Coleridge's "poetic" faith. There is no element of "walking by faith, not by sight." One's faith is easily compatible with sight, since it is all theatrical pose.

Myers shifts the perspective slightly. He tropes the phenomenon of Goth-sectarianism, recreational religion, and makes it depend after all on metaphysical realities. But there is still no faith required, because here one simply sees the god one worships. On the contrary, as at the end of "Horror Show," it takes faith (kidding oneself) to believe it's not real!

As for the god of this religion, Myers seems very alert to the associational resonances of the name Tsathoggua. Crucial to punceptual analysis, a contribution of Jacques Derrida, is the fact that the "meaning" of a word is what it makes us think of when we hear it. It "means" what it reminds us of. And this includes puns and, which is practically the same thing, homonyms. Lovecraft knew this when he advised young Rimel to change "Dreams of Yid" to "Dreams of Yith," since "Yid" would convey a crude anti-Semitism to many readers. Gary Myers has listened carefully to the associations of "Tsathoggua/Sadoqua" and tried to include them, not exclude them. The result? The toad-god is Sat, the real, being. He is sated with obscene revelry. And he is enthroned on the sadism of his people.

Horror Show

by Gary Myers

1.

Lisa looked up from her drink to see a young man standing on the opposite side of her table. He was tall, slender and good looking in a quiet, intellectual way. His features were open and friendly. His black Miskatonic University T-shirt was his one concession to the club. Except for this, he looked as much out of place here as Lisa herself.

He pulled out the chair and sat down. "I was supposed to meet some friends here tonight, but they're running a little late. Then I saw you sitting by yourself, and I thought you looked like you could use some company. My name's Aaron."

"Mine's Lisa."

"You're not one of the regulars, are you, Lisa?"

"Does it show? No, I'm not a Goth, if that's what you're asking. I've never been here before. I probably wouldn't be here now, except that a friend of mine made me come. She thought it would be good for me, or something,"

"And has it been? Good for you, I mean."

"Not so you'd notice. But it's probably my own fault. I knew it was a bad idea when my friend suggested it. But when she promised to show me around and introduce me to some kindred spirits, I hoped it would be OK. But my friend disappeared soon after we arrived, paired off with some vampire wannabe for a few hours of mutual bloodletting. Fortunately, I brought my own car. But now I don't know whether I'm supposed to wait for her or leave her to find her own way home."

"I can see how that would be annoying,"

"And that's not the half of it. There's also the little matter of the kindred spirits I was supposed to meet. That's the part I found depressing,"

"Oh? Why is that?"

"Do you have to ask?" Lisa waved her hand around the room. "Just look at them! Clothes black, as if they just got back from Queen Victoria's funeral. Hair dyed black too. I know, because I saw the roots growing out. Faces white from staying out of the sun, or at least painted to look that way. And the expressions on those faces! I swear, they must spend hours in front of a mirror to get that perfect blend of pained intensity and melancholy boredom. But none of it's real. It's all play-acting and make-believe. Underneath it all they're just ordinary people like you and me, just ordinary people trying to forget how ordinary they are."

"I'm not saying you're wrong," said Aaron, smiling, "But after all, what did you expect?"

"Expect?" The question surprised her. Until that moment she had not been aware that she had expected anything. And yet "You're right. I guess I was expecting something, something a little deeper than a Byronic pose, I was hoping that the pose had a meaning, that it was the outward reflection of something inward and very real. That's it. I was hoping to find people who were a little more real than the rest of us. People who knew a thing or two about life, and who faced up to it anyway without flinching. People who celebrated darkness because the world is dark and they were at home in it . . . "

Here she broke off, suddenly embarrassed by the sense of her own words.

"God! Where did all that come from? I hope it's just the wine talking. Otherwise I'd have to believe that underneath it all I'm just the like the rest of them."

"Not like them," said Aaron. "Not many of them would have the brains to recognize that there might be something bigger than themselves, or the heart to try to find it. These people are playing at being something they're not. This club is where they come to play. But they aren't the only people, and this isn't the only club. Listen. Our friends have stood us up. Why not let me take you someplace and show you something a little more real? That is, if you're interested."

Lisa hesitated. She had not come here to be picked up. Still, the evening so far had been a total bust, and this was the first promising offer she had had.

"I am interested," she said. "When do we start?"

2.

Twenty minutes later, Lisa drove her car at Aaron's direction into the old industrial district, between blocks of dead factories and empty warehouses that industry had abandoned. The buildings loomed like tall black cliffs over the half-lit streets. The upper windows were blind and dark, the lower ones bricked up as if to repel a siege. The walls were defaced with torn bills and spray-painted slogans. It was almost a shock to find cars in such a place. But there they were, parked along both sides of the street in ever increasing numbers.

"Park where you can," said Aaron. "We won't get much closer than this,"

Lisa pulled into a space between a new BMW and an old VW Beetle. But it was not until they had gotten out of the car and walked for a while that Lisa saw the people. They were standing in line along the sidewalk under the brick wall of a warehouse. They were mostly the same Gothic types that they had left behind at the first club, with the same white faces starkly offset by the same black hair and clothes. But their expressions of melancholy indifference were starting to crack under the strain of waiting in line. Some of them stared at Aaron and Lisa resentfully as they passed.

"The line looks pretty long," said Lisa. "Do you think we'll get in?"

"Don't worry. I know the management."

This was no empty boast, apparently. He did no more than exchange a look with the bearded giant of a doorman before the latter unhooked the chain to let him pass, drawing a murmur of protest from those in line. The doorman almost re-hooked the chain before Lisa could follow, but Aaron stopped him. "She's with me," he said. The doorman shrugged and let her pass too.

Inside looked more like a theater than a dance club. The building was only a shell anyway, a converted warehouse easily large enough to have served as a hangar for a blimp. The third nearest the entrance was quite crowded with tables and chairs, with people sitting at or milling around them. But the center, where one would have expected to find a dance floor, was occupied instead by a sort of stage, a stepped platform maybe thirty feet wide by three tall with a black curtain hanging across the front.

Even the lighting had a theatrical look. The area between the entrance and the stage was an island of light in the midst of a sea of darkness. The area to either side of the stage, and behind it as much as could be seen over the curtain, was quite black. The invisible ceiling hung over everything like the night sky, with banks of lights shining down from the unseen rafters like so many moons and stars. The lower hall murmured with many voices, while somewhere in the darkness overhead the recorded voice of a female vocalist sang of the darkness gathering in her soul.

Aaron led Lisa to one of the few unoccupied tables, not far from the entrance and even less from the broad aisle that ran between the entrance and the stage. They sat down, and she looked around at the people sitting at the neighboring tables. In appearance they were not much different from the Goths in the line outside. Maybe they were a little more conservatively dressed, with contemporary dark clothes and glasses standing in for the more usual Victorian costume, but that was all.

Yet there was a difference, and it was not long before Lisa realized what it was. The typical Gothic air of spiritual torment and melancholy boredom was largely missing here. In its place was a most un-Gothic air of barely suppressed hilarity and eager anticipation. Lisa thought that this was probably the effect of alcohol or cocaine. There did not appear to be much consumption of either going on, but that did not mean that the attendees had not indulged themselves before coming here.

In addition to the people sitting at the tables, there were a number of others in long black robes circulating between them. Lisa assumed that they were servers taking orders until one of them approached their own table and held out an open coffee can. Her appearance was startling even here. Her face was thin and very pale, with dark circles under her haunted eyes. Her graying hair appeared to have been bobbed with a dull kitchen knife. But the startling part was that none of this appeared to be makeup. Lisa wondered how such a person had managed to get past the doorman. She was genuinely surprised when Aaron asked: "How much money do you have?"

"About twenty dollars. Why?"

"Give me ten. For the upkeep of the temple,"

"The temple? I don't understand."

"I'll explain later."

She gave him the money and he dropped it in the can.

After the robed woman moved on to the next table, she turned to him to ask for her explanation. But just then the recorded song was cut off in mid-lyric. The lights dimmed almost to darkness. The murmur of voices fell into a hush as everyone's attention was turned on the curtained stage.

3.

The performance began with all the excitement of a high
school pageant. Two black figures converged in silence on the
stage from opposite sides of the hall. They walked slowly
through the darkness in moving circles of light, in long black
robes and pointed hoods that covered their forms and faces.
They mounted the steps at the center of the stage, then went
off again to left and right, drawing the two halves of the curtain behind them. But the stage thus revealed was no less dark
than the curtain that had concealed it.

When the curtain was fully drawn, the figures returned to
stand side by side at the front of the stage. They pushed back
their hoods to uncover the heads of a man and woman so like
in appearance that they must have been brother and sister.
They were young, blond and attractive. They wore thin silver
circlets on their brows. They looked impassively over the audience to the back of the darkened hall.

Several members of the audience turned in their seats to
look in the same direction. Lisa turned too, and saw that a third
figure was standing in another circle of light at the end of the
aisle. This figure was robed and hooded like the others, but in
blood red rather than black. Now it began to walk toward the
stage at a slow and measured pace. Over the loudspeaker a
male voice intoned:

> *From the darkness Of N'Kai,*
>
> *From the shadows of K'n-Yan*
>
> *From the caverns of the earth,*
>
>   *Arise to us, O Buried One!*

The man and woman met the third figure at the top of the
steps. There it stopped between them and turned back to face
the hall. It pushed back its hood as the others had done, to
uncover the head of another woman. But where the first was
fair and impassive, this one was dark with an excited, even

exalted expression lighting her youthful face. On her head was a tall golden tiara.

Slowly, solemnly, she removed the tiara from her head and placed it in the hands of the first woman, who in turn placed it gently on the floor. She took off her robe and passed it to the man, who folded it and laid it down likewise. Nude, she turned her back on the hall, and all three began to walk toward the center of the stage. The voice over the loudspeaker continued:

> *Taking matter from the dark,*
>
> *Taking contours from the light,*
>
> *Taking body in the stone,*
>
> *Appear to us, O Hidden One!*

The light traveled with them to the center of the stage, where it now discovered two black posts standing together about five feet high and the same distance apart. The nude woman stopped between the posts and raised her hands to touch them on either side of her, while the others tied her wrists to waiting rings. When she was securely bound, the man lifted the dark cascade of her waist-long hair, and the woman produced a pair of scissors and began to cut it off above the shoulders.

Lisa stirred uneasily in her chair, increasingly uncomfortable with the way this was going. She had heard of things like spanking clubs, but she had never dreamed of setting foot in one. She was embarrassed to be here. She was disappointed to learn that this was Aaron's idea of something real. She was insulted to think that he had imagined that it would be her idea too. She got up to leave, but Aaron caught her by the arm.

"What is it?" he asked her.

"I'm not into this scene. I want to go."

"But you can't go now. The ceremony has begun. Sit down. Everyone's looking at you."

This last was at least partly true. The people around her were glaring at her in annoyance. She sat down again, and

Aaron released her arm. The voice over the loudspeaker continued:

> *The depth of Thine imponderable wisdom,*
>
> *The height of Thine illimitable power,*
>
> *The fire Of Thine insatiable lust,*
>
> *Impart to us, O Generous one!*

The man and woman each took up a thin black rod about two feet long, and began . . . But no! Maybe Aaron could prevent her from leaving, but he could not force her to witness this degrading spectacle. She closed her eyes against the sight. But she could not close her ears against the sound, the slow, deliberate sound of cutting blows on naked flesh, counting off the seconds like a metronome from Hell.

But this was not the only sound. Somewhere in the audience a single voice accompanied the blows with a shouted word or phrase. Soon other voices took up the phrase and repeated it in unison, until it was loud enough to cover up even the sound of the blows.

What was it they were shouting? It was not an English phrase, or a phrase in any language that Lisa could recognize. It seemed to be a single barbaric name repeated over and over. But the shout had grown to a ringing thunder before she could make out what it was.

> *Tsathoggua!*
>
> *Tsathoggua!*
>
> *Tsathoggua!*

Then all at once the voices and the blows fell silent. Lisa opened her eyes.

The beating at least was over. The beaters had laid down their rods and covered their heads and were backing away from the bound woman in a grotesque crouching posture. But the effects of the beating were plain to see in the body of its victim. She hung between the posts as if dead, her knees slightly bent, her head bowed below the level of her shoulders. Her back was crisscrossed from shoulders to thighs with the marks of her punishment.

Yet all this was of secondary interest. For the stage itself had changed dramatically while Lisa's eyes were closed. The circle of light had grown wider, pushing outward from the center of the stage to illumine something at the back. This was a statue in dull black stone set on a raised dais. Even without the dais it would have been as tall as a man. But the man would have been standing at his full height, while the statue was hunkered down in the posture of a toad. It was in fact the statue of a toad. Its wide mouth was calm and impassive, its round eyes closed in sleep. Only its face was fully lit. The rest of it seemed half dissolved in the darkness behind the stage.

Now, slowly, painfully, the bound woman came to life again. She raised her head to look at the statue before her, and turned up her palms in a gesture of acquiescence. The voice over the loudspeaker intoned:

> *This is our offering of flesh,*
>
> *This is our sacrifice of blood,*
>
> *This is our hecatomb of pain,*
>
> *Accept of us, O Hungry One!*

For a moment nothing happened. Then the eyes in the stone face opened into luminous slits like crescent moons. The wide mouth opened too, and a long pale tongue came whipping out to curl itself around the waist of the bound woman, who now began to throw herself from side to side against her bonds and scream uncontrollably.

4.

Lisa did not see what happened next. Her overturned chair crashed to the floor behind her, and Aaron's voice called after her in a sort of whispered shout. But she did not stop, because she did not hear him. She could not hear anything while that mad screaming was going on. She could not stop while that terrible rite was still in progress.

Outside, the sidewalk was mercifully empty. The people in line must have all given up and gone home. There was no one to pry into her distress, no one to torment her with questions she could not answer. She collapsed gasping and sobbing against the reassuringly solid brick wall.

She was still in this position when she heard footsteps approach and stop before her, and a low voice speak her name. She looked up to see Aaron, as she had known she would. But his voice had sounded tense and strange, and his face looked very pale in the lamplight.

Embarrassed, she made an effort to pull herself together, "I must look like a perfect idiot," she said, wiping her eyes. "I don't know what came over me. I don't know why I was so frightened. You'd think I'd never seen a horror show before!"

Then she added, almost pleadingly, "That's all it was, right? A show?"

He did not answer for some time, though more than once he seemed on the point of doing so. When he spoke again, the strangeness in his voice was almost gone.

"Of course it was a show! What else could it have been? Anyway, it's over now. Come on. I'll walk you to your car." 🕸

About "The Tale of Toad Loop"

Stan Sargent, author of fine tales such as "From Darker Heavens," "Live Bait," and "Black Brat of Dunwich," is a major new talent in Cthulhu Mythos writing. Here is another effort from his poison pen. In it I believe I discern a fresh and independent use of one of Lovecraft's notes (the one we dub "The Round Tower," probably based on a visit to the Old Stone Mill in Newport, Rhode Island) that August Derleth incorporated into his episodic novel *The Lurker at the Threshold*. Sargent has activated certain rich potentialities left untapped in Derleth's development of the idea. In particular he gives the "child of Sadogowah" business a new twist.

In his *The Fantastic*, Tzvetan Todorov explains what gives the genre its power of evoking a sense of eerie, almost numinous wonder: the ajar door of uncertainty. Yes, it might all be a hoax or a mistake, but then again, it might not be. . . . A classic device to this end is that of the unreliable narrator, between whom and the reader a widening ironic gap begins to yawn, since the reader eventually begins to notice important things the narrator has not, or has misconstrued. In a horror story, the narrator may tell his tale from his padded cell, like Delapoer does in "The Rats in the Walls." There is still the chance that he is merely crazy, locked up for good reason. But what if he has been confined because the "self-blinded earth-gazers" simply cannot brook the truth?

Sargent's variation on the theme is brilliant (though you might want to go read the story at this point, lest I spoil it for you). Okay, the narrator is nuts; no doubt remains on the point. But what drove him nuts? Maybe he used to be sane until. . . . Well, we'll never know now. We can only speculate . . . and shiver before dismissing what must surely be no more than pathetic delusion. Yes, that's the ticket.

"The Tale of Toad Loop" first appeared in *Nightscapes* #1 (online, Dec. 1997) and in *Dark Legacy* #1 (1998).

The Tale of Toad Loop

By Stanley C. Sargent

S o you want this old codger to tell you about Pritchy Kwik and the goin's-ons out at Toad Loop, do you? 'Though forty years is a mighty long time, I remember it clear as a bell. Mind you, there's none can give a more accurate account 'cos I eye-witnessed the better part of the whole shebang. There were those that differed with me on a couple of the finer points of events, but I was there and ain't spinnin' no fool's yarn. I got proof positive of my words if you still harbor any doubts after, and I'll show you. Let me give you some background, then we can get to the meat of the matter.

When Mazrah Mulltree first showed up here in Madlan County, I was sixteen years old. You wouldn't have recognized me; I was a strappin' lad livin' down on my daddy's farm. It's hard to believe now, but back then, the girls were crazy for me.

Mazrah seemed an okay feller at first. He right away bought up a good-sized piece of land which for years had laid idle. Word was he plunked down full payment in ingots of solid gold, though I didn't see it myself.

I asked him once why he'd left back East. He said he'd had a fallin' out with a relative, Captain Marsh, who more or less ran his hometown of Innsmouth. Mazrah up and left when he and this Marsh feller didn't see eye-to-eye.

The property he bought was mostly good pasture land, not wantin' for water. One part was wooded-over, though, down

where the Mad River curved all the way around. The river was-
n't much more than a trickle at that point, yet by looping
around it made an island we called Toad Loop. Nobody knew
it then, but the Loop was the reason Mazrah chose that particular piece of land in the first place.

Well, sir, there was a lot of clearin' needed doin' before
plantin' season, so Mazrah hired himself a bunch of us locals to
help out with the clearin', cuttin', and stump-guttin'. We built
him a one-story catslide house, two-story barn, hog pen, and
chicken coop, so he'd be in shape for Spring. Hiram Kline,
Martin's daddy, dug the hole for the outhouse.

Though the house wasn't far from it at all, ol' Mazrah never
allowed us near the Loop itself. It wasn't like the waters was
any danger or nothin', 'cos like I said, the river'd dwindled to a
creek by then.

So everything went along just fine for a couple years,
though folks felt Mazrah kept to himself too much. He up and
courted Asaph Kwik's youngest girl, Pritchy, who was considered a good catch by most. She wasn't the prettiest girl around,
though her curly whiteblond hair was much admired. Mazrah
was a good lookin', though sternfaced, man and Pritchy fell for
him right off. Next thing we heard was they was gettin' mar-
ried. Even though Mazrah didn't attend church meetin's, old
Asaph favored the wedding. If you ask me, he hoped some of
them gold ingots were still tucked away somewheres. It wasn't
long, though, before Asaph learned he wasn't so welcome at his
son-in-law's, though it gnawed his gut somethin' awful.

The couple kept to themselves exclusive 'cept for Mazrah's
monthly supply trips to town. On rare occasions, Pritchy'd call
on her folks, but Asaph said she looked kind of peaked and
down in the mouth, like she'd lost her spark, rather than like a
blushin' bride. He had to admit, however, that never once did
a bad word pass her lips either about Mazrah or his treatment
of her. 'Ventually though, Asaph and Mazrah got in a big blow
up and Mazrah forbid Pritchy's folks to visit. Pritchy was stuck

in the middle and when she chose to stand by her man's wishes, Asaph up and disowned her, sorry to say.

The first sign of other trouble came about three years after the weddin'. Folks reported weird glowin's up in the night sky directly above Toad Loop, glowin's brighter than a harvest moon. And at April's end, Quent Swiggart swore he seen a big circle of brightness, round as a dinner plate, floatin' over the island about level with the tops of the trees. Now, mind you, this was decades before anybody claimed to see flying saucers.

Most didn't take it all that much to heart. It was only logical that Mazrah would clean up the Loop sooner or later, and the lights was thought to be stump-burnin' fires reflected on the night fog or clouds. Still, there were some who whispered about the dangers of tinkerin' with the Circle.

The Circle wasn't nothin' but six rough pillars of limestone, each a foot thick and nearly tall and wide as a man. Though the better part of the island was flatter than a pancake, it raised up right in the middle to a hump 'round which the stones roosted like fenceposts. No one ever knew their purpose or who put them there in the first place. The Injuns claimed the Circle was built for some kind of unearthly critter that come down from the sky on occasion. Toadaggwa, they called it, sayin' it put the stones to questionable uses at certain times of the year. Truth is, they were scared shitless of the place without really knowing why. They gave the Loop the widest possible berth, swearin' the stones were the works of demons here long before any of the tribes. None of the whites confessed to belief in such savage superstitions, yet we all steered clear of the Loop just like the redskins did.

The crap first hit the fan when some school boys claimed they heard weird singin' and chantin' comin' from the Loop. Their curiosity got the better of them 'til they went and got themselves an eyeful — of Mazrah and Pritchy blatherin' a raft of gobbledygook while cavortin' naked as jay birds betwixt the Circle stones. Word of such carryin's-ons spread and set

tongues a-waggin'. It soured most folks on Mazrah, so's they
steered clear of him when he came to town after, though he
paid 'em no never mind. The younguns was warned to stop
cuttin' didoes anywhere near the Mazrah's land.

Things quieted down after a time, mostly 'cos there was little to be done otherwise. Hell's fire, nobody was gettin' hurt by
such carryin'-on, and Madlan County done away with witch
laws decades ago.

It was that durn Simmons kid, Steve was his name, that
kept things buzzin' by rattlin' on about how the Circle was all
fixed up with the fallen stones raised and tilted ones
straightened.

He carried on about holes the size of a man's fist havin'
been bored through the stones about a foot from the top for
ropes to be tied off and strung to the Circle's middle. Such
things worried them that listened.

It all might've just all blown over if it weren't for that
Simmons kid, who was a smart aleck bully of a redhead as I
remember him. He went and dared three of his cronies to hike
out to the Loop with him, promisin' 'em a gander at Pritchy in
her altogether. Least that's what he spouted later, though if you
ask me, he was hopin' to catch sight of Pritchy and her man
doin' things a lot more vulgar than naked dancin'. Whatever
the call, however, them boys sure as hell got more than they
bargained for when they accepted that dare!

They waited 'til after dark on Halloween as most likely for
festivities. Once they waded the creek and were on the island
proper, they swore it was rainin' real hard, which struck the
Sheriff as mighty peculiar when he heard it later, 'cos he
recalled it being clear as a bell that whole night.

The way they told it, the four of them hove up through the
mud to hide behind a crop of cat tails about ten yards from the
stones. They kept just back from the light of the bonfires
Mazrah had lit at the foot of each stone in spite of the rain.

What little they could make out didn't make much sense to the gawkers, but it sure as hell stopped them dead in their tracks.

Pritchy was nowhere in sight, though Mazrah stood out clear in the drizzle, standin' clingin' onto a rope for dear life. The oglers couldn't determine right off just what he was strainin' to keep ahold of, just that it was bound up in the ropes running from holes in the stones. Their ears told them that whatever he'd snagged was madder than a hornet; though it screeched and hollered loud enough to make a body deaf, they couldn't get a gander at it 'til Mazrah finally stepped aside, allowin' the light to shine on his catch direct.

Well, them boys was like to die of fright upon seein' what Mazrah'd snared! One fainted right off. The others claimed they saw a giant toad, ten foot long and taller than a man, sloshin' in the mud, tryin' to free itself of the ropes. That's hard to swallow, but they swore to the truth of it on the Bible. They said it had a mane of long black hair trailin' down its back and didn't croak like a toad, but let fly with screams and roars the likes of which nothin' could compare.

Up in the sky above all the commotion, they claimed a big, glowin' hole was floatin'. They said it looked like an upside down twister or a cyclone with a light inside its spinnin' innards, only there wasn't no wind like accompanies a regular twister.

All of a sudden the great toad reared up on its hindquarters, like to jump, but the ropes held it fast to earth. It cut loose with a stream of what Steve swore were words in some nasty-soundin' foreign language. Whatever it was, it had an effect.

Frogs by the hundreds poured down from the whirlin' hole, peltin' Mazrah like a plague straight from the Bible. They slammed into him or plopped down on the ground only to bust wide open like gut balloons! I'll hazard it was a hell of a mess!

Old Mazrah, well, he slipped in the muck 'til he lost footin' and fell flat on his back. He lost hold of the rope in fallin', givin' the toad an opening. That rope must have been the key, 'cos the toad snapped the other ropes once Mazrah lost his grip.

The toad turned and reared up right quick on Mazrah, pinnin' him down in the mud. They said a look of pure evil joy came over its bloated face, it's eyes shinin' all red, cuttin' through the rain and dark like fire brands.

The damn thing bent down and wrapped its big ol' black tongue around Mazrah, then sucked him up like a bug! Half his body dangled out the side of its mouth for a bit, thrashin' and floppin' up and down like a raggedy doll in agony, while the toad just squatted there, lookin' for all the world like it was fast asleep. Then, with one quick jerk of its head, it snapped up the rest of Mazrah and gobbled him whole! Must have been awful sickenin'!

Well, them boys took off at a clip, 'cept for Steve, who was so scared he couldn't budge. The way he told it later, the toad let out another stream of them weird word-noises to bring the lip of the cyclone down low enough for it to jump inside. The hole raised up, closed in on itself, and disappeared, just like it hadn't never been there at all.

With that, Simmons found his legs and skedaddled at such a pace that he nearly trampled his buddies in passing them up. He made a bee line straight for home.

Now, keep in mind that I can't vouch for any of that part 'cos I wasn't there in person. 'Though it defies belief, wait 'til you hear the rest before making your mind up final.

Anyways, Steve's daddy was waitin' up for him, and as you can imagine, he was madder than a stick! But when the kid came in soaked to the skin and scared half to death, the old man backed off. He listened to the boy's tale, then marched right over to the Sheriff's. The Sheriff wasn't all the way convinced it wasn't a case of high jinks, but he fetched old Doc Jefferys nonetheless, and together they high-tailed it out in the Doc's cutter to take a look.

They run into heavy mud as soon as they crossed to the island and saw the ground 'round the Circle was rife with frog guts, broke rope, and the ashes of several fires. There wasn't much in the way of tracks left in the drying mud, but they could make out where somethin' had been dragged from the Circle up towards the Mulltree farm. The trail led 'em right up and into the house.

Turned out it was Pritchy's pitiful path they was followin', where she'd crawled and dragged herself through the mud. She was in real bad shape, but Doc fixed her up. Problem was she couldn't seem to talk — she was in shock as Doc put it — so she couldn't say what happened. Mazrah was nowhere to be seen, which added more credence to Steve's story. The Sheriff eventually went home, leavin' Doc there for the night in case Mazrah didn't show. He never did.

The Sheriff had talks with the other boys and their families after that, and asked them to keep to themselves 'til he got Pritchy's side of the story, but that didn't last long.

Doc took supplies out to Pritchy on a regular basis after and even got one of the neighbors, Oly — that's short for Olivia — Johnson, to look in on her daily. But despite all, Pritchy's mind didn't heal up in tune with her body. Whatever'd happened must've been more than she could bear causing her mind to just close up shop permanent. When she finally started talking, she didn't make much more sense than a child, and she never did get any memory back.

A month or so later, Doc realized Pritchy was in a motherly way, which didn't bode well, what with her no longer havin' a man around. I think old Doc felt sort of fatherly toward poor Pritchy; he kept a careful watch over her for the rest of her pregnancy like one'd only do for a daughter of his own. He paid Oly to help care for Pritchy the whole time while providin' food supplies himself. Pritchy'd set her mind on havin' herself a little girl, so Doc bought her a pretty little doll that was all dressed up fancy like a princess for when the baby arrived.

When Pritchy's time finally come, Oly fetched Doc herself, but as she told later, she refused to stay and help with the birthin'. She claimed Pritchy'd been heavin' up seaweed and foam, which scared Oly silly. So Doc sent her home, knowin' she wouldn't be any help while in such a state.

Nobody ever saw Doc alive again after that. It appears sometime near dawn, he slipped an envelope under the door of the Sheriff's office, then went home direct and shot himself dead. He put a 12-gauge to his head and, well, that's all she wrote! Ain't that a fine howdy-do?

Unbeknownst to Doc, the Sheriff was out of town, though, and the deputy didn't feel he should read the letter since it was marked "personal" for the Sheriff. So he just cleaned up the mess over at Doc's and waited for the Sheriff to get back.

A week later, I come into town and heard a bit of what had happened. I'd known Pritchy all through grammar school, though we was never close, so I couldn't allow for her being all alone out there with a brand new youngun. I loaded some food goods in my wagon and headed out to see how she was copin'.

I s'pose you could say the situation hit home with me, When I was just five, my own mother died givin' birth to my sister Marcella. When we lost Marcella, too, a few days later, it hit me so hard that I wasn't right for months. 'Though there was nothin' could've been done, I felt I should've done more to save little Marcella at least, like I'd let her down. So when I heard about Pritchy and her new baby, it struck a close chord.

I knew somethin' was wrong as soon as I passed the barn and saw livestock strewn out on the ground like they'd been slaughtered, the dead bones picked clean as a whistle. The Simmonses were my neighbors, and Angus had told me some of what his son said about a monster toad. I got to admit to sweatin' a mite more than usual recallin' that story while standin' there in the yard lookin' at them bones.

When nobody answered my knock, it was plain somethin' was wrong. The door was part way open, so I let myself in, callin' out so Pritchy'd know who it was. The baby was whimperin' somewhere in the back part of the house, which took some of the edge off my nerves, at least at first.

The minute I pushed the door wide, the most sickenin' smell I've ever known hit me right in the face. It was enough to gag a maggot! I right quick stuffed a hanky over my nose, hoping I could keep my lunch. I swear it was gawdawful!

The curtains were all drawn tight in the sittin' room, so I found myself stumblin' through in only half-light. The furniture was all smashed and tossed ever'which ways, which gave another real sickenin' pull to the pit of my gut.

I came upon what was left of Pritchy in the bedroom. Lord, what a hellish sight! It was obvious she'd been dead for days, with half of her layin' draped off the side of the bed. The way her arms and legs was splayed-out all a-kilter, it looked like she'd exploded from the inside out. Before I could cover her up with one of the bloody sheets — and I ain't proud of this — the sight and the smell got me so bad that I barely made it outside before gettin' sicker than a dog. It must have been fifteen minutes before I could drag myself back in there, and only then 'cos I heard the baby squallin' somewhere towards the back of the house.

I still felt mighty queasy, but I just had to find that child. So I went 'round to the back of the house, feelin' a mite too unsteady to go inside again.

When I opened the back door, somethin' about my own size shot out of nowhere and busted ass 'round the corner of the house towards the barn. It must have been hiding in the spring room off the kitchen. Damn thing was so quick I hardly got a decent look at it, but I did note it was trailing a blue blanket from somethin' it was totin'. I tried to fool myself into believin' it'd been a young bear or great big ol' dog, but I knew it was somethin' a lot worse. And I knew too that it had the baby 'cos the cryin' sounds was now comin' from out by the barn.

I'm ashamed to admit I took my time chasin' after it. I wasn't about to stroll right into whatever might be lurkin' 'round that bend, so I strode clear of the house to get a good look before goin' any further.

There wasn't nothin' waiting there, so I figured it must've gone on into the barn to hide. I wasn't too all-fired inclined to traipse in after it, but I kept hearin' cryin', this time from the barn. I knew I'd have to bite the bullet sooner or later, and I feared later'd be too late.

All I could figure was that the Simmons boy's toad must've come back. Seein' somethin' like that could well cause a body to suicide, though Doc had never been the type to leave a helpless mother and child alone. I guessed the toad had ate the livestock in the yard, then went for what was in the house. After tearin' poor Pritchy up, it must have been full, or maybe it had other plans for the little one. Regardless, I was bound and determined nothin' bad was goin' to happen to that child.

The barn stood quiet as a stone inside. I should note the stink didn't trail from the house into the barn. And all I could hear was the squeakin' of the plank boards as I stepped, and believe you me, I was scared plumb shitless.

Being that time of year, the barn was chock full of hay, and that meant scores of hidin' places. The best places to hide were in the loft, where it'd be dark and hot as hell, all that fresh-cut and packed hay generatin' a shitload of heat, up there.

So I hove up my courage and climbed the wood ladder I'd nailed to a support beam while workin' on the barn just three years before. The sun was settin' and, what with failin' light and hay dust, it wasn't an easy search. By the time I got to the back of the loft, all I had to go by was a few pencil lines of light comin' in between the boards of the walls. Lucky for me, I managed to find a workin' lantern, otherwise I might have fallen through the trap door down twenty feet or more from the loft to the cattle stalls below; probably would've broke my damn neck in the process.

Mazrah'd known enough to allow tunnels through the bailed hay for ventilation, so I ended up pokin' my head down a bunch of dark holes while listening for any kind of noise anywhere around me. Considerin' the bails were stacked twenty high, there were lots of tunnels. When my ears caught some whimperin' noises, I crawled through a dark square of tunnel right to the heart of the hay pile to look for its source. Breathin' wasn't any too easy in there and, on top of that, I had to keep movin' for fear of catchin' the hay afire with my lantern.

After crawlin' straight towards the back of the barn for a while, I came to an empty space that by all rights shouldn't have been there. I held the lantern up high and saw a scene I could hardly accept!

I can see it in my head just as clear as glass even now. Lord Almighty, I never seen the likes of such a thing! It must have been ten, twelve feet from top to bottom and at least fifteen feet deep and long. It brought to mind a wasp's nest, hanging there from the back wall of the barn like that.

The more I looked at that conglomeration of mud and hay, the more it 'minded me of a mud dauber nest; a wasp nest hangs free, but this thing didn't. From where I was standin', I counted three rows of cells, six to a row, tunnelin' up and inside at an angle. The entrance hole to each cell looked big enough for a man to crawl through, but I wasn't about to find out. Like I said, I ain't never seen nothin' to compare.

I parked my lamp on the end of a pitchfork I'd found propped up against the wall and shoved it up into the holes one at a time, figurin' I'd find out what was inside without puttin' myself at risk. All 'cept the last held chickens that looked dead though they was still breathin'. Next to 'em lay a group of what appeared to be frog eggs like one'd see in a pond; the difference bein', these were bigger than basket balls. They were all wrapped in some sort of gut sacks, and things was movin' around inside 'em. In the final cell I recognized Old Champ, a good ol' neighbor dog, layin' there in place of a chicken. It was terrible troublin' to me.

I soon realized I hadn't been far off comparin' the nest to a mud dauber's. You see, daubers look just like regular wasps, but they sting bugs instead of people, even when they're pissed off. The sting knocks the bugs senseless so the daubers can stuff 'em in the cells of their nest with new-laid eggs. The par'lyzed bugs get eaten by the newborn daubers, and I had an idea that was to be the fate of the chickens and Old Champ alike. It gave me a nightmare vision to think of such vicious critters scatterin' all over creation!

I looked real hard for a place where the nest builder might be hidin', and before too long I located two big holes in the hay, one on either side, about ten feet from the nest. The bails'd been broke apart around each hole, then patted down to hide the openings. I've seen toads doing that very thing in order to have two or three escape routes from their burrows. I piled a couple hay bails over each of those holes to block them up, then crawled back out to the main floor of the loft. Then I plugged the hole I'd come out of and climbed back downstairs again.

Sure enough, the bails on the main floor had been stacked up from floor to ceiling in order to hide a tunnel of mud stretchin' down the wall from above. I guessed the critter's lair must be secreted in the hay 'neath the nest somewheres.

After scoutin' around outside a bit, I found where a hole come out under the barn. With the inside escape routes blocked up, the only way out had to be down the side of the barn and out that hole.

I figured I'd scare the bastard out by tossin' rocks up against the barn wall. I might have come up with a better plan in time, but the sun was settin' and pretty soon I'd have only the light of my lantern betwixt me and that hole. I threw a bunch of rocks and waited with fork in hand to see what commenced.

When I heard the baby cryin' like the dickens, I breathed easier, knowin' the little feller or gal hadn't been stung as yet. Some loud thumps followed, along with a sound like somethin' scurryin' full chisel down the inner wall of the barn. The baby's squalls changed to more of a whimpering, and it struck me all of a sudden that there could be more than one of them monsters lurkin' in there. But it was a bit late for worrying about that.

After a time, somethin' poked its head up the hole and crawled out real slow, clutchin' a blanketed bundle to its breast. When it sniffed at the lantern, I got my first good look at it.

It appeared to be a great bloated toad, but the size of a grown man and nowhere near so big as the Simmons boy reported. Its kisser was plug ugly and put me in mind of a bat. The skin was all warty like a toad, and I was surprised to see the bumps made some kind of weird design on its back. For a bonus, it had a light coat of curly, white-blond fur streamin' from its head down over the design. Rearin' up on all-fours, it stumbled towards me on its hind legs like a drunken sailor! Its waddle blowed up ever' now and then like a bullfrog's, but I couldn't make out if it made any sound 'cos the baby seemed to gurgle and coo whenever the waddle deflated.

My skin was crawlin', but none of the rest of me could've moved. When the toad was about seven, eight feet from me, I raised my fork up ready to strike, but Toadaggwa, or whatever it was, was too fast for me.

A pitch black snake of a tongue shot out its mouth and, before I knew it, the fork was snatched from my grip and I was knocked face down in the dirt. The toad slammed down on top of me. I rolled over quick to grab it by the neck, but the loose leathery waddle under its chin wouldn't allow for no real choke hold. We wrestled and thrashed back and forth for quite a spell, with me staring into its half-closed scarlet eyes most of the time.

I must've been bleedin' like a stuck pig from gettin' bit all over a whole raft of times — it had a mean set of teeth for a toad! It held me down fast with its stubby foretoes, and I felt its ice cold breath on my face when it finally stung me with the tip of its tongue. I was later told it had a sack of poison growing on each side of it where shoulders should have been. When the feeling started drainin' from my body, I was convinced I was a goner for sure.

Then the whole world exploded in deafenin' thunder! I thought I'd come to Final Judgment! But the thing I'd been strugglin' with fell off me, and somehow I overcome the poison in me enough to run at top speed to grab the baby. Ever' part of me was screamin' from pain, but I snatched the bundle up and kept goin' as best I could go in my feeble condition.

I ran like a madman 'til the world turned black and caved in on me. Despite it all, though, I somehow made sure my little charge was safe. When the Sheriff caught up with me, he said I was singin' a lullaby to what I cradled in my arms. As it turned out, what I'd read as thunder was actually the blast of the Sheriff's shotgun as he blowed that monster back to Hell!

For a time after, I wasn't right in the head at all, and I'm willin' to admit to it. I was half dead from shock and toad poison, yet they still had to knock me out before they could take the baby away from me.

I spent close to six months in the hospital, then I was brought here. I owe my life to the Sheriff, I don't deny, but he's long dead now and, damn his soul, it's his lying that's kept me locked up here ever since.

Even the Sheriff had trouble acceptin' the contents of Doc's note, least ways at first. He'd just got back to town and read the note when he heard I was on my way out to see about Pritchy. In the note, Doc declared Toadaggwa was the real sire of Pritchy's child, Mazrah havin' planned it that way without her knowin'. It was the awfulness of the couplin', Doc claimed, that blanked out her mind.

The note contended Pritchy'd been beyond help when Doc left, as the half-human baby'd not been born so much as it'd eaten its way out of her. Doc didn't have it in him to kill the child even then, so he charged the Sheriff to do it for him. Doc wrote that it was more than he was capable of handlin', so he decided to end it all.

Hopin' to head off any panic among the locals, the official tale the Sheriff gave out afterward was that Pritchy had caught some terrible, fatal disease from Mazrah, and Doc had kept it secret from ever'body includin' Oly, even after Mazrah died of it. Pritchy died from the disease after a stillbirth, then when the Doc realized he was infected too, he shot himself. It was a hundred percent bullshit, but it was easier to swallow than the truth, so folks accepted it without question.

The only other person who knew the truth was the Sheriff's deputy 'cos he helped burn the house, the barn, and all their contents "to prevent the spread of infection." You can't tell me the neighbors don't suspect somethin' more though, since a week later they hammered the Circle's stones to powder and dammed the river up so it didn't loop around no more.

I never did figure what possessed the Sheriff to get me labeled insane so's I'd be kept in this nut house for the rest of my life. Nor can I see these head shrinkers believin' monsters could beget offspring with a human woman. Even if such were possible, how could they give credence to any tale of a baby that growed to six feet in under a week? It don't make no sense unless they're the ones who's crazy!

I sure as hell ain't idiot enough to get myself all but ruined for no doll, but that's what the Sheriff claimed I did! Hell, that thing butchered my looks so bad my face is only fit to scare snakes now! Would I allow that to happen over a doll? A man'd have to be insane to do such a thing!

I can see from your face there's need for that proof I promised, solid proof that can't be ignored. I got it, or rather her, right here. Now, can you look at this pretty little baby here and still tell me Pritchy birthed some half-breed monster? I've been takin' care of her since that very day, and there ain't nobody can convince me she ain't a real live flesh and blood baby!

Ain't she just an angel all dressed up in her pretty little princess outfit? And she's never once been a bit of bother or noise in all these years. Bless her tiny soul, little Marcella here's been the best sister a boy like me could ever hope for! 🕸

About "The Crawling Kingdom"

From the pages of *Midnight Shambler* # 3, July 1996, comes a tale by Rod Heather, editor of *Lore* magazine. The story provides a good example of how to write a Mythos pastiche (a good thing, not a bad one). It rings true precisely by ringing changes on familiar themes. On the syntagmic axis, "The Crawling Kingdom" takes us places we have been before, or at least we think so at first, because we seem to recognize the route. And we are right: it is a well trod path of narrative logic. But then we start to notice that our surroundings are disquieting for their subtle unfamiliarity. They are not quite what we expected. This is because Heather has reshuffled the options along the paradigmatic axis, the axis of substitutions. He has shifted the kaleidoscope a notch. Though it sounds a simple enough trick, many never seem to learn it. The Scylla and Charybdis for a Mythos writer are to rehash the same old stuff and to depart totally from the old paths, so that the result is unrecognizable.

What Heather has done is to exploit a familiar and yet neglected theme from Mythos fiction: the ominous croaking of frogs, like a Greek chorus rekekekexing their interpretation of the action to the reader. Only this time, they are not merely the herald of doom but are that doom itself. Heather has moved them from being the appetizer to being the main course. The link is a natural one: combine Derleth's froggy choir with Smith's Tsathoggua!

The Crawling Kingdom

By Rod Heather

alls.

I am surrounded by walls now. Many would find this a comfort, these silent, surrounding walls, equating them with a vague sense of security. No limitless depth to fathom, no distracting dimension to contemplate. There was a time when I, too, would have felt an indelible security behind these four walls. The conviction that I need not be concerned with what lies beyond their stolid surface. The simplicity of two dimensions.

It was during my stint as a reporter for the *Beckham Bulletin* that I met Dr. Wilum Von Helmer and that simplicity was shattered forever. That was when the comfort of ignorance was washed away forever, wrenched away like a pall revealing the cadaverous reality beneath.

The doctor was a retired biology professor from Beckham College, who had kept himself locked away from public view in his remote mountainside cabin. Locked away ostensibly to study the indigenous amphibious inhabitants of the untamed Appalachian hinterlands. My assignment for the weekend was to do a short "Residents In Focus" piece about him. I wasn't exactly inspired by the assignment, but the additional money I would earn could conveniently pay a few bills come month's end. I decided, also, that the doctor should at least prove a shade more fascinating than, say, Tommy Shea the pharmacist, whom I profiled the month before.

The street address given me by my editor was One Old Rural Highway. I had just financed a new car — a 1989 Volkswagen Fox — and this address incanted visions of unkempt dirt roads and lake-size puddles. This put me off, but with slanted mouth firmly fixed and a sense of journalistic duty I lumbered to my car and was off.

The August heat was in full swing, and the road roiled with shimmering streams of hallucinatory water. What havoc this illusion must play on heat-parched trees! If, that is, trees can perceive such things. I do not doubt this contrivance as much as I did before my interview with Dr. Von Helmer.

The roadside became increasingly desolate. At last I came upon a shadowed dirt road which cut off from the main Interstate and headed deep into the ascending countryside: Old Rural Highway.

The going was tough, and I crawled along gingerly in hopes of saving my new shocks a bit of the inevitable wear. The road snaked through a shady forest of Pitch Pine carpeted with rusting needles. A feeling of serenity came over me; a feeling I remember had always accompanied being surrounded by nature, where the roaming wind animates the surrounding branches and the sweet sound of unfettered wildlife reaches a sublime pitch.

How I do miss such things.

After driving for close to half an hour, I came upon a lone mailbox standing on the side of the road. The number *one* had been painted boldly on its surface, and at least a week's worth of mail hung out of its yawning mouth, some pieces had fallen to the ground and from there had been wind-swept into the surrounding bushes. I turned up the steep driveway and proceeded to the large silhouette that was Dr. Von Helmer's cabin.

At the same time, I was surprised by the more-than-accommodating size of the place, and appalled by its shocking disarray. One would think it had been abandoned for years — rusting tools littered the grounds, an untended garden of roses invading the surrounding natural scrub, broken or cracked window panes left unrepaired. Yet upon closer scrutiny I could hear distinctly over the tranquil breezes a spoken litany emanating from the back of the house. The heat was suffocating and I immediately longed for the crisp chill of the car's air-conditioning. Only the hope of obtaining a cool beverage prodded me on toward the back of the structure, the vague conversation a veritable harpy's song.

That's when I became aware of the chirping. The day was getting late, and I remembered my boyhood summers spent at Uncle Bobby's farm in Tennessee and how the frogs around the cow pond would start to sing as evening approached. Not the song of angels, surely, but the chorus struck a familiar chord in my mind. It was rather pleasant.

I paused to wonder what it was about these unattractive creatures that took hold of Von Helmer's interest for such a long time. I remembered hearing from my editor that the "old fart" hadn't even been seen in town for over six months, and then only to buy supplies. Assembling all of the knowledge I possessed about those warty little creatures, not one point caused me to raise an eyebrow.

"Hello?" I called to the large screened-in porch sticking out of the cabin's back. Above the tin-sounding conversation, which I could now discern as coming from a radio, I heard a slight shuffle and the distinct clink of a glass. The radio was abruptly silenced. I waited, then called again.

A shadow crept slowly toward the door. A figure took form through the silvery mesh: a shock of unruly white hair, two cautious, scowling eyes investigating my appearance, expressing what I imagined to be a combination of curiosity and fear. "Who are you?" the figure whispered.

"I'm with the *Beckham Bulletin*, Dr. Von Helmer. We're doing a piece about interesting residents of Beckham, and you were at the top of the list."

I thought I detected the shadow of a sardonic smile. "Mmm, was I?" A breeze brought toward us the singing of the frogs and the doctor quickly lost his smile. The old eyes seemed to tremble. "Come in, come in!" he whispered frantically.

I climbed the stairs and entered the side of the porch. The porch had been transformed into a small apartment, leaving the rest of the house virtually unused. It was large and boxy, filled with books, charts, and an impossibly littered desk. A disheveled cot was pushed into one corner. There were very few shadows apart from those beneath and within the old man's eyes. Those eyes ignored me for a long moment as we stood in silence. He seemed confused, lost in thought. A sudden sense of nerves filled me with the need for speech.

"Um, what we're planning, doctor, is a short feature describing your studies. What about the frogs in Beckham is interesting? A bit about your teaching at . . . "

"Studies! It's been over two months since I've studied anything, young man. I am, in fact, hoping to move from here in the fall. I'm hoping to get to New Hampshire, Merrimack, New Hampshire."

"Really. Um, well, when this feature sees print next week, you'll still be a resident, so that's okay."

He suddenly turned toward me and gazed deeply into my eyes. To my utter surprise, the sharp sting of Jack Daniels singed my nostrils. Not only was he turning out to be an enigmatic eccentric, but he was probably a raging alcoholic as well. With trembling hands he indicated a chair. I sat down. Hastily, he stumbled to a corner of the porch that was littered with empty bottles of various intoxicating paramours. What a life it must be to be isolated in the middle of the woods and forever drunk. I felt a deep sense of pity as I watched his trembling hands pour two tumblers of Jack. I gazed with distaste at the unwashed glass handed me, then took a cautious sip as he sank into a ratty wicker armchair.

"So, you don't like our fair Beckham, eh?"

"Beckham's fine," he sighed, "it's . . . weather is all. Gets me itchy." I could not stop my eyebrow from rising to this strange rejoinder.

"The weather? I see . . ."I was beginning to falter. He exhaled loudly and, without so much as wrinkling his nose, took an inhuman gulp of Jack, which would've sent me convulsing to the floor.

"Um, okay," I sighed pretending to sound interested. "And what about the weather don't you like?"

Leaning his chin on his open hand he rolled his eyes and moaned.

He gazed at me for a moment and his troubled eyes seemed to clear. He genuinely smiled. "Yes, yes — boring. You want the real story, don't you? The one that will please your editor. It is a story that will alarm you, that will spill into your sleep like formless nightmare. A nightmare of vision — and of sound." He paused, seemed once more to listen. "A nightmare that will haunt you during daylight," he whispered then to himself, "that will make you afraid of the dark. Yes, that's the kind of story that will fascinate your readers. I've just the thing for you."

I could not speak. Something in his words strangely disturbed me. I took a sip from the glass, one that shocked my tastebuds. He reclined deeply into the chair, and looked for a long moment past the confines of the porch . . . into the swaying pines.

"Now, I want you to listen attentively to every word," he said, pointing a trembling finger at my face. "Let me tell my story all the way through." It was not a request — it was a command.

I thumbed the record button on my mini-recorder, and he began his tale.

"I had, as you said, been studying. There's more diversity up here than you people could imagine: *Scaphiopus holbrooki*, some of the Rana species, which is mostly what you hear calling out there now. There's *Bufo americanus*, *Acris crepitans*, *Hyla chrysoscelis* . . . I even think I heard *Bufo valliceps* up here that one time!" His eyes had grown dreamy as he canted this litany of names. "Frogs, my boy! Toads and frogs. They're everywhere!"

He paused to listen to the sounds from outside. "I've been studying the little critters ever since I retired from Beckham," he slowly continued. "I've watched the males wrestle each other over three foot stretches of territory, heard them time their mating calls specifically to drown out that of a rival. They are really — well, you'll find few creatures in nature as remarkable. Uglier than sin, though, eh?" He leaned into his chair smiling. "Actually, they're quite beautiful."

His subtle hostility was not aimed at me, I think, but at the outside world who mocked his passion. As he spoke, the calls of the various species died down, as though spellbound by the doctor's adoration. Perhaps there was more of a story here than at first I imagined.

"Ever since the spring thaw I've been out here documenting the times different species come out of hibernation, when they start breeding, and even possible congenital defects caused by pollution. One of the biology labs had a bad chemical spill over at the college a few years back." He frowned momentarily at the memory. "Anyway, I have volumes of notes put together. Perhaps some day I'll even be able to get them published, eh?"

I don't think he expected an answer. His gaze never left the woods beyond the screens. Nevertheless, I managed a patronizing smile and nodded.

"I had been out recording the call of the male Leopard Frog this past June when suddenly, surprisingly, it began to rain. Thick clouds came down off the mountains. Sheets of cool water fell from the sky. Oh, you should hear how excited the little fellows become in the rain. As if it signified a breeding

free-for-all. The Leopard Frogs, the Pickerels, the Woodhouse
Toads . . . and, as I've said, I'm absolutely certain I heard the
trill of a Southern Toad that day. They all struck up into a veritable symphony, relishing the fact that they were in absolutely
no danger of desiccation. And all I could do was hide for cover
under a big ol' Silver Maple and drip!

"Well, as the rain was completely unexpected, I was of
course unprepared. My jaunts sometimes took me as far as five
miles into the woods, far from home for an old codger like
myself. My equipment was out in the rain with the toads, most
likely ruined. There I stood shivering and cursing right in the
middle of this bustling amphibian orgy."

He rose, empty glass in hand, and wandered to the mesh
wall. I could suddenly sense his loneliness, the loneliness of an
outsider. He turned and looked at me, as if he knew my
thoughts, and grinned. "It went on tirelessly with no end in
sight. I stayed under that old tree for a good twenty minutes
before deciding to brave it and dash for home. The deep black
sky showed no sign of clearing, and it was getting late. That's
when the thunder started. Loud majestic booms burst from
deep within certain of the larger cloud masses. I fancied them
celestial belches.

"Within minutes, the lightning and wind came as a mur-
derous team. The wind churned the trees into an angry, lashing
gauntlet that whipped at me, driving me onwards. I had been
up there during storms before, but never have I experienced
one with as much conviction.

"I tripped and stumbled amid the now blaring assembly of
calls, howling wind and deafening thunder, running virtually
blind for over an hour. Then, just as suddenly as it had started,
the wind let up and the storm downgraded to a steady downpour. There's nothing quite like the woods in the rain," he
weirdly whispered. "It's serene. It's supernatural.

"I was lost. I kept on in the direction I thought was right.
And then I heard . . . the change. There was still the trill of the

Leopard, the lamb-like bleating of the Pickerel. But now, through the rain and din, I could hear something more. Something low, almost a rumble. Lightning still flashed in the sky, but between the corpuscations a constant glow reached out from within a thick grotto ahead.

"There were . . . people . . . in that stand of trees, strangely enough. They were singing — or chanting — slowly. I couldn't make out just what about, so I crept up with careful footsteps and looked through the dense thicket."

He raised a trembling hand, as if to indicate the scene. "There, in a small clearing, several folks stood around a small wavering fire. How they had managed a fire in such beastly weather I could not imagine. There was something about the motion of those flames that did not seem natural. It seemed a living entity, somehow aware of those who surrounded it. Reminded me of old Moses's burning bush. They all wore sweeping black cowls that covered their faces, which at first I took for rain gear. They were all holding hands in a circle around that central flame. They were so engrossed in their ritual that they paid no notice to the flashes of lightning above, or to the few mottled Bull Frogs that plodded about their feet bellowing their deep 'jug o'rum' call. Nor did they pay mind to the large black thunderheads moving down off the Appalachians toward the very spot on which they now stood; we were clearly in for another lashing.

"As I said, I couldn't make out what they were saying. Now that I moved closer I understood why. Their tone was low and their cadence slow . . . almost hypnotic, now that I think of it. But in point of fact they were not speaking English. Nor were they speaking Spanish, nor French, German, or Russian — certainly none of the Asian dialects. Those each have at least a recognizable tone, something that betrays them in even the most general way. No, this was nothing I had ever heard before. Slurred verbal mixes of impractical letter couplings and weird contractions. I was at a loss, but at the same time couldn't pull my eyes away. The scene beguiled.

"One large portly fellow wore a peculiar bronze talisman around his neck. I squinted through the brush and almost gave up the ghost right then and there when I realized it was a toad dangling on that chain! A beaten-bronze toad, stippled in the light of the fire.

"I became aware that another dramatic cloudburst would occur at any moment. I could feel the storm without having to look up at the dark sky — a certain unease in the air. Yet I was transfixed. I had to see what was going to happen next. My sense of caution kept me in my hiding place.

"As the chanting grew louder, the agitated frogs and toads of the woods began to call louder and louder. Almost as if they were chanting along with these cloaked loons. The 'jug o' rum' of the Bull Frog, the loose banjo twang of the Green Frog, the chanting of both the amphibians and this strange group seemed to twist into something frighteningly similar. Then he looked up, just as a large singular boom tore from the heavens.

"He looked up and his hood fell back behind his neckless head. I could only scream. He had the protruding eyes of a toad! The boom from above not only signaled the beginning of yet another downpour, but drowned out my cry as well. Or so I thought until his horizontal pupils locked onto mine.

"The fire weaved and wavered as forks of lightning kicked across the sky. The chanting ended and the toad-eyed man continued to stare. He didn't attempt to alert the others, who either had not heard me or paid no mind to my presence, but simply stared. Stared and smiled. It was a wide, toothless smile I shall never forget. It haunts my sleep nightly. And, damn it, no amount of this blasted booze can rid me of that horrible stare. I've tried, god, I've tried.

"The storm was now directly above. The wind blasted us with a fury that nearly knocked the chanters from their feet. And that's when the . . . that monster arched his malformed head to the sky and croaked in rough and fractured English, 'Tsathoggua is come.' I shall never forget that hideous name!"

He covered his face with shaking hands. His fear was contagious, and I found myself trembling with uncanny sensations. He lowered his hands from his haunted eyes and continued in a whispered voice.

"Then it happened, that which has caused my sanity to drain away like the rills of rain at my feet. The clouds overhead began to boil. Rain fell in torrents. The seething clouds lit up with a sickly green pallor. Then came the licks of lightning, queer in form, like mammoth frog-like tongues unfolded from the heavens. They lashed down toward the weird conclave. At first I thought the group had fallen, struck by lightning. I feared I might be next. But then I noticed the tongues of fire were still visible, that (I swear!) they began hoisting the chanters up into the clouds one by one! And the ones who still remained just stood there so very calm, as if they wanted to be taken. As if it was some destiny not to be denied. The sky went about eating them all!

"The talisman-wearer was the last of the dozen or so to be snatched up. Still he fixed his cold batrachian stare on me as I squirmed and grimaced in absolute terror. He sensed my loss of sanity, and, slowly removing the talisman from around his neck, he tossed it in my direction. A thick tongue unfolded over his toothless smile and delivered him up into the sky with an ear-splitting, apocalyptic roar."

* * *

We sat in silence for a little while. Then he rose and bade me follow him to face the wavering mesh. The sky had darkened, and a cool wind approached from the now-silent woods. They somehow seemed to reflect the chaotic horror of the tale he had just told me.

"I woke up here, on the porch. And from the looks of me, I must've crawled on my belly through the mud the whole way home. I have no recollection of the journey, of how I got here at all. I hoped and prayed to dismiss that night as a nightmare — until I found the talisman around my neck. I thought I had dropped the thing in all the confusion, but there it was, around my neck, itself almost like a frog tongue holding me captive as if I were a fly.

He produced the relic from nowhere, like a sleight of hand artist, and held it up to my wide unblinking eyes. As it dangled and caught the porch light I could make out filigrees of etched runes wholly covering its surface. The amphibious simpering came to us from the woods. The noise stung at my eardrums, each note a venomous dart. Was the old man drunk? Was I? I wondered for but a second, then glanced down at the bottle not half empty. The old man began to laugh a throaty cackle. Thunder rumbled from some distant place.

The wind began to rise. Von Helmer stood before me, dangling the daemonic talisman in front of my face. He seemed to understand its disturbing effect on my nerves, but at this he merely laughed. For the first time, I noticed his wide toothless mouth. I ran from that porch, tumbling along the side of his house, in the dark, amid the ominous batrachian chorus. The strange quality Von Helmer's eyes began to take on struck me suddenly, as suddenly as did the greenish flashes of lightning that illuminated the distant Appalachian range.

I leapt into my car and rushed headlong down the rain-slick road that was Old Rural Highway, never to return.

* * *

Well, I certainly could never go back to the *Bulletin* with a story like that. They've been calling me these past few weeks, wondering where I am, but so far I've stuck to my story of researching some big scoop. But I don't think they are buying it. I'll have to come up with something else soon. I just can't cope with leaving the house. Whenever I peek out from behind the curtains, all I find is those dark, autumnal clouds crawling predatiously along the horizon. Maybe the weather in Merrimack would be better — if I could get that far.

Money is low . . . can't remember when last I ate (grocery boy won't take my checks anymore) . . . booze is almost gone. It doesn't really help anyway. Feel like it's a stakeout, always being watched. Damn frogs so loud I can't hear anyone prowling. Unless that's why they're making such a ruckus. So here I sit, here with all the lights off, here behind these thin, brittle walls. 🕸

About "The Resurrection of Kzadool-Ra"

Just as Alfred Hitchcock used to cast himself in a cameo role in his own films, the ancient priests and scribes who compiled the Hebrew Scriptures were not above the temptation of intruding themselves into the pages of sacred writ, as if the sculptor of Mount Rushmore had snuck his own kisser up there with the four presidents! We meet a fascinating range of material in the Bible in which priests are the protagonists. One can see the self-aggrandizing redaction of the priesthood nowhere better than in the Book of Chronicles, a tendentious rewriting of the earlier histories of Samuel and Kings. Events are rewritten to increase the prestige and importance of the temple priesthood. The Priestly source of the Pentateuch tends to recast history the way it ought to have been and must have been from the sacerdotal standpoint.

The best and the worst of the Old Testament can be chalked up to priestly redaction and composition. The cautionary tales like that wherein Uzzah is blasted to atoms for daring to touch the Ark of the Covenant without appropriate ritual preparation (2 Samuel 6:6-8), or where Nadab and Abihu are struck down for screwing up the incense formula (Leviticus 10:1-3), were put about by the priests to keep the underlings in line. Others reflect internecine power politics, a lower order of priestlings (the Korah Guild) jockeying for a higher position and getting slapped down by the Aaronide hierarchy, jealous of their professional perks (Numbers 16:1ff; 17:1ff).

On the other hand, a number of Psalms (e.g., 16, 50, 63, 133, 134, 137) reflect a profound, even mystical piety cultivated by the priesthood who, after all, had the leisure to retain "right-mindfulness" if so inclined.

Perhaps because such priestly functionaries and underlings are ideally positioned as focal characters to convey the ironies of priestcraft and religious hypocrisy, a whole sub-genre of Dunsanian and pseudo-Dunsanian fiction centers upon them. In this way, stories like Dunsany's "The Sorrow of Search," HPL's "The Other Gods," Lin Carter's "The Acolyte of the Flame," and Smith's "The Holiness of Azedarac" recapitulate the Priestly stratum of the Bible even while turning it on its head, poking fun at the very priestcraft that spawned the Bible's cautionary tales.

Vester's "The Resurrection of Kzadool-Ra" belongs in this genre. In fact, a form critic reading this story might take it as a genuine piece of cautionary propaganda put about by the priesthood of Zothique against "false" worship. See what happens when you yield to the temptation to undertake an interdicted religion! Yat-san, tired of being a small fish in a big pond, decides to become a big fish (or a big frog) in a small pond. The moral of the story? "He who humbles himself shall be exalted, but he who exalts himself shall be humbled" (Luke 14:11).

And note this: Vester has hybridized his Klarkash-Tonian lore. This is the first tale of Zhothaqquah in Zothique! It premiered in the pages of *Chronicles of the Cthulhu Codex* # 4, 1987.

The Resurrection of Kzadool-Ra

by Henry J. Vester III

The shadows of dusk had lengthened noticeably while Yat-Shan had been engaged in the Lukar Ritual, and in the cleansing of the altar afterward. As a final act of obeisance he lit from a brazier, a long-burning joss and placed it before the image of Qualosh-of-the-Abyss, the eyeless god whose shrine he had been responsible to service that afternoon. Yat-Shan was pleased that he had discharged his duties with such skill and reverence. Surely the abbot, Del-Manphar, would soon begin to take note of his fidelity and attention to fine detail, and assign him to some of the more prestigious deities instead of all the relatively minor gods whose acolyte he had been since his initiation a full month ago. He did not expect, of course, to be Warder of Thasaidon or High Steward of Ronn-Zimm in so short a time, but he had thought his devotion to the gods would, by this time, have earned him at least an occasional assignment in the Pits of Xxax. Yat-Shan bowed thrice before the face of Qualosh and stepped from the shrine into the deepening twilight.

Yat-Shan had come to Nashir, City of the Sleeping Gods, after having completed a long and painstaking apprenticeship at the Temple of All Gods in Shulkarong. It had been his dream since a lad to learn the Rite of Nine Spiders, to climb the steps

before the altar of the goddess Yahoonda, and to quote from the
Testaments of Carnamagos as the new moon thrust its horns skyward above Mount Neeshra. His erudition had won him the
post of Apprentice Devotee at the Temple of All Gods, and that
background of scholarship and devotion to the gods had stood
him in good stead through the year of arduous memorization of
hundreds of rites, ceremonies and liturgies, not to mention the
commission to memory of thousands of passages of sacred writ
from the eighty-one holy books and scrolls recognized by the
Temple. He had been most assiduous in his studies, ever thirsty
to learn of this obscure god or to perform that arcane rite. He
had even been severely reprimanded by the High Priestess
Herself for having asked to know the rituals of the forbidden
worship of Zathogwa. (he had stopped asking thereafter, but
his curiosity had in no wise diminished). And during that year
of scholarly application he had considered no other post for his
future service than that which he now held: Curator of Deities
to the City of the Sleeping Gods.

Yat-Shan clutched his robe more tightly about his spare
frame and glanced skyward with a start as the evening wind
began to hiss over the high city walls, laden with its burden of
sand and detritus purloined from the Quarry. The young
Curator cursed himself for being slow enough be caught out-of-
doors during the passing of the Southern Wind which as all
knew, blew every evening through the Quarry, from which no
good thing any longer came. Since the Quarry had been
declared Anathema by the Holy Ecclesiarch after the last God's
image had been taken there from a thousand years before, all
manner of unwholesome and profane things had taken lodging
in its several caverns, crevasses, and crenellations. On every
night of every year could be heard uncouth whimperings,
gorge-raising gibberings, and voices-which-were-not-quite
arising from that place. By day it seemed but an ordinary
quarry — an ugly, unhealing wound in the flesh of the earth.
But beneath the bone-pale face of G'beesh, the moon god, that

wound festered with a sentient putrescence — a colony of the unholy made up of every mad djinn, lost ghoul, and foundered soul which had ever been drawn to that desanctified place. Yat-Shan had heard the Priests, Stewards, and other Curators speak of the fathomless pool at the bottom of the Quarry, and of those things which may have made their homes therein. None had ever seen a sign of habitation or any indication of life (if that term may be here applied) in or about the pit. None doubted, however, the source of the wind-borne howlings and whisperings, nor did any approach that unhallowed place by day or by night. It was well known by Ecclesiarch and neophyte alike that the Southern Wind carried in its ethereal fingers the essence of uncleanness from the Quarry, and it were less than advisable to be out-of-doors until it had passed.

Yat-Shan, knowing rather more of such matters than he really liked, lost scant time in finding a passageway which led off from the open street along which he had been walking. He entered quickly into a covered alley in the hope of finding unlocked one of the many doors which lined the lichen-crusted walls. He tried each door on either side as he made his way toward the end of the alley (avoiding certain doors whose aspects he particularly disliked), and, near the alley's end wall, was rewarded by the angry squeal of long-disused hinges and a gust of cool air from the building's shadowed interior. Without waiting even to light a candle, Yat-Shan stepped into the darkness and closed the ancient door behind him just as the first few questing fingers of the Southern Wind insinuated their way into the mouth of the alley. Now calmer, Yat-Shan reached into the folds of his ceremonial garments and withdrew a small candle from its pouch, along with a bit of iron and a piece of flint. Coaxing a spark onto a pinch of tinder, Yat-Shan soon lit the taper and began to take stock of the place which sheltered him. Most of the temples, shrines, libraries and mausolea of Nashir communicated with one another through intricate webbings of hallways, tunnels, and even bridges in some instances. The

Curator little doubted that he would be able to make his way
back to the abbey by travelling from building to building in the
general direction of his destination until he came upon a structure or a thoroughfare which he recognized and could use as a
landmark. Holding the candle high above his head, Yat-Shan
peered about him in the enclosing gloom, searching for a door
or hallway which would take him in the direction he desired.
The feeble flicker illumed only the area immediately around the
door through which he had just passed, and so the young curate
was obliged to follow the wall to his left in the hope that it
might provide egress from that veritable cavern of a room.
From a source which he could not determine Yat-Shan heard,
now and again, the moanings and whimperings of the Southern
Wind as it swept around the temples, spires, and pillared porticoes outside. He quickly suppressed a mad impulse to laugh-
ingly taunt the searching spirits of the wind, and silently continued his own quest. He could discern no identifying features
of the vast enclosure in which he had taken refuge, save those
of its immense size and great age. The huge stone blocks which
formed the walls had not been employed in Nashir's architecture within the last thousand years — not since the closure of
the Quarry a millenium ago. This, then, must have been one of
the oldest surviving buildings in the city. Yat-Shan realized,
with some unease, that these stones had come from that place
which was now a haven for all manner of unclean things.
Shaking such unhelpful notions from his cowled head, the
priestling raised his candle yet higher and approached an
arched entryway which appeared to lead in a promising direction. Having passed through the archway and moved some distance down the lightless corridor, Yat-Shan encountered a
wooden door of such antique design that he knew that this was,
without question, one of Nashir's first-erected structures. He
put forth his hand to test whether the portal was locked and
was startled as the entire barrier crumbled to dust under his
touch, burying his sandalled feet beneath a mound of fine, des-

iccated powder. Yat-Shan kicked and stamped as much of the
dust from his feet as he was able and stepped into a chamber
into which penetrated a murky half-light through a crystal skylight in the ceiling above. Wishing to prolong the life of his
candle, he extinguished it and replaced it in an inner pocket.
The room in which he now found himself was not a large one
and had as its central feature an altar of sorts upon which lay
an irregular mass which had long since been obscured by the
sifting dust of centuries. Unable to resist the command of his
great curiosity, Yat-Shan approached the dais, stepped up to the
altar, and began brushing away the blanketing deposit. The
configurations of the hidden shape at first confused the
Curator, for its contours were strongly suggestive of a massive
skeleton, vaguely man-like. The discovery of a human skeleton
would hardly have surprised or discomfited Yat-Shan, for he
was more than passingly familiar with rites which required the
participation — willing or otherwise — of persons whose mortal forms (or portions thereof) were deemed to be fit oblations
to this god or that. But not only was this skeleton clearly not
that of a man, woman, or child, it was not composed of bone at
all, but rather of some dark, smooth stone so finely wrought
that each smallest joint and skull fissure was intricately articu-
lated. Yat-Shan used his kerchief to brush away the last of the
concealing dust and stepped back to better view his discovery.

The shape upon the altar, apparently in semblance of the
repose of death, was, indeed, an ebon skeleton of unearthly size
and shape. Standing, it would have been half again as tall as
Yat-Shan and at least thrice as broad in the shoulders. Its feet
and hands terminated in claws fully as long as a man's fingers,
and the bones of a short tail appeared to depend from the base
of the beast's oddly-formed pelvis. The willow-thin bones of
huge wings seemed to be folded beneath it, but obscuring dust
made any certain identification impossible. As startling as were
all these attributes, most startling to Yat-Shan was the aspect
of the skull and facial bones which seemed to combine the most

repellant features of bat and snake in appallingly realistic composite. As the thing had obviously not been a sacrifice, Yat-
Shan had some difficulty ascertaining the meaning of his find
until he recalled a chapter from a little-studied text which he
had surreptitiously consulted during his apprenticeship in
Shulkarong. That time-eaten scroll, *The Heresies of Gvada-Reesh*,
had dealt — in veiled fashion — with the worship of
Zathogwa, outlawed by all proper and wholesome gods before
ever the first human drew breath to scream. Gvada-Reesh had
declared that Zathogwa had once fathered an offspring through
a female of the race of serpent-beings which had ruled the earth
prior to man's tenuous dominion. That offspring, Kzadool-Ra,
had offended its dread sire by some unspecified act of cosmic
betrayal and had been summarily incinerated in the devouring
wrath of Zathogwa. All that had remained, claimed Gvada-
Reesh, was the lithic skeleton of the creature which soon
became, itself, an object of worship by certain heretics of
Zathogwa's sect. Those apostates had all vanished unaccount-
ably over the span of a single night, and the location of the subject of their adoration — this very skeleton — had been
unknown since that night. Yat-Shan knew not whether any of
his ecclesiastical brethren had knowledge of this shrine or of its
vast theologic potential. The multitudinous possibilities fairly
danced in his imagination, and he was hard-put to decide
which to allow his fancy to embrace. In an instant, though, one
prospect perforce took on life and strength and dimension of its
own which far outstripped all lesser notions. Stepping up to the
head of the altar, Yat-Shan's eyes delved into the monstrous
empty sockets of the son of Zathogwa. In that moment he
determined to carry out a most bold and heterodoxical act: to
offer worship to Zathogwa, the Outcast God, and to importune
that deity to accept his fealty and his priesthood. He reasoned,
from his wealth of knowledge of the ways of his offspring this
would be the ideal locale from which to make obeisance to
Zathogwa, for a portion of the god's cosmic awareness must

always remain in this place. Having thus conceived so venture-some a plan, Yat-Shan determined not to procrastinate so much as an hour, but to act immediately before timidity prevented him.

The cleric stepped down from the altar and withdrew from his robes all of his remaining candles and the means by which to ignite them. There being little, if any, reliable information regarding the favored rites of Zathogwa, Yat-Shan was obliged to draw upon his years of study of the ways of the gods, and devised what seemed to him to be an acceptable ritual and liturgy. The feeble glimmers of his five little candles were, now that the setting sun had altogether disappeared, the only light in that mausoleum-shrine. He placed a taper at each of the four corners of the altar, and set the fifth on the floor at the feet of the huge relic. Yat-Shan knelt in the dust of centuries and, sprinkling a bit of incense now and again into the candle's flame, swayed back and forth intoning selected portions of the timeless litanies of Zothique, the last continent of an old and dying world. Tiny puffs of fragrant smoke arose before Yat-Shan, and these he inhaled and blew downward onto the floor of the shrine, signifying his devotion to Zathogwa, who dwelt in lightless places far below the surface of the earth. Yat-Shan sang of endless caverns, and of the spaces between the stars, and of the sentient winds which whispered in those spaces. He sang of Zathogwa's ancient exodus from a young galaxy long since gone to ashes, of his advent upon the infant planet Earth, and of the veneration and exaltation he had received from this world's races, human and pre-human alike. When he had sung and recited holy writ for a respectable length of time, Yat-Shan drew forth a small ceremonial knife and, without the barest hint of hesitation, carved into the flesh of his left palm that for-bidden sigil by which Zathogwa's minions inscribed his infa-mous name.

The Curate raised his dripping hand high above his head and, screaming out the name of the proscribed deity, smote his open hand with great force upon the shrine's marble floor. Yat-Shan had not known what to expect at the conclusion of his adorations, but he most certainly had not expected that which met his eyes as he lifted his head and smarting hand from . . . where? The surface from which he lifted his hand was hardly that of the floor of the shrine, but seemed to be one of natural igneous rock. Peering about him in the semi-gloom, Yat-Shan realized that he was no longer in Nashir at all, but had been removed to some underground place. The sulfurous fumes which burnt his throat and eyes, and the dim, red glows cast by scattered pools of bubbling magma served but to certify his belief that he had been transported to the subterranean realm of Zathogwa the Abhorrent. A low rumble behind him — somehow more like a snore than a growl — brought him instantly to his feet and facing the direction from which the sound had emanated. Out of the shadows of huge stalagmites lumbered that which had heard the prayers of Yat-Shan. The being projected an aura of incalculable age and wisdom, and of powers gained on worlds long lost in space and time. It closely enough resembled the representations drawn by Gvada-Reesh that Yat-Shan harbored no doubt that this entity was, indeed, Zathogwa of Cykranosh, object of his earnest supplications and sire of the travesty which lay upon an altar some untold distance above him. What startled Yat-Shan more than his uncanny transmigration, more even than the distastefully heterogeneous aspect of the god's face and strangely sloth-like body, was the size of the deity before whom he now stood. For Zathogwa was but small in stature, a good deal less tall even than the cleric himself. It ambled out of the shadows into the light cast by the nearest lava pit and squatted back upon its ample haunches to gaze upward into the face of its devotee. It opened its battish muzzle and gave vent to a most prodigious yawn, revealing triple rows of needle-sharp teeth. It blinked its bright yellow eyes sleepily and finally spake.

"I am the god Zathogwa, whom you have entreated," it chittered. "I will accept now your sacrifice," and therewith fixed its eyes upon Yat-Shan's left hand.

Knowing not what other to do, the Curate closed his eyes with a shudder and extended his bloodied hand to the beast-god. Zathogwa stretched forth its three tongues and lapped long and vigorously at the congealing blood. Just as the priestling was certain that he could no longer contain his rising gorge, Zathogwa ceased grazing and licked its furred lips with obvious appreciation.

"Your prayers and your sacrifice have been found acceptable to me," it spake. "Long, long has it been since I have had worshippers on this planet. You may ask a boon of me, O man, nor be you timid in your petition, for the form which I am now content to assume belies the considerable powers which I command."

Yat-Shan bowed himself to the rocky floor of the cavern and replied to his god thusly: "I wish only to serve thee, O Terror of the Depths, and to give thee the exaltation and sacrifice which is thy due. None in the world above any longer revere thy name, and thy temples have long ago been given over to neglect and desecration. Allow me, therefore, to be thy High Priest and Ecclesiarch, and thou shalt not want for prayer and oblation so long as I draw breath."

Zathogwa closed its eyes and considered briefly before replying, and Yat-Shan was momentarily affrighted that he might have offended the divinity with his rash request. But his trepidation was groundless, for the sleepy little god granted Yat-Shan's desire and more besides. As Zathogwa spake to Yat-Shan and described the honor to be bestowed upon him the Curator very nearly swooned with the joy which filled his soul. Never, in all of the eighty-one holy texts, had he read or ever heard of a similar glory to be granted the servitor of any god or goddess.

"Only of this one thing must thou take care, O man," warned the deity as it shambled sleepily back into the cavern's far shadows, "that thou offend me not in the manner of thy predecessor, or a like fate shall be thy portion . . ."

Yat-Shan heard these words but dimly through the ecstacy of his elation, but they troubled him not at all because of the skill and perspicacity with which he always discharged his sacred obligations.

While still wrapped in the elysium of his bliss, Yat-Shan felt himself to undergo a bizarre disembodiment in which he could not discern whether he had ceased to exist in the world or whether the universe had altogether dissolved into nothingness around him. That absolute remission of all physical impressions was abruptly replaced by an acute heightening of every familiar sensation, as well as the addition of powers of perception which had never before been his. He clenched a fist and felt great talons dig into this palm. He opened his eyes and found that he was able to see perfectly well in the formerly stygian darkness of the chamber to which he had been returned. The first object which claimed his attention was his own body which lay upon the dusty floor of the shrine, unmoving and already attracting those vermin which are not held to be overly scrupulous regarding that upon which they feast. Yat-Shan raised himself from the stone slab upon which he had found himself. He stood and was amazed at the height from which he looked down upon his old, discarded physical self. He opened his muzzle and offered a howl of praise and gratitude to his new sire: the god Zathogwa! For it was true — he had been granted the astounding ennoblement of kinship with his god! He was Zathogwa's new son, and endowed with the restored form and all capacities of that first, ill-omened offspring. He spread first one great wing and then the other, taking pleasure in the ripple and tension of the mighty sinews in his back and breast. He strode to the center of the room, peered up toward the crystal skylight, and leaped starward. Gaining speed with each powerful stroke of his wings, Yat-Shan burst through the skylight with another joyous howl, scattering its silvery crystal shards to the darkness like the remnants of exploding suns. He climbed higher and yet higher into the evening sky, now come alive for him with his sharpened senses and preternatural vision. He stretched forth his membranous wings to their fullest extent and soared upon the Breast of Night, all the winds of the firmament there at his call and command. Far below him, Nashir seemed to cower at the base of Mount Neeshra, the city's shadows flecked here and there with an occasional lit window or flaming altar. But no more for him the cities of mere humans, for was he not now of the race and family of gods? No longer would he call himself by his trifling, human name. Let the cosmos of gods and spirits know that one of their number lived again! Kzadool-Ra had returned! Through his augmented vision and other, less describable senses, Kzadool-Ra beheld objects, beings, and events invisible to earthborn eyes. He discerned clearly the face of G'beesh, the moon god, as he peered impassively down upon Zothique. His august expression seemed, perhaps, a bit less impassive as he noticed below him the form of one he had thought long since vanished into that oblivion shared by mortals and immortals alike. Kzadool-Ra howled a greeting to G'beesh and sped onward. He hovered over the Quarry and saw the lost spirits and unclean creatures which dwelt therein. Later, perhaps, he would deign to pay them a more personal visit in order to make himself known to them and to accept their homage. But now he continued his flight, passing over the hills of Tinarath and downward to the forest beyond. Unlike the desert about Nashir, the forest was fairly teeming with life. Deer, birds, and woogras were plainly visible to him, as were the woods' less salutary denizens such as lamiae, vampires, and the chance ghoul here and there. As he glided over the vast wooded expanse he espied a lambent, golden glow moving through the forest beneath. He hovered again, his colossal vans treading the night winds effortlessly, in order to see what manner of being or natural wonder might cast so glorious an effulgence. The aureate splendor seemed to move from tree to tree as it neared an open meadow, pausing at each momentarily before moving on to the next. Kzadool-Ra positioned himself above the clearing so to afford himself the best possible view of the emerging phenomenon. The shimmering radiance hesitated for an instant at the edge of the meadow, then stepped forth into Kzadool-Ra's full vision.

A being beyond all earthly beauty stood there revealed. There were no words in any human tongue to praise the splendor of that face and form, for no human mind could conceive or contain any experience of that transcendent refulgence. The son of Zathogwa was utterly ensorcelled by her, nor was he ignorant of the identity of the being who had so enthralled him. Both his human knowledge of gods and goddesses and his own quasi-divine perceptions concurred in the certainty of her identity. She could be no other than Yahoonda, the Elk-Goddess, warder of all things sylvan from time immemorial. Unable to further restrain his allurement, he descended to earth and stood before the goddess. He was grieved that his throat was no longer shaped for speech, for he wished heartily to speak to her the words of adoration which filled his heart. And she, in her turn, seemed to recognize him with a similar affectionate regard but was disinclined or, perhaps, herself unable to speak. But no need of words had these two divinities, here met in a mystic wood of an aged, fading planet. She put forth her hand and stroked his muzzle, igniting in his eyes the flame of an irrepressible ardor. Kzadool-Ra reached out and drew her to him, fanning into wilder flame that flicker of her own passion's spark. And they two proved, in that meadow, that the differences between gods and mortals may not be so vast as some would have men believe.

When their tryst was at last ended, Yahoonda, wordless, glided back into the depths of her beloved forest, leaving Kzadool-Ra standing, greatly fatigued, in the glade. He watched until her last faint golden gleam disappeared from his view, and then leaped to the air once more.

Returning by the route he had come, he was cresting again the hills of Tinarath when a prodigious explosion all but cast him down from the sky, and Zathogwa appeared before him in the awful splendor of his terrible wrath. No longer was he the sleepy little god of the depths.Now he towered above Kzadool-Ra in his rage, and his voice was like unto the rendings of worlds.

"O faithless son!" he roared, and the hills of Tinarath trembled in their terror. "Thou hast again taken to thyself that which is mine alone!"

Kzadool-Ra could but roar and howl in the extremity of his confusion and fear nor, it seemed, was any protest of his intelligible to his enraged sire.

"My great love for Yahoonda is a matter of cosmic history," Zathogwa thundered, "As is her own prediliction to take what lovers she will. I may not forbid her, but thou I have forbidden."

Kzadool-Ra bellowed forth his innocence through ignorance, but to no avail. As he watched, hovering, the image of Zathogwa expanded until it filled the entire sky, hiding even G'beesh's wide-eyed face from his view.

"That fate which claimed thee in ages past findeth thee once again, O perfidious one, nor shall any death relieve thee so long as I shall dwell upon this mote of wetted dust."

Thus saying, Zathogwa pointed a gargantuan claw at the paralyzed Kzadool-Ra and spake that word which, in the language of gods, signifies a flame. Kzadool-Ra felt his bones begin to warm, and then to burn within him with a searing, torturous fire.

* * *

Del-Manphar, the kindly old abbot of Nashir's priest-caretakers, continued to pace the cold floor of his spartan sleepchamber. His concern regarding his young protege, Yat-Shan, had grown steadily since the setting of the sun, nor could he safely send forth a party of searchers for him. The spirits of the surrounding desert often prowled the streets and tombs of the city by night, perchance to encounter any vulnerable souls upon which to feast. Nothing, therefore, could be essayed until dawn. He greatly feared that such malignant spirits as they might have made off with the young Curator of Deities, cutting short what had promised to be a most illustrious calling and career. He stood before his chamber's single window and gazed out toward the constellation of The Dragon's Brood, seeking some solace from the stars. Of a sudden he beheld a flaming mass appear in the sky and plummet toward the desert below. Had the flare come out of the constellation of Eenash, or even that of Shonn-Ramm, he might have been able to interpret such as an omen favorable to the safe return of Yat-Shan. But the elder cleric sighed, disheartened, for the streaking blaze had come from neither of these, but out of that portion of the night sky called Nib, which was utterly devoid of so much as a single gleaming star. Del-Manphar watched the dying coruscation fall to earth-ward, flashing down across the hills of Tinarath to disappear into the abhorred Quarry. This final portent the aged abbot took to be a very ill omen indeed, and he slept but poorly by reason of the particularly dolorous lamentations which arose from the pit that night. 🕸

ABOUT ROBERT M. PRICE

Robert M. Price has edited *Crypt of Cthulhu* for twenty years. His essays on Lovecraft have appeared in *Lovecraft Studies, The Lovecrafter, Cerebretron, Dagon, Étude Lovecraftienne, Mater Tenebrarum,* and in *An Epicure in the Terrible* and *Twentieth Century Literary Criticism.* His horror fiction has appeared in *Nyctalops, Eldritch Tales, Etchings & Odysseys, Grue, Footsteps, Deathrealm, Weirdbook, Fantasy Book, Vollmond,* and elsewhere. He has edited *Tales of the Lovecraft Mythos* and *The New Lovecraft Circle* for Fedogan & Bremer, as well as *The Horror of It All* and *Black Forbidden Things* for Starmont House. His books include *H. P. Lovecraft and the Cthulhu Mythos* (Borgo Press) and *Lin Carter: A Look Behind His Imaginary Worlds* (Starmont).